Copyright © 2021 Olivia Hayle

All rights reserved. No part of this publication may be distributed or transmitted without the prior consent of the publisher, except in case of brief quotations embodied in articles or reviews.

All characters and events depicted in this book are entirely fictitious. Any similarity to actual events or persons, living or dead, is purely coincidental.

The following story contains mature themes, strong language and explicit scenes, and is intended for mature readers.

Cover by Ana Grigoriu-Voicu, books-design.com.
Edited by Stephanie Parent
www.oliviahayle.com

OLIVIA HAYLE

PROLOGUE
VICTOR

If there's a will, there's a way.

And there's most certainly a will. It's in the hands of attorney Robert Tirsch, sitting by my grandfather's oak desk. He ignores the pack of vultures watching him and keeps his eyes on the will. Searching for a way out of this, perhaps.

I lean against the bookshelves, breathing in the familiar scent of leather-bound books and dust. It didn't matter how often the maids tried to clean this room. Grandfather always drove them out.

My aunt shifts in her chair. "I think we'd all appreciate if we could get this done soon. Today, preferably."

Mr. Tirsch clears his throat. Looks from the document in his hand to her. To my cousins crammed onto the old Chesterfield sofa. And then, finally, his gaze comes to rest on me.

That's when I know.

Nothing as trivial as the grave will stop Grandfather from micro-managing St. Clair affairs.

Mr. Tirsch presses a handkerchief to his forehead. "Let's begin, then. Thank you all for gathering here today for the reading of the last will and testament of Richard St. Clair. As you're all aware, this is not how we usually inform beneficiaries of the contents of a will. But the testator left specific instructions, and his lawyers have decided to honor those wishes."

He clears his throat, eyes refocusing on the will in front of him. Must be easier to face than the room's eager anticipation. "Richard St. Clair leaves half of his assets, excluding real estate, to his daughter, Mrs. Charlotte Reece, as quantified in liquid cash, stocks and bonds."

My aunt draws a breath. It echoes in the crammed office. "Did you say *excluding* real estate?"

Mr. Tirsch blots his forehead again. "Yes."

Dignified, fifty-eight-year-old Charlotte Reece doesn't turn around to glare at me, but I know she wants to. There are only two main beneficiaries to this will. Her, and me. My grandfather only had two children. With my parents gone, I inherit my father's lot.

"The other half of his assets, including real estate, will be left to the child of Richard St. Clair's late son, Victor St. Clair."

So, he gave me the house.

The old bastard gave me this place, the house that was my prison and solace for years. Maybe I can finally get someone to dust this room.

My aunt rises from her seat, but a nervous head shake from Mr. Tirsch stops her in her tracks. "There is, however, a requirement placed upon Mr. St. Clair. It's most unusual."

I cross my arms over my chest. "What is it?"

Mr. Tirsch's eyes lock with mine. He shrinks, fidgeting with the paper in his hand. "The estate will be held in a trust by the bank until Victor St. Clair is married, after which he will formally inherit the house. If he has not changed his civil status within two years, the trust will revert to Mrs. Charlotte Reece. As I said… most unusual."

"You're not serious," my aunt says. "Is that it? No explanation? Nothing?"

One of my cousins shoots me an incredulous look. I keep my eyes locked on the attorney and my face blank.

Grandfather is requiring me to marry to get the house.

Did he really think it would have that strong of a hold on me?

"There's a line included in the will, yes. It was Richard St. Clair's wish that his grandson Victor would carry on the family name." Tirsch gives me a look that's half-fear, half-apology. Perhaps I should have been nicer to him on the phone when he called about this meeting.

Carry on the family name. Marry.

For a few seconds, no one in the office makes a sound.

Then I start laughing. It's the first time in forever I've felt this lightheaded. Of course my grandfather is requiring this of me. He's not done making judgements about me and my life or using me as a pawn. He's thrown down the gauntlet, gambling that he knew just what this house means to me.

Marry to keep it. Don't and watch it go.

And I have two years to do it.

1

CECILIA

"The usual, for your boss?"

"Yes. Go light on the mayo this time, please."

"He didn't like it last time?" Ryan asks.

I give him an apologetic shrug. "For what it's worth, I thought it tasted amazing."

Ryan chuckles, hands a blur behind the counter. Smoked salmon, rocket, capers, cream cheese and a small amount of mayo on gluten-free bread. We chat the whole way through, about the latest addition to his family. A pug named Lucy.

"My wife loves the Beatles," he says with a grin. "So Lucy it was."

"Does she have a diamond-encrusted collar?"

"Do you think I'd still be making sandwiches if she did?"

I laugh. "You have a talent… so yes!"

"Oh, you flatter me." He hands me the finished sandwich, wrapped in plastic. "Here you go. I hope he likes it."

"Oh, I'm sure he will." I wave him a cheery goodbye, the footlong made to Victor St. Clair's exact specifications tucked under my arm. I stop by the corner shop and get him his coffee. Dark roast, Colombian beans, no sugar, no cream.

I make it back to Exciteur Consulting with four minutes to spare before Mr. St. Clair's meeting ends.

Stacey, the new security guard working the lobby, is on duty by the electronic gates. Awesome.

I wave at her. "Hi!"

She smiles and motions me ahead of the line of employees waiting to pass through the electronic gates.

"Thank you. You're the best."

She winks. "Only for the top floor."

The elevator I hurry into is only half-full. The chatter dies down as soon as I hit the button for the thirty-fourth.

Yes, I think. I work for executive.

The corridor on the thirty-fourth is quiet when I arrive, my heels against the stone floor the only sound as I walk past executive offices. Two are empty conference rooms. One is the CFO's office, the other the COO's. Two are in-house attorneys.

And then, at the very end of the corridor, is the atrium I call my home. Mason is at his desk. His fingers still on the keyboard as he sees me. "They're not back yet."

I breathe a sigh of relief. "Awesome, thank you."

My keycard unlocks the door with the gold-rimmed sign of CEO and it swings open on automatic hinges. I put his lunch and coffee on his desk. Keyboard to the left. Lunch to the right. His neat stack of papers to read for the day are well out of the way of any potential food stains.

Perfect. Just like every other lunch I've prepared for Victor St. Clair over the past couple of months.

I make it back to my desk in the knick of time. The elevator dings and I look up at Mason. "Showtime," I mouth.

They sweep through the hallway a few seconds later, side-by-side, two conquerors returning from the battlefield. Eleanor, the COO, nods a cordial hello to Mason before entering her office.

My boss does no such thing. The sharp cut of St. Clair's jaw is all I catch before he's gone, unlocking the door to his palatial office. It clicks closed behind him.

The corridor is silent once again.

I drop my shoulders and meet Mason's gaze again. This time, he's grinning and pretends to wipe sweat off his forehead.

He's Eleanor's assistant and I'm Victor St. Clair's.

I know Mason would never agree to switch jobs, despite the pay gap between us. And I understand.

It's been a year since Tristan Conway left and Victor St. Clair took over the position as CEO of Exciteur. As the major shareholders of the company, Acture Capital can appoint leadership at will.

But did it have to be St. Clair?

Working for Conway had been a breeze. A pleasure, even. He'd throw an occasional joke my way and I'd done the same to him, always with a hum of courteousness running beneath the surface. I got stuff done. He appreciated that.

Victor St. Clair is nothing like that.

He speaks as if there's ice in his throat, chilling the words on the way out. The glacial blue of his eyes is devastating when they're turned on you in disapproval.

I fear that above all else.

I've been his assistant for eleven months, three weeks, and two days. I know that because I have a timer on my computer counting the days. I'd sat here, eleven months, three weeks and two days ago, and overheard a conversation between St. Clair and Conway.

Conway recommended me.

St. Clair doubted I'd last the month, let alone a year, but he'd give me a shot. He'd made it sound like he was doing me a favor.

Well, I'd lasted the month, and in eight days, I will have lasted an entire year. Take that, St. Clair.

When that year is done, when I've won my one-sided bet with my devil boss, I'm out of here. I've been polishing my resume for weeks and I have the latest version right here on my desk. It needs more fine-tuning before I can send it out to companies across the city. Anything and anywhere away from St. Clair's orders. A job with normal hours and free weekends, with enough time to spend on my own business.

The one I've wanted to start for years.

Mason clears his throat across the hallway. He's gesturing toward the elevators, a smile on his lips.

"Oh!" I half-whisper. "Thank you!"

"Go!"

I put my computer to sleep and hurry down the corridor to the elevators. The staff kitchen a few floors down is busy, but most people give me space.

"Hey, Cecilia," Barry calls out. "How are things up at the ice palace?"

"Chilly," I say.

The others laugh, and I grin back, sticking my falafel wrap in the microwave. Do I have two minutes? I decrease the timer to one and a half.

"Do you have time to stay down here with us?" Amy asks. "Susan brought in cookies for the sales department and we swiped a few."

"You guys are the best, but I have to head back up."

"He can't force you to eat at your desk."

"Oh, he hasn't," I say. "I doubt he thinks I eat at all."

The others laugh again and I look at the microwave. Twenty seconds. Nineteen. Eighteen...

I'm walking so fast I'm almost running toward the elevators with my half-heated wrap in hand. It's a risk, but St. Clair should be busy with his lunch. He always takes at least ten minutes to finish...

My heart is pounding when the elevator doors finally open to the thirty-fourth floor.

The sight at the end of the corridor makes it stop dead.

St. Clair is not in his office. He's standing next to my empty desk, his face frozen in harsh lines, inspecting a piece of paper.

I force myself to take the steps forward. My heels echo

with each painful step, and it doesn't sound smart or fierce. It sounds ominous.

When I reach the desk, St. Clair looks over at me. His eyes are flat blue. "You weren't at your desk."

"I was heating my lunch." I raise my falafel wrap up as proof. *Here, Judge. Exhibit A.*

His gaze drops to it and he frowns.

"Is there anything you need, sir?" I ask, because the best defense is a good offense.

"There is no lettuce on my sandwich." He flips the paper he's holding over. A copy of my newly minted resume, swiped from my desk. "What is this, Miss Myers?"

The backs of my thighs hit the hard edge of my desk. "My resume."

"I can see that. Are you planning on leaving Exciteur?"

It's been a while since I was on the receiving end of his gaze. That much intensity isn't meant to be directed at one person. Ever.

"I'm considering it," I murmur, and brace for the worst.

It doesn't come.

St. Clair's eyes narrow in thought and he sweeps his gaze over me, from head to toe, in a way he never has before. He puts my resume down on my desk and gives me a long, final look. It sends a shiver down my spine.

"Interesting," he says.

He heads toward his office. The door shuts with finality and I release a shaky breath. Across the hallway, Mason is staring at me with wide eyes.

What the hell do I do now?

―――

The other shoe doesn't drop the day after. Or the day after that. St. Clair continues to send me emails with no content, only orders typed as efficiently as possible into the subject line.

Push my four o'clock meeting.
Reschedule my Denver flights.

Still, I can't believe my idiocy. To leave my resume out on my desk, amongst my other papers... I almost deserve to be fired. But still, I hope he doesn't. Not only because I need this job and the money it provides, or that being fired will make it harder to find a new one.

But because I still haven't lasted a year, as the timer on my desktop likes to remind me, and beating that shiny, ticking little thing has become a life goal. Two weeks left, and then I'll have worked a full year for Victor St. Clair. I suppose my life will feel empty afterwards, meaningless, even. What do I do when I'm not fighting a war with my boss that he doesn't even know he's in?

Victor likes to work undisturbed for a few hours every afternoon. Any meetings I can delegate, I do. Any conference calls that are not strictly speaking necessary, I decline. So I'm confused when he calls me into his office at five p.m. on Friday.

I know he's not close to slowing down. A Friday afternoon means nothing to St. Clair. I've lost count of the weekends I've spent working, helping St. Clair with projects, booking obscure plane tickets, sorting out his calendar.

I push back my chair and straighten my pencil skirt. Glance at Mason's empty desk. He's left, because Eleanor didn't require him to stay longer. She cares about employee satisfaction.

I wonder what that feels like.

Victor is sitting at his desk, back straight, eyes on his computer.

"Sir?"

"Have a seat, Myers."

Nerves dance in my stomach, but I do as he says, sitting down on the chair opposite his desk. "I'm sorry."

He looks at me from his computer. "What are you apologizing for?"

"My resume?" I ask. "You saw it? I know I shouldn't have had it in the office."

"No," he says, "you shouldn't have."

"I recognize that, and I'm sorry. Won't happen again." I'm about to start cold sweating beneath my silk blouse.

Victor raises an eyebrow. "Despite how unprofessional that might have been," he says, "I didn't call you in for that."

"Oh."

He leans back in his chair and looks at me in that full, scrutinizing way he'd done the other day. That's twice in a week. I bear the full brunt of Victor St. Clair's intensity, unsure if I'll survive a third time.

"So you want to quit," he says.

"No," I say. "I mean, I might in the future. This has been a terrific job, truly. But I think I've learned all I can in this position. So I'm thinking of finding another job, one more challenging, so I can continue to grow. But that's in the future."

"Right. Well, that's excellent."

I stare at him for a long moment, my heart pounding like I've run a marathon. His words don't make sense. "It's... excellent, sir?"

"Yes. I have a new job proposal for you."

"You do?" He has never expressed anything but disdain or a complete lack of interest in me. Had I managed to impress him? I do everything he asks of me and a lot more he doesn't.

"Yes. It's unorthodox."

"Unorthodox?"

He braces his hands on the desk. "You know that my grandfather passed a few months ago."

"Yes, I do. I helped arrange his funeral."

"Right. Well, he left a will."

"Oh."

"A will with certain... stipulations."

This I understand. "You want me to coordinate with the lawyers?"

The lines of his face deepen. "No. I've already tried that for the past half year. They won't budge."

"Oh. Well, I'm sorry."

His jaw works. "My grandfather's will stipulates that to gain access to my inheritance, I must be married."

"Married, sir? Is it legal to include that in a will?"

"I doubt it," Victor mutters. His hands clench tight around the edge of his desk. "But the old bastard got his lawyers to agree somehow. They filed every available loophole to make sure my inheritance is contingent on my civil status."

"Wow. I'm sorry, sir. I imagine that's difficult."

St. Clair is never going to marry. I know that from working a year with him. Hell, I'd known it after working for him a week. He dated like a tomcat. Over the past couple of months I'd set him up on dates nearly every week.

Not to mention there wasn't a woman in this world who'd tolerate the long hours he worked. The man had even spent Christmas Day in the office and forced me to answer his emails remotely.

And then there's the issue of his personality, of course.

"It's ridiculous," he says. "But as it so happens, I've decided to do it."

"To get married, sir? To whom?"

"I'm glad you asked, Miss Myers," he says. There's a hint of humor in the ice blue of his eyes. "To you."

2

CECILIA

"You want me to marry you?"

Victor meets my gaze. I've never looked at him for this long before. It's terrifying. "You want a new job."

"Not as your wife."

"Marrying me would get you out of this office."

"Yes, but not away from you."

St. Clair blinks once and then his usual scowl breaks, lips curving. Something glitters in his eyes and damned if it doesn't make me more afraid. "I always knew you wouldn't last a year."

My hands curl into fists, nails digging into the meat of my palm. "Six days from now," I say, "I will have worked for you for an entire year."

"Well, then you have nothing to lose."

The man is serious. There are a billion reasons why this is a bad idea, but as I grope for them, I say the first one I can think of. "But you're not the marrying type."

The same half curl to his lips. "This would be a marriage in name only, Miss Myers. We would not actually be in a relationship."

"No. Right. I would never... of course not."

"You'd be compensated handsomely for your time," he

says. "You're in quite the bargaining position here, Miss Myers. How much do you want for agreeing?"

"I'm not going to marry you for money."

"You worked for me for money," he says, voice dropping. "You already trade your time for money. I'm asking for very little of your time for this contract. Only your name, signature, and one year of not being able to marry anyone else. It's a far better bargain than the job you're currently at."

Victor St. Clair is infamous for driving a hard bargain, and he doesn't relent until the other party accepts. I know. I've listened in on more than one of his negotiations, when he pesters and coaxes and intimidates until the person across from him folds. And then he walks away, victory glittering in his eyes, having doubled his fortune.

I just never expected to be the one on the other side.

"But... it's marriage," I say, in a brilliant stroke of verbal genius. "It's not the same as a job."

"We can decide it is. Come on, Miss Myers. What do you want?" He leans back in his chair, eyes narrowing as he studies me. "An entirely new wardrobe? A year of traveling around the globe? There must be something you want, more than simply out of your current job."

"You're really doing this. You're buying a wife."

He snorts. "If I was trying to buy a wife, I'd go online. Plenty of people in the market for a green card. No, I want a contract. I want someone I know, someone I can trust to follow orders, who is organized and reliable. Someone who understands exactly what this is."

"So you thought of me."

"Well, you submitted your resume."

"Not intentionally."

"Does it matter?" he says. "You said you wanted away from me. Well, you won't have to work for me anymore."

I stare at him. "But I'd be *married* to you."

"You'd have your own bedroom, bathroom and space in

my apartment. Your own set of keys. We'd barely see one another."

"I'd have to live with you?"

St. Clair's jaw ticks. "One of my grandfather's rules. I'm aware of how… unorthodox this is."

"Who on earth was your grandfather?" I shake my head, his desk turning blurry. "No, sir. I'm not going to marry you. I can't. I won't."

"You can," he says, "and you will."

"That's not for you to decide."

"No, it's up to you," he says, and I know not to trust him, but I look up anyway. He's braced his hands on the desk and ice-blue eyes lock with mine. "This is the chance for a new life, Miss Myers. Leave Exciteur. Make enough money from this deal to do whatever you've ever dreamed of. If you want no contact with me, I'll make sure it's minimal. You'll be married to me for a year and not a day longer. After all, you've lasted one year with me already. What's one more?"

I stand on hollow legs. His words make no sense, and yet they do, and that's why I have to leave. Because I know Victor St. Clair gets what he wants.

And he's not getting me.

"I'm sorry, sir. But I'm not interested."

"Take the weekend to think on it. We'll discuss it further on Monday."

I force the next words out. "No, we won't. I'm not interested."

"Of course, Miss Myers. We'll see where we stand next week."

I shake my head, more to myself than for him, and head for the door. The bleak, impersonal atrium that is my office has never seemed so welcoming before.

"One more thing."

I pause, fingers on the door handle. "If you're asking me to be the mother of your children too, then the answer is no to that as well."

Silence stretches out between us, and I want to apologize for the words, but I don't. Because they're true. Because who is he to demand this of me?

St. Clair's gaze feels heavy. "Not quite. I need you to sit in on the seven p.m. with Tokyo. I need notes taken on the suppliers."

"Oh," I say. "Well... okay."

———

The next day is slow, as Saturdays in October can be, but in all the best ways. My best friend comes over to my tiny studio apartment and I've arranged an obscene amount of nail polish for us on the coffee table.

I keep them in a lazy Susan made out of clear plastic and arranged by color. The bottles form a perfect rainbow from pink to beige to red and then to black. Just looking at it makes my heart happy.

"He did not say that," Nadine says.

"He did. I can't believe he did, but I swear to God, it happened."

"His *wife*?"

"You know I wouldn't lie."

"Only if it's about eating chocolates I buy for myself."

"I've only done that twice. I was on my period."

"And I'm still salty." Nadine throws a pillow my way and I catch it, clutching it to my chest. "His wife? He really wants you to marry him?"

"Yes."

She shakes her head, braids flying. "All for an inheritance? That's the part I don't understand. You've told me time and time again how rich this bosshole of yours is. Why would he go through all this trouble?"

"That's what I don't understand either. If it wasn't St. Clair, I'd think all of this was a practical joke."

"He's not just pulling your leg, then."

"He looked dead serious." I compose my face into a poor imitation of his, staring at my best friend with eyes I'm trying to make smolder. "Nadine," I say. "You already trade your time for money, working as my assistant. Trading your name for a year should be an easy decision."

She blinks twice before breaking into laughter. "The man is a sociopath. Or a psychopath. I can never remember the difference."

"He defies all labeling," I say. "Perhaps he can get his own disorder."

"No, that would probably please him too much. Having something named after him." Nadine shakes her head and leans back on my couch, stretching out her leg so it rests against mine. "Did he at least offer you anything in return?"

"All kinds of things. An apartment. Money. A year of travel. And, listen to this, a new wardrobe."

Nadine chuckles. "Right, because if money or an apartment wouldn't sway you, some new designer dresses sure would."

"Of course. I am but a simple woman, after all."

"Men," she sighs. "Maybe you can milk this for a few days. Let him buy you an expensive purse before you turn him down. This is your chance to squeeze the bastard for all he's worth."

"That's you," I say. "You can do that sort of thing. You know I can't."

She rolls her eyes. "You can, Cece. Stand up for yourself. This man has been nothing but demanding for over a year. He's had you work overtime, on weekends, on holidays. He's specified and respecified his lunch order fourteen thousand times. He's made you cry! But when he had you planning the funeral for his grandfather? You didn't see him shed a single tear."

"I don't think he's capable of emotion."

"Wouldn't it feel great to skim some money off the top? Leave him behind with lighter pockets?"

I knock her knee with mine. "You're the devil on my shoulder, huh?"

She grins back. "Always. But level with me. Are you considering it?"

"Of course not. No way."

She reaches for a bottle of bright blue nail polish. "Did he say how much he was offering? I might be interested."

I groan. "Be serious."

She laughs, unscrewing the top, and starts to lazily paint her pinky. "I'm a struggling artist. He could finance all of it. Imagine the kind of studios I'd be able to show at! I'd trade my last name for that."

"You, the least traditional person I've ever met."

Nadine winks at me. "I have to keep you on your toes."

"Well, mission accomplished." I reach for a pale pink nail polish. "I didn't think you'd go for the blue."

She stretches out her hand and admires her nails. "I'm working on *Charity* right now, for my seven virtues series. It's turning into an abstract seascape. This is almost the exact color I'm using."

"How's it going?" I ask. She's been sending her portfolio to art galleries across the city. After a decade of slowly, painfully building a name for herself, Nadine's finally at the point where she could exhibit.

But so are a lot of other artists.

She sighs. "It's going terribly. Most galleries don't respond. Some are interested, but not in *this* particular series. It's like trying to win the lottery."

I unscrew the top to my nail polish. "At least you have your classes at the art center, right?"

"Yes, but teaching kids to collage is only *just* enough to pay the bills, and definitely not enough to host an exhibition." She shakes her head, admiring the nails of her left hand. "But one thing at a time. Hey, speaking of difficult topics. When are you finally quitting your job to start your own company?"

I groan, leaning my head against the couch. "Hit me where I'm weakest!"

Nadine laughs. "You need to be pushed here, though. How long have you worked on your business plan? Perfecting names, logos? You even have paperwork filed you haven't sent in yet!"

"It's too big of a risk. I need to have a job at the same time, or I could lose everything, all the money I've saved. You know most new business ventures fail."

"But some don't, Cece. If anyone's going to make it work, it would be you."

"You have too much faith in me."

"No, you have too little. Now's the time. Besides, you'd also be working for yourself, not Victor St. Clair. How ironic is it that he has the word *saint* in his name?"

I snort. "Very."

She nudges me with her knee. "So, you're not going to marry him. But take the opportunity to leave your job, at least. In six months' time, I want to see you as the CEO of your very own virtual assistant firm."

"I have learned a lot, working for Exciteur," I admit. "I've even learned a lot from Victor St. Clair."

"Great! Take that and run. You don't owe the man anything."

I smile, looking down at my nails. "Will you help me design my graphics?"

"Of course I will! You know it'll be a success. Your vision is too good not to be."

"Thank you," I say. Truth is, I have full faith in the idea itself. A company where people can purchase tasks is brilliant. Need your plane tickets booked? Send the info to us and we'll do it for you. Need to research the best dog grooming business in Seattle? We'll send you an itemized list in an hour. Need to negotiate with your cable company? We'll handle the phone call.

Clients could have a subscription or pay one-off fees. It's

convenient for them, and it's convenient for me and my imagined hires, who could be located all around the country.

People like me who love organization and research.

Clients who have too little time and too many tasks.

The idea itself is sound. It's the execution I'm afraid of messing up, because if I've learned one thing from my time as an assistant, it's that business rarely runs smoothly.

Nadine and I spend the rest of the afternoon lazing about before we get ready for the evening. With her, there's no telling where a night out will end, so I've given up planning. I put on a short black skirt, tuck a silk blouse into it and run a brush through my brown curls.

"Winged eyeliner!" Nadine calls. She's doing her makeup in my living room, sprawled on the couch.

"Yes, Mom!" I call back, but I do as she says, and the effect is striking. She'd helped me perfect the technique a few months ago and since then it's been my go-to going out look, making my green eyes pop.

"Can you imagine?" I call. "I received my first proposal today. I feel like a character in a Jane Austen novel. Turning down unwelcome proposals of marriage!"

Nadine pops her head into my bathroom. "Yes. And then, just like a Jane Austen protagonist, you're going out to down martinis at Temple."

"Practically afternoon tea, my dear."

"Think your suitor will come calling?" She bats long eyelashes. "Leave his calling card?"

"If that's his business card, I don't want it."

She disappears back toward my couch. Our dresses are laid out on my single bed, wedged in the corner of my tiny apartment. I return to my makeup. We work in silence for a few minutes.

"Oh my God. Cecilia. Oh my God!"

"What?" I peek out of the bathroom, only to see her standing in her underwear by the bed, her phone in hand.

"I just got an email from the Francis Hunt Gallery. They're inviting me to exhibit with them!"

"Nadine, that's amazing! Are you serious?"

"Yes. This is… yes. Oh goodness. I'm going to have to find money, though. Artists pay half of the exhibition fees."

"They do?"

"Yes. Oh, Jesus. It costs several thousand dollars to exhibit there. But it's such a good opportunity."

I sink down onto the couch. "Really?"

"Yes. Most artists will make it back, based on sales. I might? But I don't have that money." She puts a hand on her flushed cheek, breathing deep. "But somehow I'll have to get it. Extra shifts, I suppose. Collage classes all night long!"

I nod, feeling hollow inside. Because I already know the best way to make her professional dreams come true, and just maybe, go after my own in the process.

"We'll find a way," I tell her. "This is your dream."

3

CECILIA

My hands are shaking around the coffee cup. Dark roast, Colombian beans, no sugar, no cream. Just like he wants his coffee. Only this time, he'll get it with a side of victory.

I glance in the elevator mirror. My usual composed appearance gazes back at me. Brown hair brushed back into a low bun. Pink blush, brown eyeliner, nude lipstick. A gray pencil skirt and a white blouse. I look like an assistant to a high-powered man. For years, that's been my job. Helping someone else be on top.

Perhaps it's time I look like a business owner instead.

Money for my own start-up, money for Nadine's art, and one more thing. The thing he's going to hate most of all.

Mentorship.

I don't like St. Clair, but he's the best at what he does. He negotiates like it's his native tongue. He cuts costs and grows profit margins. I've learned more from him over the past year than I did from Tristan Conway before him. It just hasn't been as easy.

Mason's desk is empty opposite mine. Eleanor doesn't require him in until seven thirty, so it's just me and my early bird devil in his office. I wonder what world-conquering moves he's already made.

Fired an entire Exciteur department? Bought another company? Invaded Portugal? Tristan did things tactfully, if a bit bluntly.

St. Clair is ruthless in comparison.

I knock on his office door and it swings open. He's seated behind his desk, legs crossed and a dossier of papers in his lap. The blue shirt he's wearing is the exact color of his eyes.

He's impossible to look away from.

My hand shakes harder and I flex my fingers, gripping the coffee cup tight. This is a transaction. I don't need to think about why he's doing this. All I need to focus on is what I'll gain. I've been given a chance to change my life and that of my best friend. Nadine has been a brilliant, struggling artist for a decade.

This is her big break.

St. Clair looks up from his dossier. "Good morning, Cecilia."

I didn't think he knew my first name, and he *never* says good morning. This isn't a good sign. This means he's done his homework, like he always does before negotiations. Only this time I'm not the one who'd done the research for him.

"Good morning," I say. Force my legs to move and put down his coffee.

"Excellent. Thank you."

I stare at him. He's never thanked me for anything.

St. Clair looks back at me with cool determination. "Have a seat and let's continue our discussion from last week."

If I let him, he'll take control of this conversation. I've seen it happen too many times before.

I grip the back of the chair and look him straight in the eyes. "I have three conditions."

He sets his dossier down. "Name them."

In my head, I hear the sneer of *gold digger*. But the ruthless businessman in front of me doesn't let the opinions of others bother him. I've seen him squeeze his suppliers or customers for every dime they're worth. If he can do it, so can I.

"I want double my yearly salary, and half of it upfront."

The sharp cut of his jaw dips once in a nod. "Agreed."

So I'd asked for too little, but even this amount feels like a dizzying sum. For Nadine's art exhibit and my start-up.

"My second condition. There's an art gallery I want you to patron."

One eyebrow rises. "To patron?"

"Yes. Go to the Francis Hunt Gallery a couple of times," I say, clearing my throat. "Attend an opening and buy a few paintings, invite some of your famous friends. Create some buzz, you know."

He gives another nod. "Fine. Specify all of that in the contract and I'll look it over. Is that all?"

"One more thing," I say. "I want you to mentor me."

Victor St. Clair stares at me. "You want me to do what?"

"Mentor me," I repeat, hands tightening around the back of the chair. "When you're not at Exciteur, you run a successful venture capitalist firm. Well, I'd like to start my own company, and I want your advice."

His lips turn down. "You want me to be a silent partner?"

"No. I don't want you to invest." Not when I know just how ruthless he can be. There's no way St. Clair is coming close to owning a piece of my new business.

"You want my time," he says.

This is going to be a hard sell. "Yes. I want you available once every week for the year we're married, to ask you any questions I have about my business. I want your unbiased, professional assessments."

"You want to start a business."

"Yes."

His eyes narrow. "Do you know anything about running a business? Anything at all?"

"I have a BA in business administration," I say. "I worked

at several firms before Exciteur, and I've seen how both you and Mr. Conway work up close. I'm ready for my own start-up."

I have no idea if I'm ready.

But business is all about faking it till you make it.

St. Clair reaches up to adjust his tie and the tone of his voice is arctic. "You made it clear you wanted away from me, Miss Myers. Not to negotiate for more time with me. No. I'll double the amount instead. Two hundred thousand and patronage of an art gallery."

"No," I say. Tasting blood and feeling ready to bolt.

He raises an eyebrow. "No?"

"No. We can make our question-and-answer sessions once every two weeks. But they're happening, or you can find yourself another bride-for-hire."

Our eyes lock, the ice-cold blue of his freezing. I want to run to the safety of the corridor outside his office, to my desk and my half-eaten breakfast sandwich and Mason's kind eyes.

But I stay and I watch him the way he's watching me. The way he's taught me. "One two-hour session a month," he says, jaw tense. "And two fifteen-minute shorts. You're to schedule them with my new assistant."

"All right."

"Is that it, then? Or do you want me to sponsor another one of your friend's businesses too?"

There's a dryness in his tone I haven't heard before. But then, this might be the first conversation we've ever had where he isn't speaking in monosyllables. "No, that's all."

"Then that's it. Congratulations, Miss Myers. You're about to get married. I'll have my lawyers send you documents to read. Pre-nup and standard clauses." He opens the dossier on his lap again, dismissing me. "Make the arrangements. You know my schedule."

I let go of the chair. "I do. Should I coordinate with your lawyers for the marriage license as well?"

"Yes."

"Irving or Hardmann?"

"Irving." He closes the dossier with a smack and reaches for his coffee. "Send my eight a.m. in directly when he arrives."

"Yes, sir. Will do." Just like that, I've agreed to marry my boss. "Courthouse?"

He's returned to his work, eyes on his screen. "Yes. Book a time midday, if you can. I want to avoid traffic."

"All right."

My cheeks are still flushed when Mason arrives. He stops in front of my desk, and his smile fades as he sees my pinched expression. "Hey, Cecilia. Everything okay? You didn't get fired, did you?"

I give a half-laugh. "No. Not exactly."

No, I have a wedding to plan.

My own.

4

VICTOR

My hand tightens around the phone. "Yes. I'm sure."

Irving takes a deep breath on the other line. "Mr. St. Clair, large portions of this contract are unenforceable in court."

"I realize that."

"The deal you're making here is... well, beyond the scope of the law."

That's a fine way to put it. Paying someone to marry you isn't illegal, but it's not covered by standard clauses.

"I'm aware," I say. "But I want it written up. Make it look legal."

"Sir, I—"

"I'm not deceiving Miss Myers. She is well aware of what she's agreed to. The point of the contract is to ensure we both uphold our ends."

"Right. Yes."

"It's between two individuals," I say. "Phrase it like I'm giving her a gift of one hundred thousand dollars. Half at one date, the other half at the end of the year. Don't mention the marriage."

"I'll do as you say," Irving says. Another pause on the phone, and I look up at the ceiling. He'll say something now, like he always does, that I'll have to dismiss.

He's a good family lawyer. One of the best in the city. He'd been my father's once, as well as my grandfather's. No doubt he was one of the lawyers consulted on the ironclad marriage requirement in the will.

But he couldn't help sharing his opinions on things that had nothing to do with the law.

"I spoke to the lady in question," he says, and there it is. The censure in his tone. "She's a responsible, motivated young woman. I think you've chosen well, St. Clair."

"But?"

"But it's clear she doesn't understand why you're doing this. I think sharing the reason behind it would help her come to terms with the decision."

"She's already agreed."

"She's agreed verbally," he says. "But she hasn't said yes to you in front of an officiant yet."

I run a hand along the stubble on my jaw. He has a point. Until I have the deed to my grandfather's house in hand, I can't look away from this.

From her.

"Noted," I say.

"Good. I'll draw up the contract and send it to you by the end of the day."

We hang up and I stare at the inbox on my screen. Organized and sorted, and near empty. Miss Myers handles most of my communication. My correspondence. My schedule.

She has since the first day I stepped into Exciteur to take over for Tristan. The bleeding hearted fool stepped down, all because he was dating one of the company interns.

Wasn't even an HR violation.

"To make her more comfortable," he'd told us partners. "I want it all to be legitimate."

His loss. Exciteur was at a position of near global dominance in the consulting world and if he didn't want to be at the helm of that ship, there were plenty of people willing to fill it. Like me.

Miss Myers had come with the position, just like the decor of his office. A mousy young woman who'd never had her hair out of place, who dressed like she wanted to be invisible, to blend in.

And now my wife to be.

I run a hand over my face. Sleeping had been hell for the past week, as it is when the memories are at their worst. Not to mention the ticking time bomb. Months had passed since the reading of my grandfather's will.

I wish I could let it go.

That I could buzz Miss Myers in and tell her she's off the hook, she doesn't have to marry me, go ahead and quit and live her life crocheting, reorganizing her bookshelves or whatever else she did for fun.

But I can't.

Because then the damn, fucking house will pass to Charlotte, with her garish colors and talk of flipping houses. She'll strip the place. Tear down Grandfather's office and throw out all of his books. Install a pool in the rose garden.

There'd been a time I wanted to burn the place to the ground.

And now I'm willing to marry my own assistant to get it. If Grandfather could see me now, I don't know if he'd laugh or curse me out for finding a loophole in his will.

He'd probably do both.

My mind runs through the list of women I'd been on dates with over the past six months. More than I'd ever dated before. More than I ever wanted to date again.

It had been moronic conversations about moronic subjects with women who barely knew me. Socialites and businesswomen and even a few models, all of whom agreed to dates after they heard my name. But pretending to be interested in anything long-term was beyond me.

So.

Miss Myers. Cecilia. With her prim blouses and her smart efficiency. Who had talked back when I made her the offer.

Who had come into this office and negotiated with me, standing her ground, even if I suspected she'd fold like a house of cards if I'd pushed.

She'd found a backbone beneath all that pale silk.

Far more annoying was the fact that I'd need to hire a new assistant, one who'd need training. Which meant I'd be operating without a limb for a few months.

A soft ding on my computer announces new events added to my schedule.

Wedding. 1 p.m. Office of the City Clerk. Attendees: Cecilia Myers (confirmed), Victor St. Clair (pending).

I tick the box to confirm my attendance. RSVPing to my own nuptials. It almost makes me smile.

Then my calendar pings again.

Pre-wedding dinner. 7 pm. Salt. Attendees: Cecilia Myers (confirmed), Victor St. Clair (pending).

I lift my phone and press the single digit that connects me to my assistant.

"Yes?"

"Come in here," I say.

The office door opens moments later and Miss Myers walks in. Her hair is in a low ponytail today. Gray pants and matching blazer. She looks like an assistant.

My fiancée, ladies and gentlemen.

"What do you need?"

"You scheduled a pre-wedding dinner," I say.

Her hands twist in front of her, but she meets my eyes. "We need to talk."

"About what? There's no agenda attached to this meeting."

"Not about business. About us. We're practically strangers."

I frown. "We're not."

"What's my first name?"

"Cecilia," I say. It feels odd on my tongue.

"Where do I live?"

"From the fifteenth onward, you'll be living on 5th Avenue. With me."

She shakes her head, and there's a fire in her eyes. It's the same one she'd showed when she negotiated with me. "I'm not marrying you like this. We need to sit down. Talk about the year ahead. About expectations and, and… rules. Limits. You can afford to take one night off work."

I lean back in my chair. Perhaps I can, if she'll show me more of this side of her. "Fine."

"Fine," she echoes. "There's nothing else?"

"No."

She nods and turns, and my eyes do something they've never done before. They trace the lines of her body and imagine it beneath the fabric. Does she have dimples at the base of her spine? Her pants are loose, but they stretch over a firm ass as she walks.

The door closes behind her and I stare at it for a few seconds. Miss Myers.

I must be losing my mind.

Salt is my standard restaurant for business meetings. The kind that are better had outside of office environments, where a glass of wine or four butters up clients, suppliers and everything in between.

I don't know whether it's funny or ironic that Cecilia booked Salt for our talk, but I'm tiring of answering emails on my phone while I wait for her.

"Another gin and tonic, sir?" the hostess asks.

"Yes."

She bats her eyelashes and takes my empty glass away.

I glance at my watch. She's seven minutes late.

And Miss Myers is never late.

I'm halfway through my second gin and tonic when she shows up, weaving her way through the tables with flushed cheeks.

Her hair is down.

For an entire year, I don't think it ever has been. It falls in curly sheets of mahogany around her face, framing pink cheeks and a soft mouth. She's wearing makeup, too. Has to be. Because she hadn't looked like this in the office.

I would have noticed.

"Sorry I'm late." She misses the waiter hurrying to pull out her chair and has a seat. She notices him a second later. "Oh no, did I beat you to it? I'm sorry."

"Not a problem, miss. Can I take your coat?"

"Yes, please, that would be lovely." She shrugs out of it, revealing a dark blue silk blouse. Several buttons are undone and I glimpse a sliver of a lace bra. "Thank you."

"Of course. I'll be right back with the menu."

She beams at him like he's discovered a cure for cancer. The smile disappears when she turns her focus on me. "I'm sorry. The subway stopped between two stations."

"You took the subway here."

"Yes, it's a quaint little invention." But then she remembers herself, and her brief flash of humor fades. "I don't think I've ever been to Salt. I've just scheduled it for you. You know, I've spoken to the maître d' a hundred times and not once did I picture him having a moustache like that."

My lips turn down. "Miss Myers, you said you wanted us to talk."

"So I did," she says, opening the menu. Her hands grip it tight. "I've always wanted to try the mushroom ravioli they have here. You wouldn't know how it is, of course. You don't like mushrooms."

I stare at her for a long moment before Irving's words ring back in my head. The wedding is in two days. I need her to say yes, which means I can't simply ask her why she wanted to meet tonight. I need to woo her.

We're still negotiating.

"That's right," I say. "I've never been able to get over the taste of earth."

Her eyes meet mine over the edge of her menu. "Let me guess. You're going to have the beef wellington with a glass of the 2006 Merlot?"

"Yes. You know that, yet you accuse us of being strangers?"

"I know some of your likes and dislikes," she says. "Doesn't mean we genuinely know each other."

"Fair enough. Well, tonight I'm an open book. What do you want to know?"

She lowers her menu. "You're an open book."

"Sure."

"You're the furthest thing from an open book I've ever seen."

I run a hand through my hair. "Well, I'll make an attempt. If you need this to feel confident going forward, then I'll do it."

"To feel confident?"

"Yes. With the marriage."

"The marriage," she murmurs. "Well, I do have some questions. What about—oh. Hello."

The waiter gives us an apologetic smile and asks for our orders. I give him both of ours, asking for a bottle of the 2006 Merlot.

We'll need more than just a glass for this.

"Your question," I prompt her.

Cecilia's cheeks heat up. They do that often, it seems. Another thing I hadn't noticed. "You're very private, but now you want us to live together. How is that going to work?"

I resist the urge to sigh. "Like I said, you'll have your space and I'll have mine. The apartment is big enough for both of us. It'll be fine."

It'll have to be, because I don't have a choice. Besides, all we need is that she's officially registered at my address. I can always sleep at a hotel if it gets too much.

Exiled from my own apartment. Christ.

"Would I move my stuff in?"

"The things you need, yes. But the place is fully furnished. I'll pay for warehousing the rest of your stuff for the year."

Cecilia nods. Her hands curve around the stem of her wineglass. Slender, pale fingers and sheer nail polish. No rings on any of her fingers.

"How will we explain this?"

"Explain?"

"Yes, to people around us."

I shrug. "There's no one in my life who will ask questions. You can explain it however you like to yours."

Her gaze locks on mine, eyes widening. "Really?"

"Yes. The contract specifies nothing about secrecy. You can tell your friends it's a marriage of convenience, if you like. Doesn't bother me."

"Well, that's not… okay then. I guess I'll see when I get to that. It's not a simple thing to explain."

I nod, though it seems easy enough. Unorthodox, sure, but a business transaction after all.

"People at the company might gossip."

I shrug again. "Only if they find out. Besides, none of them will say anything to me."

"No. No, I suppose that's true." A half-smile plays at her lips.

It bothers me. "What do you mean by that?"

"Nothing," she says, shaking her head. "It's just… I didn't know you were aware of your reputation."

"My reputation?"

"Well… people are afraid of you."

I snort. "Only because I can have them fired."

"Yes," she says. "Only because of that little detail."

When the food arrives, my beef looks as good as it always

does. I'm here often enough that they don't have to ask for my preferences anymore.

"Fresh parmesan?" the waiter asks. Cecilia nods and we both watch as he grates a fresh block over her plate. They exchange smiles when he's done, like he's just climbed Mt Everest instead of doing his well-compensated job.

"Let me know if you need anything else," he tells her.

"I will. Thanks again."

"Of course." His gaze slides to me. "Enjoy your evening, sir."

I've been to Salt more times than I can count, and I've never seen this level of service from them. They're typically brisk. Businesslike. Not personable.

"He's nice," Cecilia says. She bends closer to her food and takes a deep, appreciative breath. A tendril of dark hair falls from behind her ear and curls at her neck. "You're missing out here, St. Clair. Mushroom or no mushroom, this pasta smells amazing."

I frown. "Sticking to what I enjoy is a solid strategy."

"Yes," she murmurs, "and God forbid you don't have a strategy when you eat."

There it is, the fire, and I stare at her while she cuts into her pasta. She'd said that people are afraid of me. Is she?

We eat in silence for a while, but then she straightens, eyes meeting mine. "So… what about other people?"

"Other people? The ones you wanted to tell?"

She turns her wineglass around by the stem. "No. I mean, I don't expect you to be celibate for a year. Are we both allowed to date? Your lawyer sent over the contract, but it didn't mention dating."

"Dating is allowed, for both of us. But I'd prefer it to happen outside of my apartment."

"Right, and the same would go for you?"

I have to agree to that. Fair is fair, after all. "Yes."

She nods, skewering a ravioli and lifting it to her lips.

They're glossy tonight, reflecting the single lit candle between us on the table.

Does she date?

A week ago I wouldn't have been able to answer that question. Now, with her in front of me in an half-buttoned blouse and glossed-up lips, I don't know. Not sure if I want to know, either.

"There's one thing I can't quite figure out."

I cut into my steak and swallow the comment that comes naturally. *Only one?*

"Why do you want your inheritance so badly? You're already wealthy," she says. "So why go through with this?"

Her words betray an ignorance of my world that would make another man smile. They just make me annoyed. Because on the surface of things, she's right.

There's being rich, and then there's wealth, and my grandfather had the latter. He'd kept the St. Clair family fortune intact over decades. The fortune my father had helped shepherd. The fortune I've heard the story behind over and over and over again for my entire life.

But I don't need it.

I can live a life better than most with what I have, what I've worked for. The fortune is hard to let go of, but not impossible.

"It's not just money," I say. "There's a house, too."

"A house?"

I reach for the collar of my shirt and undo the top button. "Yes. It's on Long Island."

Cecilia rests her chin in her hand, gaze on me. "You won't get it if you're not married?"

"Exactly. My grandfather had certain... ideas. I'm sure this is his way of ensuring they're followed, even from the grave."

Her voice lowers. "I'm guessing our contract wasn't a part of his plan."

"Probably not." I reach for my wineglass, watching the deep red swirl. "How were the mushrooms?"

"Earthy," she says, "and delicious."

"You dressed up for tonight." My eyes drift down, to where the tight skirt curves around her form in a way the straight pencil skirts never do at work.

She smoothes a hand down her blouse. "Oh. I'm going out after."

"You're going out. Where?"

"To a bar." Her cheeks are flushed with life again, eyes alight. "My best friend insisted on a bachelorette party."

I stare back at her, at this woman I've only ever seen as my assistant, with plump lips and long, wavy hair.

She'd accused us of being strangers.

Maybe we are.

5

CECILIA

One year after I started working for Victor St. Clair, I hand in my official letter of resignation. I also marry him.

So it doesn't feel quite like a victory when I reset the timer on my computer desktop to zero, starting the count for another year with him.

"You can still back out," Nadine murmurs by my side. She's been a rock over the past week, steady with advice and jokes and zaniness.

She thinks I've lost my mind.

She's also promised to be there with me every step of the way.

"I'm not planning to," I say. I'm wearing a dove-gray dress. White had felt wrong. Jeans had felt wronger still. So I'm in my gray office dress and my black work pumps at City Hall.

I'd always wanted to get married outdoors. Close to where I grew up, in the park. Next to the lake. When I was a child my mother and I often sat there and watched the swans, me reading and her meditating.

Somehow the contrast to today steadies me.

This isn't a wedding. It's a contract signing and a way to get what I need.

Nadine will put on her art show. I'll start my own company.

"If it's what you want, then you can do this. I know you can." Nadine stands on her tiptoes and rearranges my headband. "He's just a man, and he can't fire you anymore. Remember, he's the one who needs you."

"For a house," I say, and we both smile. The idea of Victor St. Clair subjecting himself to marriage to inherit a house feels ludicrous.

And steadying. It means that beneath his sharp words, he's human. Surely a true sociopath wouldn't care about a house, right?

Then again, I haven't seen it. Maybe it's the actual house F. Scott Fitzgerald lived in and he wants to convert it into a multi-million-dollar museum.

I shake my head. "Let's get out there. He's waiting."

My hands are sweating as Nadine and I leave the ladies' room. We walk down the empty and impersonal hallway to the room where they're waiting.

St. Clair turns at the sound of the door. He's in the same suit as always, and thick, dark-blond hair rises over his forehead.

He frowns when he sees me.

Had he been expecting white? Or that I'd magically transformed into one of the models he regularly dated?

Well, screw him. He needs something. I need something. This is a business deal, just like the ruthless ones he spent his entire life making. After two years doing the dirty work for Tristan Conway and Victor St. Clair, I've finally learned something.

It doesn't matter if it's ugly. What matters is that it gets done.

"This is my friend and witness, Nadine Willows."

St. Clair nods to Nadine and buttons his suit jacket. "This is Steven. He'll be our second witness."

The man to his right gives me a curt wave before putting

both of his hands behind his back again. They're standing over five feet apart.

So, not a friend, then.

A smiling, middle-aged man walks in, glasses perched on his nose. "The happy couple!" he says. "I'm honored to be here today."

I look from him to St. Clair's stoic face and laughter bubbles up in my throat. It's nervous and panicked and probably more than a little hysterical.

"You must officiate a lot of these?" Nadine asks. "Several a day?"

Our officiant laughs. "Yes. But I'm always honored. Ready to get started?"

I turn to St. Clair. His name is Victor, though I've never called him that. The man I've hated and cursed mentally for the past year. He's dictated my weeks and my weekends, my holidays and my vacation. Or lack thereof.

He gazes back at me, blue eyes reflecting the lighting overhead. Beautiful features on an otherwise relentlessly masculine face. Sharp jaw and straight nose.

There's steadiness in his eyes.

Not encouragement. Not kindness.

But steadiness, the kind I've learned to read over the past year. The one that means he's reliable in all of his self-serving, business-oriented glory. Once given, he doesn't break his word. I've seen him follow his agreements to the letter.

"Cecilia?" he asks.

The sound of my first name rings out between us, stretching taut in the silence of the dusty City Hall room.

I take a step forward. "Yes," I say. "We're ready."

There are some moments you'll remember forever. Signing my name next to Victor St. Clair's on the marriage license is one of them.

It might not be a traditional wedding. There are no speeches or supportive parents, no ushers, no flower girls, no wedding party. But there is the same one sentence I've heard over and over again.

And it falls over us like a scythe.

"I now pronounce you husband and wife."

The words ring in my head in the awkward silence that follows. Spin on repeat as St. Clair thanks the officiant, as Nadine makes small-talk with Steven.

Victor gives me a professional nod and reaches up to readjust the collar of his fitted shirt. "Well done."

"Um, thanks. You too."

He motions for the door and I follow him, walking out of the room where my fate has just been sealed. My head feels dizzy. Topsy-turvy. The deep-green carpet beneath my feet has probably been walked by thousands of couples before us. Had the brides been happy? Laughing and crying?

I wonder if any of the couples had known one another as little as Victor and I do.

If any of them had liked each other less.

"How are you feeling?" Nadine whispers.

I give her a smile. It feels wobbly.

Victor strides down the steps from City Hall with Steven beside him and I hurry to follow. Drizzle hangs in the air and New York is gray, the heavy clouds above multiplying in the glass panels of brutal skyscrapers.

It's the kind of day I long to be anywhere but here.

Nadine and I catch up to Victor by the curb. Steven walks briskly down the sidewalk. "He's going to get the car," St. Clair says.

"To get the car," I murmur. "Steven... Oh. He's Steven Daugherty. Your driver."

St. Clair nods, glancing up at the sky like he considers the rainy haze a personal affront.

Nadine clears her throat. "I'll give you two a minute. Congratulations, Victor."

He looks surprised, but then gives a single nod. I don't know if it's in thanks or acknowledgement.

We stand there in the drizzle. Husband and wife, after one of the shortest engagements in history.

"Well…" I say. "What happens now?"

"I have interviews lined up for your replacement."

I nod. That's a safe topic. "You can send the shortlist over to me, and I'll look them over for you. I know what you need."

His eyes slide to mine. "I will."

"Good."

"Steven will take you to my apartment to settle in. Have him drive any things you need from your old place. You have the numbers to the movers I used last. Fix everything and charge it to my account."

"Right. Thanks."

He nods again and just like that, I'm dismissed, another thing checked off his schedule. Get married at one, investor meeting at two.

He hails down a cab with a single raised arm. It stops in front of him and he looks at me over his shoulder.

Neither of us has words, it seems.

"Thank you," he says.

Our eyes hold for another long moment before he nods, like he's confirmed something, and disappears into the cab. It drives off and leaves me on the curb, my best friend a few feet away, beneath a New York sky that wants to evict us.

"Are you okay on your own?" Nadine asks. Her voice sounds like it's coming from far away, through a fog, but I nod.

"Sure. I've got… Steven."

"I can help you move tomorrow, I think."

"You've got work," I say. "Don't you dare take one of your precious vacation days for me."

"I can call in sick," she says. "I've been working on my fake sniffle."

"You're the worst actress in the world. No, go ahead. Thanks for being my witness."

She pulls me in for a hug and I wrap my arms around her tightly, with her deep-red peacoat and the scent of coconut from her hair. Normalcy in this sea of chaos.

"You're brave," she whispers.

"Or foolish," I whisper back. "I haven't decided yet."

"Both, Cece. You're both. Just like me."

I have to blink rapidly. "At least this will make for a great story one day," I say.

She nods. "We'll have to practice it a few times before we tell it around the dinner table with our real husbands."

"Do a few trial runs."

"Yes. We have to get the pitch just right."

I chuckle, and she gives me a broad, bright smile, the one that's Nadine to a T. All of her passionate, artistic self. "I should have just married you," I tell her.

"Still an option," she says. "Once you're divorced from St. Clair here, I'll swoop right in."

"I love you, you know."

Her eyes soften. "I know. Love you too, Cece. Now get in this car before you give your new husband's driver an aneurism, and call me later."

"I promise. Prepare yourself for fifteen pictures of his apartment."

"You mean a FaceTime video tour, right?"

"Sorry. Yes."

I get into the dark, leather interior of St. Clair's private car. Steven says something from the front, but I don't catch it, turning to wave to Nadine. She gives me a single wave back, her hair drawing up tight from the drizzle, as we're already halfway down the street. City Hall looms large behind her.

Now it'll always be the place I got married for the first time.

"I'm sorry," I say to Steven. "I didn't catch that. What did you say?"

"Please fasten your seat belt, Mrs. St. Clair."

Mrs. St. Clair. That's me now.

I'm Mrs. St. Clair.

My hands shake as I do what he says, so I lock them tight together on my lap. He doesn't say another thing to me during the drive to Victor's apartment on the Upper East Side. It's good, because with my spiraling thoughts, I don't know if I'd be able to respond.

The address is familiar. I've ordered a hundred airport pickups and taxi appointments for St. Clair from his home. I've sent home his dry-cleaning, I've coordinated with his housekeeper. I've calculated the time it would take him to walk to different restaurants to cut down on wasted time, as he liked to call it.

Also known as any time he couldn't be productive.

My new husband isn't human. But then, I'd known that for a long time.

I'd just never thought I'd get to see it up-close and personal.

Steven leads me past a stone-faced doorman and through a grand lobby. He hands me a keycard.

"Floor eighteen," he says. "The code is eight, five, five, eight, three."

"Thank you."

"I'll be on standby for you all afternoon. Just call when you want me to drive you to your old apartment." Steven inclines his head and heads off with brisk steps.

"Thank you!" I call. "For everything!"

He falters and then raises a gloved hand. "Of course, ma'am."

I manage to operate the fancy elevator. I even manage to walk down the single hallway on the eighteenth floor and stop in front of a black door. No keyhole. Just a keycard reader, a fingerprint scanner, and a keypad.

Eight. Five. Five. Eight. Three.

The door unlocks with a soft click and I push it open, walking toward my fate.

6

CECILIA

Victor St. Clair's apartment is a testament to quality.

The polished hardwood floors, the thick wool of the living-room rug, the giant cloud couch built around a sixty-five-inch TV. There are no exposed cables. No knickknacks spread on random surfaces. No fridge magnets, no smudgy handprints on the mirrors, and definitely no plants on the windowsills.

It's a space to look at.

Not live in.

I walk around the place on tiptoes, as if he's waiting around a corner. He's not. I know he's not. But his presence is everywhere, lingering on the smooth surfaces and polished edges.

It feels like walking through a museum. The only thing missing are the bored attendants, sitting on fold-up chairs in the corners, ready to tell you off for taking a photograph. I peek into a room that looks like a near replica of his office at work. Similar desk. Similar chair. I wonder if he has an assistant who looks like me hiding somewhere, ready to pop out and do his bidding.

Maybe she did the smart thing and turned down his proposal.

The interconnecting rooms span an apartment of at least two thousand square feet. Or so I think, until I see the staircase.

I'm afraid to snoop.

I'm also too curious not to.

Besides, I have to find the guest bedroom that'll be my home for the next year.

A year.

I can't let myself dwell on that. A year is too long. I'll take this in months, instead. Weeks, perhaps. Days, most likely.

The staircase leads to a second story with a long, elegant hallway. On one end is a half-open door. The other is closed.

I inch toward the half-open one and peer inside.

Bingo. The bedroom is big, but not master-bedroom big. A queen-sized bed in the center with a beige bedspread that looks ironed and pressed.

I run my hand over a desk in the corner. It looks like a hotel room. Does he have a lot of guests over?

Is this where the women he dates have to sleep? Booted out of his bedroom when he's finished, relegated down the corridor to this place?

The windows open up to a view of the park and I sit down on the bed, looking out at the fall foliage, the bright oranges, reds and yellows.

It feels like taking a deep breath.

Drinking a cool glass of water.

I can live with this view. I can spend my time in this room, working at the desk that feels like it belongs in a hotel, sleeping in the large bed, showering in the giant adjoining bathroom. I can spend my weekends at Nadine's or party with our friends. And during the days, I'll work on my start-up. My very own firm, selling virtual assistant hours to entrepreneurs.

A voice echoes below.

I freeze, listening. Are those footsteps? Why is this place

so big? I walk softly over to the open door, and the voice rings out again.

"Miss Myers?"

It's not Victor's.

I head downstairs and come face-to-face with a woman in her mid-fifties. She's dressed smartly in all black, her blonde hair in a short perm.

She smiles when she sees me. "There you are. I hope I didn't wake you from an afternoon nap?"

"No, not at all. Bonnie?"

"That's it. It's a pleasure to finally meet you, Cecilia."

I shake her hand. "Likewise. From all of our emails, it feels like I know you already!"

"Well, you do! It's a good thing he's had the two of us to organize his life for him. You've been one of his best assistants, you know."

"Oh, thank you."

"I'm sorry I wasn't here when you arrived," Bonnie says. "The ceremony was quicker than I expected. I trust it went well?"

"Uh, yes. It did."

"It's okay if it was difficult," she says. Her smile is professional, but there's genuine kindness in her eyes. "I work for St. Clair, and I'm loyal to him, which means I'm loyal to you too now. But that also means I won't inform on the two of you to each other."

I sink down on one of the kitchen chairs. My limbs feel heavy, too much adrenaline and excitement for one day. "You know why we married, then. I wasn't sure what he'd told you."

"I do. Would you like some tea?"

"Yes, please."

"Earl Grey, or herbal?"

"Earl Grey, please."

She nods and I watch her move around the pristine

kitchen, opening drawers without knobs. "He informed both me and Steven," she says.

"Right. And his lawyers."

She nods.

"I'm sorry, I'm sure what you must think of me. I promise you I'm not— "

Bonnie holds up a hand. "I don't think anything, dear. I think you're a talented assistant, the best he's ever had. I think the both of you found yourself in a position to help one another. It's only fair that you get compensated for that. God knows he's not the easiest to work with, and now you're married to him! As far as I'm concerned, you deserve every penny."

The frankness stops me dead, and then I burst out laughing. Bonnie joins in. "I can't tell that to *him*, though," she stage-whispers, a fond smile on her face.

I smile at her. "What would he do without us, do you think?"

"Without us keeping his world in order?"

"Yes."

"His blood pressure would spike," she says, pouring piping hot water into a mug. Steam curls in the air above it. "No, I don't think he could survive without us."

I accept the warm mug from her. "Thank you."

"I've been wanting to meet you for a long time," she says. "I never imagined it would be under these circumstances."

"No, I didn't either. But I've wanted to meet you too."

"Thanks for emailing me about the switch from still to sparkling water the other month." She moves to the refrigerator and opens it with a flourish. "I make sure we're always fully stocked when he wants it."

The refrigerator is a piece of art. Everything is stacked, labeled, organized. It belongs on a curated Instagram feed. It belongs in a frame.

"Bonnie," I say.

"Yes?"

"You're a magician."

She laughs, shutting the stainless-steel door. "No," she says. "I'm the domestic version of you."

"Well, I have to thank you, too, for emailing me about Reubens. I added that to his lunch rotation at work."

"Did he like that?"

"Yes."

"Good. I've been trying to get him to eat more variety for years. I cooked a dish with quinoa two weeks ago, and well..." Bonnie gives me a half-smile. "I'm not doing that again."

I laugh, because it's all too easy to imagine. "I don't think he has any idea how much we smooth his way."

"I think he does, but he doesn't know how to acknowledge it." Bonnie has a seat opposite me and reaches for the breast pocket of her black shirt, pulling out a notepad and a pen. "Now, I want to know what you'd like to make the guest room on the second floor feel more like your home. Steven and I are here to help. Do you want us to come with you and pack?"

Steven and Bonnie are in a league of their own. Bonnie chats. Steven is stone-faced. But between the three of us, we pack up most of my things in cardboard boxes that Steven had stocked inside the trunk of Victor's car.

It's clear that he only hires the best, and with the two of them, he's found the cream of the crop.

"This is lovely china," Bonnie says as she packs the vintage green set my mother had bought for me at an antique sale. It's going in the boxes for storage.

Storage, because I won't need most of this for an entire year.

I'm trying to think of it as a gap year. A fun, experimental year, as I fold linens I won't need and decide which books I won't read for the coming year. Like going to camp. A camp led by an asshole with a personality disorder, but a camp nonetheless. Business camp. I'll finally get my start-up off the ground.

"The men are here from the moving company," Steven says. He's rolled up his sleeves, but otherwise he looks as emotionless as usual. I wonder if Victor is his role model.

"Excellent," Bonnie says. "Should we start with the couch?"

I nod. "Yes, sure. Do you need help? Oh. No, okay then."

Steven bends and lifts at the same time as a mover walks in, bearded and with two other men to help him.

It takes them fifteen minutes to have all my furniture out of the studio and inside a moving van. It takes Bonnie and me half an hour to pack the rest, the things I'm bringing to Victor's apartment.

And just like that, my old life is sealed up, all in one day.

"Please let me buy you guys pizza," I tell both of them in the car. "You took time out of your day to help me. Please."

Steven shakes his head and Bonnie's voice is firm. "Absolutely not. We're working, dear."

"Even so? I can't tempt you with a slice of pepperoni?"

She chuckles. "No. Not unless you'd rather eat that for dinner instead of the food I've prepared at home, in which case I'll gladly order you pizza. Just let me know if there's a restaurant you prefer."

I sink down in my seat. There's so much here I haven't considered. That they're staff. That I'm... not, not anymore. I'm their employer's wife.

I can't even think that thought.

"We'll eat at St. Clair's," I say.

Steven drops us off outside the apartment building that is now my home. He idles, turning around to look at me. "I'm heading to the storage facility to see that everything's gone all right with your delivery. Would you like me to take photos of the unit they've assigned you to while I'm there, Mrs. St. Clair?"

I blink at him. "Um. Yes, please. I appreciate it. But I'm not Mrs. St. Clair. Please call me Cecilia."

He gives a hesitant nod that makes it clear he'll do no such thing.

I spend the rest of the afternoon unpacking in my bedroom. Putting my toothbrush in the marble en-suite and hanging up my clothes in the giant closet. My eyes keep flickering to the view of Central Park from this angle, the forest of trees with their leaves ablaze in color. I can't believe this is my view now. From my bedroom. In my boss's apartment.

It's late when I venture downstairs. Bonnie is cooking, a black apron around her waist. She smiles when she sees me. "Is it feeling more like a home up there?"

I nod, sitting down at the kitchen counter. "Yes. This smells amazing. What are you making?"

"Lobster ravioli."

"*Lobster* ravioli?"

"Yes. It's one of St. Clair's favorites."

I take another deep breath of the intoxicating scent and glance at my watch. He never leaves the office before seven. "I can't wait."

In truth, I have no idea how I'll react when he comes home.

Home. My husband. Victor St. Clair.

I rest my head in my hands, the full weight of the day crashing down on me like a tidal wave. I've signed a contract. I've gotten married. And I've moved, sitting in an apartment that is nothing like me, so far removed from everything I've ever known.

And the man I'm waiting for to come home is the man I despised just two weeks ago. The man who is now single-handedly bankrolling my new start-up and launching my best friend's art career.

"I imagine it's a lot," Bonnie says softly.

I nod, unable to speak.

"I'll make sure you get pepperoni pizza for lunch tomorrow."

I give a weak laugh. "Thank you."

"Of course. For what it's worth, I've known St. Clair for years. He'll stay true to his word. And if he doesn't," she says, raising her spatula in warning, "he can kiss his homemade lobster ravioli goodbye. I'm not opposed to burning them if he upsets you in any way."

I laugh. "You know, I sometimes gave him decaf coffee when he annoyed me at work. He didn't notice. It was my small act of rebellion."

Bonnie's eyes widen, and then she laughs too. "Decaf?"

"Yes. Tiny, perhaps, but I know he'd have hated it if he knew."

She laughs again and my own laughter grows, half-hysterical and half-sane.

The front door slams shut.

I try to stop giggling, but I'm still wheezing when footsteps sound in the hall. They're familiar. I should know, having spent a year ruled by their comings and goings down the office corridor.

Victor St. Clair stops in the vaulted doorframe of his kitchen. He looks between me, still giggling, to where Bonnie is smiling by the stove. Suspicion blooms in his eyes.

"Welcome home!" I say. It's over the top, but what's the worst thing he can do? Fire me?

He steps into the kitchen and puts his briefcase on the counter. "Hello, Cecilia."

He's still in the fitted, navy suit from our ceremony, but his dark blond hair isn't in its usual neat waves. It's tousled, like he's run his hand through it repeatedly. It's been a stressful afternoon for him, then.

I don't know if that makes me feel better or worse, that marrying me wasn't stress inducing for him but work was.

"I moved into the guest room upstairs," I say.

He nods, eyes on the papers he's flipping through. "Right."

"Steven and Bonnie were invaluable. They helped me pack up my old apartment, and Steven drove all my stuff to the storage unit. I couldn't have done it without them."

Victor makes a humming noise. "Good."

"Yes. How was the rest of your workday?"

Blue eyes land on me. "It was a disaster. I had to spend over two hours on the assistant candidates HR prepared."

"Oh," I say. That explains the hair.

"I have a shortlist of three who might be passable." He slides a document over the marble counter. "Call them tomorrow for me. You'll be able to tell which one is best."

I look down at the three unassuming names and phone numbers on the piece of paper. You might leave St. Clair's employ, but you're never really out, it seems. I flip through the resumes of three people who have no idea what they're in for.

"I wired the money to your bank account, as per the contract. It should be there tomorrow."

"Uh, yeah. Thank you."

Victor shuts the briefcase with a loud snap and turns to the stove. "Lobster ravioli?"

"Yes. Ready in five," Bonnie says.

This is my time.

I clear my throat and Victor turns back to me. I have no idea what he thinks of me sitting here, in his kitchen, in his house. Perhaps he expects me to live in my room and stay out of the communal areas.

"Yes?" he prompts.

"I'd like us to schedule a meeting about my start-up. I want to present what I have and get your input."

His mouth tightens. "You should have everything in order before we meet. Treat it like I'm a true potential investor."

"I know. I have most of it in order."

"I find that hard to believe," he says. "When would you

have had time to work on it? While you were my assistant? I doubt it."

It takes effort not to grit my teeth, not to back down. "So you were aware of all the late nights and weekends I worked. I wasn't sure."

"I paid you to be available."

"On Christmas? On my birthday?"

His eyes narrow. "Yes."

"Well, I did have time. Not much. But I carved it out, and I'm ready to present it to you. Next week?"

"I'd ask you to check with my assistant, but I don't currently have one."

"No," I say. "You married your last one."

Victor slides his briefcase off the counter, eyes locked on mine. They burn again. Like they did in his office when he first made me the offer. Like they did in the restaurant when he took in my outfit.

"Call the shortlisted candidates tomorrow," he says.

"If you schedule a meeting for us next week," I say.

"Fine."

"Great."

Keeping his eyes on mine, he speaks to Bonnie over his shoulder. "I'll eat in my office. I have work to catch up on."

"Of course, sir."

He gives me a farewell nod, and I return it, like two knights just finished with their duel. Then he walks out of his kitchen and disappears down the hall toward the home office I'd glimpsed earlier today.

I sag against the kitchen counter. Confronting Victor St. Clair is becoming a hobby, and I don't know if it's one I enjoy.

Bonnie sets down a plate in front of me and the scent of fresh pasta and lobster washes over me. My prize and my reward.

"Good on you," Bonnie says.

"Will you eat with me?"

She glances down the hall, weighing her options. Then she nods and grabs a plate of her own. "Of course, dear."

And that's how I spend the night of my wedding. Eating delicious, expensive pasta with Victor St. Clair's housekeeper, adrenaline leaking out of me with every bite, as my new husband works in his office.

7

CECILIA

Victor and I find a routine in the coming days. It's as beautiful as it is simple. It's avoidance.

He gets up earlier than me. I hear him in the mornings, lying in my too-big, too-soft bed, listening to his feet in the hallway that connects our two bedrooms. They always disappear down the staircase.

He starts off by going to his home gym. Either he works out alone or has one of his twice-a-week sessions with a personal trainer. I know, because I'd scheduled and paid the appointments.

Forty-five minutes later on the dot, I hear him return up the stairs and the door to his bedroom shuts. Showering, I suppose.

It's odd how I know a person's life so intimately when I know so little about the person himself.

Victor is gone every day, from seven in the morning to eight or nine in the evening. When he returns, he heads straight to his office, eating his dinner at his desk. I want to ask Bonnie if he started with the dinner-at-his-desk routine when I arrived, but I don't dare. I don't know what I'd do with that information. Be pleased? Offended?

The apartment is most always empty when I start my day,

and it is now too. I've explored more in the days since I arrived. I even went so far as to lift one of the dumbbells in his home gym and nearly dropped it on my foot.

There is personality in this space. It's just hidden well. Like the bottles of wine in the wine cooler. The books scattered around the living room. None of them are fictional. They're all biographies of great men and women of ages past, or books written by contemporary business leaders. Books he reads.

Today, I spend the morning working on my business proposal for Victor, interrupted sporadically by texts from Nadine.

Some are more welcome than others.

Nadine: Your mother will come to town at some point, you know.

Cecilia: I know.

Nadine: You know she's my favorite person.

Cecilia: Ouch. You're banned from getting pickles off my burgers.

Nadine: That's a disproportionate response. I know you'd never keep me from pickles. Aaaaanyway, what are we going to tell her about you and your new HUSBAND?

I smile at my phone. Thank God for Nadine and her use of the word *we*. She doesn't know about my intentions to use the money yet, or about Victor's patronage of her art gallery.

Cecilia: I have absolutely no idea what I'm going to tell her. She'll freak out. I'll have to prepare a list of crazy things she's done herself.

Nadine: Good one. Nothing says don't-care-about-me-marrying-my-boss like pointing out the one time she parked outside of a fire department.

Cecilia: Deflect, deflect, deflect. I learned it from the best!

Nadine: I don't know if you're referring to me or your mother, but… yes. Good strategy. I'll be there with you, you know. If you want me there.

Cecilia: I always want you with me.

Nadine: You're never getting rid of me!

Nadine: I should be free on Friday. Can I come over and see Mr. Bosshole's apartment then? Pleeease? I need to know you're not his captive. Is he monitoring your texts? Tell me the exact color dress you wore to our junior prom. If it's correct, I know you're safe.

Cecilia: Friday's perfect! Mustard. It was an awful look. Thank you for making me relive it.

Nadine: You looked cute.

Cecilia: Liar.

After making myself lunch from the well-stocked fridge, I go out for a run. It takes me four-point-five seconds to make it to Central Park. It's just across the street, and then I'm there, pounding on pavement under fall foliage. Dry leaves crunch beneath my feet and I breathe in deeply.

I got this. I just have to keep my eye on the prize. A year living in this place, barely ever seeing Victor, with time to spend every single day working on my business. He gave me the opportunity of a lifetime when he proposed, and I'm going for it. Accept the open door. It's what he would have done.

I return, sweaty and breathless, to see Steven walking through the lobby. He's carrying a giant blue package, complete with a dainty white ribbon. His face is a mask of concentration.

I hurry across the marble floor. "Do you need help?"

He shakes his head, but when he tries to hit the elevator button with his elbow, the package wobbles.

I press it. "Let me. Are we going up to Victor's apartment?"

"Yes. Thank you, Mrs. St. Clair."

"Call me Cecilia, please." It's difficult to see him over the giant box, but not impossible. I meet cautious brown eyes. "How old are you, Steven?"

"I'm twenty-three, Mrs... ma'am."

"How long have your worked for Victor?"

"Two years." He looks from me to the gilded walls of the elevator, like he's not sure we're allowed to talk.

"Do you enjoy your job?"

His eyes turn suspicious. "I do, ma'am."

The elevator door opens and I hurry on ahead, using my keycard to open the front door. "That thing looks heavy, too. Are you sure you're okay?"

"Yes," he says, but he grunts as he hoists it up and steps through the front door.

The hallway is filled with presents.

They make an obstacle course on the floor. Every size and shape, some wrapped, some not. The explosion of gifts stretches all the way into the living room. The coffee table is filled with so many flower bouquets it looks like a garden patch.

"What's this?"

Steven sets the box down. "Wedding gifts."

"*Wedding* gifts?"

Bonnie answers, emerging from the kitchen with a clipboard in hand. "Welcome home!"

"Um, thank you." I toe off my dirty running shoes and run a hand over a silver packet. "All these arrived today?"

"Yes. There's been a steady stream." She taps her pen against the clipboard. "I've started making a list of all the senders. I took the liberty to order a stack of thank-you cards that will be here tomorrow, and I'm compiling all the senders' addresses."

"The senders? Who sent these?"

"Oh, a ton of people. I'll run through the list with you in a second. Steven?"

"Yes?"

"Will you please go down and get the latest bouquets that arrived?"

His shoulders sag, but he nods and leaves the apartment without another word. I wonder how many times he's ridden the elevator today.

I lift a small, white gift box with a gauzy bow and turn it over in my hands. In my old workout leggings and messy ponytail, I feel like an ogre next to this pristine display of wealth. "There's no name on this one."

"Hmm? Yes. Some have put their cards inside the present, rather than on the outside." She shakes her head. "Understandable, for privacy reasons, but it doesn't make it easy for us."

There's a giant heart of roses. As in, real cropped roses arranged in a cardboard heart, colors of pink and purple and white. I lift the attached note.

Mr. and Mrs. Victor St. Clair,

Congratulations on your wedding! We hope you're both taking the time off for a much-deserved honeymoon.

The card is signed by a bank. Not a person. A bank.

I lower it. "Bonnie."

"Yes?"

"A bank sent us flowers?"

She nods. "Your marriage got out, I'm afraid. It's public record, and there are a lot of people who want to be on Mr. St. Clair's good side."

"They're sending us gifts as business investments?"

"Some, yes. Some are by St. Clair's family friends."

"Family friends," I murmur.

Bonnie unfolds a large paper bag and places it between us. "Would you like to start unboxing, dear?"

My eyes glaze over as I look at the sheer number of deliveries. Some are stacked five high. "I'm not sure Victor would like that."

"I've checked in with him," Bonnie says, handing me a pair of scissors. "He wants them taken care of."

I reach for a black and white packet. "Well, in that case…"

Bonnie is an organizational wizard, and I love efficiency. It takes us five minutes to work out a flawless system.

Unbox the gift. Add the gift-giver's name to her list. Take a picture of the gift for our records. Recycle the wrapping paper.

Or, in my case, save the really beautiful bows and ribbons in a separate box. Bonnie smiles when she sees me do it.

"For future gift-wrapping," I say.

"I do the same thing at home."

I lift the hand-blown glass vase I've just unwrapped and turn it around.

"Wow," Bonnie says.

"Yes. Is it just me, or does it look like…?"

"It does. Unfortunately, it really does."

"Who sent us a phallic-shaped vase?"

She laughs, reaching for the packaging I discarded. "One of his business partners. Carter Kingsley. What are you going to do with that?"

I look around the sparse, modern hallway. There's nothing

on the console table except a round mirror, braced against the wall. It's clearly a design mishap.

"Here," I say, placing it on the table. "This spot is screaming for some love."

Bonnie's lips twitch. "Prime placement."

"Yes. It's the pride and joy of our home."

"Where all guests can see it."

"We should include that in our thank-you note," I say. "Let them know we're proudly displaying it."

Bonnie laughs again. "I'm so glad he chose you to marry. I'd be doing this with anyone he picked, of course, but I don't think I'd have this much fun with anyone else."

My chest tightens. "Thank you. You've been so welcoming, you know. So helpful. Thank you for making this easier."

She smiles. "Well, I can only imagine all of this is overwhelming. I'm not one to speak ill of anyone. But I think we both know where St. Clair's flaws lie, and well... it can't be easy."

"That was a great way of putting it." I reach for a box with a familiar logo on the side. It's one I've seen in high-end catalogues all my life and never once come face-to-face with. "Have you noticed how many of these cards are addressed to the happy couple or to Mr. and Mrs. St. Clair? I don't think they know my name."

"I think many of them," Bonnie says, "are shocked he married at all."

"That was my reaction when he asked me. 'You? Getting married?'"

She shakes her head. "That was probably his own as well."

I unwrap the Hermès leather wallet, embossed with the designer label and the St. Clair name. The kind of money these things must cost...

"The Winthorpes sent this over," I murmur. The family is legendary in this city.

Bonnie nods. "They were good friends with St. Clair's parents."

I turn the wallet over. Wondering if I should or shouldn't pry, and knowing which instinct will win. Best to give in straight away. "His parents aren't around, I've gathered."

"They passed a long time ago."

I nod. "Well, it's awfully kind of them to send him this, then."

"You," Bonnie corrects. "These are all gifts to both of you. They're hoping, I think, that he'll become someone like his grandfather or his parents were. Social, affable. The St. Clair name used to be well-known in these circles."

I glance at the notecard and the name Winthorpe. "He won't like all this."

"No, I don't think he will."

"Maybe seeing the phallic-shaped vase will cheer him up."

Bonnie chuckles and hands me a baby-blue box to unbox. "Somehow, I doubt that too."

I unwrap the Tiffany box with careful hands, but what's waiting for me inside isn't delicate in the least. It's a saber. I grip the heavy handle and pull the gleaming blade out, brandishing it.

"Someone sent us a gazillion-dollar sword."

Bonnie looks over. "Ah. A champagne saber. The household already has two of those."

"I'm not surprised." I lift it up, still sitting cross-legged in the hallway in my workout clothes. *"En garde!* Is there no one here to challenge me?"

The front door swings open to reveal Victor. His suit is dark with raindrops, hair tousled and damp. He looks from me to the saber, eyes narrowing.

"We're taking care of our wedding gifts," I say. I lower the saber, but with no fancy sheath at hand, I tuck it safely back in the blue Tiffany box.

"I can see that," he says. "All of this arrived today?"

"Yes. There should be more incoming tomorrow," Bonnie says. She gets up and carries the kitchen chair back, disappearing down the hallway.

Victor steps closer and a wet, Italian leather shoe appears next to my legging-clad knee. "Well," he says. "The assistant you recommended was shit."

I look up at him. He looks enormous from this angle. Twenty feet tall, at least. And both Bonnie and Steven have left me alone and at his mercy.

"Sarah is not shit," I say. "She came highly recommended and has the perfect temperament for the job."

"She didn't pick things up quickly enough."

"No, because she's still learning. I'd been working with Mr. Conway for a year when you took over as CEO, so you didn't have to deal with that. She's had three days."

He frowns down at me. "Well, I told her to pack her things. She isn't likely to come back."

"No, I guess not. Does that mean you're calling the second candidate on my recommended list?"

"Yes. Brian."

"Brad."

"Right." He steps past me and disappears into the kitchen without another word, and so I reach for another present. I've just snapped a picture of it when Victor appears again.

He has a beer in hand and the rained-on suit jacket is gone. In its place is another of his crisp, white shirts. He starts to roll up a sleeve, inch by inch. "She didn't color-code my calendar the way you did."

"Sarah?"

"Miss Fleming, yes."

"Well, and I hate to point this out again, she *had* only been there for three days."

"I need you to train the next assistant." He takes a swig of his beer, a furrow in his brow. "I've been getting calls of congratulations all day with no one to screen them. I don't know how the hell our marriage got out."

"Well, don't look at me. I didn't call the tabloids."

"I didn't think you did." He leans against the wall and looks from me to the assortments of goods spread out around us.

I clear my throat. "Well, you're just in time to see me open our final gift."

"Because that will make my day better." He bends and grabs a card lying on top of a cashmere blanket. His face harden as he reads. "I haven't spoken to these people in a decade."

"Well, that's nice," I say. "That they'd send something."

"Sure. Not like they're kissing ass or anything."

"There might have been some of that. Your bank sent us flowers."

Victor snorts, taking another sip of his beer. "Have your pick of this crap."

"Are you sure you don't want another champagne saber for your collection?"

"I'm sure." His gaze drops to the gift in my hand. Right, I'm meant to open it. I undo the ribbon and carefully lift the lid, unwrapping layers of silk paper. At its heart is an envelope and scrawled on the front is *Mr. and Mrs. St. Clair*.

"Who's it from?" Victor asks.

"I don't know. Who sends a wrapped envelope?" I open it and pull out a thick card with the same scrawled writing. The letterhead makes my throat close.

"It's from Acture Capital."

Victor groans. "Read it."

"Victor. We were both pleased and surprised to hear the news. Congratulations are in order, it seems. To celebrate, you're both welcome to dinner on Saturday the twenty-fourth at the Conways'."

"Who signed it?"

"All three," I whisper. "Tristan Conway, Anthony Winter, and Carter Kingsley."

The partners in his venture capitalist firm, and one of

them used to be my boss. I'd worked side by side with Tristan, organizing his inbox, his work schedule, his life.

And now I'm invited to dinner at his place.

"Damn," Victor mutters. "I thought this would be a quiet, private thing. I see now that it's not."

"No," I say. "Doesn't seem like it."

He runs a hand over his jawline. The rain in his hair has started to dry, leaving it a tousled, half-curled, dark blond mess. It's a side of him I've never seen at work. Pissed off, sure. Aggravated, often. But not looking at me with calculation, the sleeves of his shirt rolled up to display muscular forearms.

"We can go," he says. "It'll get them off my back, answer some questions, and we won't interact with them and their girlfriends again."

"You want me to come," I say. "To meet your co-founders?"

He nods. "Yes. People know. We're going to have to own it, even if it's not in a big way. You want me to frequent an art gallery, right?"

"Right."

"Well, that'll go over better if we're seen as a couple. You love the art, I'll buy a ton of it to please you."

"Pretend to be a couple," I murmur. "Will Tristan Conway be there? At the dinner?"

His eyes narrow. "Yes. It'll be at his place."

I swallow, meeting the unforgiving gaze. For so long, what I'd wanted was to be brave, to dare, just like these men did. To go after my dreams of running my own company. I've given up ever earning Victor St. Clair's respect.

But I didn't want Tristan Conway to ask me why I'd married his successor and have no answer.

"Will you tell them?" I ask. "About the reason why we married?"

"No. I don't want anyone to know about that apart from us and the staff."

His voice doesn't broker questions. But I'm already sitting on the floor in my old sweaty gym clothes, and he's still here, leaning against the wall like we're hanging out. Any dignity I had is gone.

"How come?" I ask.

He looks from me to the line of gifts that litter the floor, sweeping his gaze from one to the next. "I don't want anyone to know my grandfather wrote a clause like that into the will."

"Oh," I say. "I understand."

He clears his throat and pushes away from the wall. "Take what you want from all of this up to your room. Throw out the rest."

"I'll donate what we don't want," I say. "Bonnie and I are writing thank-you notes tomorrow. Do you want—"

"No. Sign them for me."

"All right."

"Will you come into the office? When Miss Fleming's replacement starts."

"You're asking me to train your new assistant? And attend a dinner with your co-founders, pretending I'm now your wife."

Ice-cold blue eyes meet mine. "You are now my wife."

"The point still stands, though. You're raising the requirements."

His eyes narrow. "Yes, I am."

"Then you're going to have to up your ante."

"Fine," he says. The word is spoken through clenched teeth. "I'll give you my entire Sunday to work on your start-up. Give me everything you have so far and I'll give you my thoughts."

"Thank you," I say. "That will be perfect."

He tosses back the rest of his beer and turns to the kitchen. "Wedding gifts," he mutters. Then his eyes snag on the console table. "Why the fuck is there a glass dick on my hallway table?"

8

VICTOR

The house is empty and quiet, just like it had been when its occupant was still alive. But it hadn't been this dark.

I look at the windows on the second story, and even up to the small, round one in the attic. All dark.

I spin the key around in my hand once, twice, before taking the steps up the old porch. The door creaks when it opens. I can't remember it ever doing that before. There'd been a time when Grandfather would call Stanley's name at the top of his lungs and the door'd be fixed in thirty minutes. Or, if Stanley had the day off, he'd march off to the gardener's shed himself to get the oil.

Now the house smells dusty and shut-in. The bank hasn't been here to keep the place clean and aired, and no wonder. Why would they?

I turn on the lights as I go, walking past the double-staircases in the hallway and into the dining room. The giant table is empty. We'd once been many people around it on the holidays, but when I lived here, there had been only me and him.

I make my way upstairs and pass the room that had been mine without looking inside. The door to his study is half-open, the way he liked to keep it. Half-open to let people know they could come in if they needed to talk to him. But half-shut to signal it would be preferable if they didn't.

That was one of the many business and life maxims he liked to spread around him, always told in the same crusty voice, damaged from a life of whiskey and smoke. He'd let those tidbits drop like jewels, expecting me to treasure them. To live by them.

I push the door open and turn on the lights.

His office looks as it did the day we read the will. The giant oak desk in the middle of the room with the leather inlay, the bookshelves that line the walls. Two large windows open up to the giant oak trees on the property, clothed now in darkness.

I run a hand over the desk's surface. The jade ashtray is empty. It would have had half-smoked cigars in it had he been here.

I look at the drawers in the desk. Eeny, meeny, miny, moe… I pull one open at random.

Papers are neatly stacked inside. His handwriting is unmistakable. Lists. Lists of everything, and for everything, as was his way.

The heading on the top one reads *Spring Plans*, and the first item on the list reads *Schedule regular lunches with Victor in the city*.

I shut the drawer again.

I might have gained the legal right to this house, but I can't sort through the belongings of a man who had been intensely private, his shadow moving over my shoulder.

I can't do it.

And I can't have anyone else doing it either.

I walk to the door, and from a habit that's nearly twenty years old, I look at the framed picture that hangs next to it. The only place in this house where my mother and father are present.

They're on either side of my brother and I. Smiles abound.

Phillip has his arm around my shoulders, and my stupid fucking grin is missing two front teeth. I look happy. I also look like a fool, unaware of the tragedy heading our way.

I've always hated that picture. Hated it for what it makes me feel. Hated it for being the only one of my family that my grandfather allowed in the house.

I shut the door to his office behind me. No need to keep it half-open anymore.

Steven is still in the car in the driveway, and he fires up the engine when he sees me. We're out of there without a single word spoken and the house on Granview disappears in the rearview mirror.

His house. My house.

A house with too many memories.

And a house that won't simply be blown out and torn down and transformed because my aunt wants to have an open-planned kitchen.

The house I'd married to get.

If someone had told me I'd go to such lengths just a year ago, I'd have laughed. I lean my head against the leather headrest and close my eyes.

Married to Miss Myers, who is more than meets the eye, it seems.

She's funny in a dry, careful way. From the looks of it she's charmed my housekeeper, a woman who'd been nothing but professional around me.

And she'd strode into my office today, dressed in the same gray pencil skirt and silk blouse combo that had been her armor, and told me she'd finished training my new assistant.

"That quickly?" I'd asked.

She'd nodded. "I've promised to be available on email for the coming two weeks if he has any questions, but I doubt he'll have many. I've left extensive written instructions."

"Excellent."

Cecilia had headed out of the office, heels clapping

sharply against the floor. But then she'd stopped and done something she never did as my assistant.

She'd turned around and given me an order.

"Be nicer to this one," she said. "Give him at least two weeks before you consider firing him. I won't train assistant after assistant because you can't be patient."

The fire I'd seen in her echoed what she'd shown me when we negotiated our marriage. The same one that had burned in her eyes when she sat in my hallway, hair curling at her temples from her workout, and told me I had to up my ante.

Marrying her had been a good decision. I liked being straight with what I needed. It was ten times better than what I'd attempted before, dates after dates with women I'd tried and failed to have any lasting interest in.

Cecilia had been surrounded by the sycophantic gifts we'd received. All from people who wanted things from me. Time. Money. Connections.

She'd worn leggings. They'd clung to shapely legs, ending just above bare ankles and sneaker socks.

I don't know why the image is burned into my mind. Miss Myers with her hair in a messy ponytail, her skin makeup free and cheeks flushed from her exercise. But it is.

And I can't seem to get it out.

Steven bids me a good night when he drops me off outside my apartment and I ride the elevator with rising anticipation. There's no telling what I'll come home to anymore. Her wielding a saber or baking in the kitchen. The silence that had once reigned supreme is gone.

Cecilia's in the kitchen when I get home. No Bonnie in sight, just her, her hair in that low bun at the base of her neck and an apron tied tight around her waist. My eyes drop down, but no leggings this time. Her legs are concealed in loose jeans. I don't know if I'm disappointed or relieved.

"Hello," she says.

"Hi," I say. It's the first time I've seen her cook here. It smells good. It smells like... "Are you making lobster ravioli?"

She turns from the stove. Tendrils of dark hair have escaped at her temples and they've curled in the heat. "Yes. I was wondering if we could have dinner."

"Have dinner," I say. "Together?"

She nods. "I got the recipe from Bonnie. I don't know if I'm really doing it justice, but it's an attempt."

She's cooking dinner for us. The two of us. "Why?"

Her lips curl into a half-smile. "We're supposed to play an actual couple tomorrow night with your business partners. If we're going to pull that off... well, I'm sorry to break it to you, but we need work."

"We need work?"

"Yes. If you look at the two of us interacting right now, not a single person would think we're married, not to mention in a relationship."

I pull out one of the kitchen chairs. "Right. And that's a problem."

"Well, it is if you want us to seem married. If you'd rather tell your business partners the truth, then that's all right with me."

I grit my teeth. "I'd rather not."

"Well, then have a seat, eat some ravioli, and let's talk about our great love story."

I stare at her for a long moment. She looks right back at me, spatula in hand. She looks like she did when I got home the other night, only it had been a champagne saber.

It would be easy to send an email to my business partners and rain-check. Avoid them altogether for as long as our marriage lasts.

Avoid having to do... *this*.

But something draws me to the kitchen table. The lobster ravioli, most likely. It smells good.

"Okay," I say. "Our great love story."

Cecilia smiles. It's not an expression I've seen often on her,

73

and never before the past few weeks. "Do you want parmesan on your pasta?"

"Yes."

It's been a long time since someone other than a housekeeper cooked for me. She sets the plate down in front of me and grabs one for herself. "How was work today?"

I narrow my eyes at her. "What is this, really? Are we playing house?"

Something flashes through her eyes, but I can't figure it out, because she looks down at her plate. "No. There's no one here to watch us, either. I just thought it would be easier to talk over food."

Easier. It would also be private. She didn't want Bonnie here to listen to the two of us manufacture a love story out of a year's working relationship.

I taste the food, spearing two of the lobster raviolis. The sauce is great. Almost exactly like Bonnie's.

"This is good," I tell her.

She looks up. "You think so?"

"Yes."

"It's a fairly easy recipe, but I might have aimed a bit high, going for your favorite right away."

"This is my favorite dish?"

"Bonnie told me it was."

"Hmm." I do like it, and I might have made a comment to that effect once. She must have picked up on it. Goes to show just how good the staff I've hired is.

"So," Cecilia says. Her voice takes on the serious note I'm used to, the one she always had when she briefed me on the week ahead, standing with her back straight in my office.

This is familiar territory. "Yes."

"We started dating in secret, because we didn't want the HR department to find out."

"I'm the CEO," I say. "What was HR going to do about it?"

Her eyes lock on mine with something like exasperation. "They wouldn't have fired you. They would have fired me."

"Not if I have anything to say about it. And I do."

"Okay, fine. Let's just say we didn't want HR to find out because of the hassle. Because of how people were going to talk."

I open my mouth to protest, but she cuts me off before I can speak. "Victor, we can say it was because of me. That I asked you not to make anything public."

"All right. Fine."

"The real problem is when they ask us about the wedding. Why the courthouse? Why so soon?" She drums her fingers against the table, a furrow in her brow. It looks almost... sweet.

"They might think you're pregnant," I say.

Her eyes widen. "Oh. Right. And I wanted to be married first."

"We can let them make their own assumptions, Cecilia."

"But there's no way I could be..." Her cheeks flush with faint color. The kind of rosiness she'd have if we attempted to get her pregnant. Thoughts I shouldn't be having dance in my mind, of her legs in the tights, of her hair mussed and loose. Of the flash of defiance I'd discovered in her.

What would taking her to bed be like?

"No," I say slowly. "There's no way that could be true."

"So the question remains. Why did we marry?"

"Because we're in love," I say. "I don't know. The same reason most people marry."

"I don't think they'll buy that. You and me, I mean. In love."

I roll my neck. "They don't have to buy it. They just have to accept the version we tell them."

She worries her lip between her teeth, her eyes examining as she runs them over me.

"What?"

"Nothing," she says. "It's just, I think you can get away

75

with being the quiet, silent type when you're in love. I know I can play my part. We probably don't need much to convince them it's real."

"I'll drape my arm over the back of your chair," I say. "They'll see it as a declaration of love."

Her lips twitch. "They've never seen you with one of your dates?"

"No." Much as they liked to, I'd never mixed in pleasure with my business. I played poker with my business partners sometimes. We attended functions together, the occasional event. But at the heart of it, I needed them because I could accomplish more with our pooled resources in Acture Capital than I could on my own.

And they did, on occasion, have solid input on business decisions.

Cecilia brightens. "Well, then. You don't have a precedent to live up to."

I cut my last ravioli. "That's it, then. Our story's straight."

There's something like laughter in her voice as she reaches for her phone. "Well," she says. "I prepared a list of questions."

I lean back in my chair with a groan, but she ignores it, just like she'd ignored it when she was my assistant. Eye on the prize, that's Cecilia Myers.

"Questions?"

"Yes. Where did you grow up?"

"They won't ask us any of this."

"No, but I'm expected to know it about my husband."

I shake my head. "Next question."

The furrow between her eyebrows is back. She scrolls on the phone, passing what must be dozens of questions along the same lines. "Fine," she says. "Where did you propose?"

"In my office. At work."

"That's the least romantic proposal story I've ever heard."

"It's also the truth," I say. "My business partners will expect it."

She chews on her bottom lip again. "You're right. It'll work in our favor, actually. To play on that."

I run a hand through my hair and consider the options before me. Going to this dinner won't be easy. It won't be fun. But it will help soften the image I know I have. An image I've cultivated and never minded before. It's also an image that, at times, makes me somewhat unapproachable.

I know. I'm a paragon of self-awareness.

Cecilia is the opposite. She makes housekeepers laugh and brandishes champagne sabers like swords.

"We got married at City Hall because we couldn't wait," she murmurs, looking down at her phone.

"We didn't want a big ceremony."

"That's right," she says. "We'd worked so closely before, too, in the office. We already knew each other very well."

"That was my argument, once," I say. "But someone said that we were strangers."

She looks up at me, a smile flashing across her lips. "Yes. Well, we were. Still are."

"We're not strangers, Cecilia."

"I don't know where you grew up," she counters. "You don't know anything about me."

"I know enough," I say, thinking of all the little things I'd noticed in the last couple of weeks. Her running habits, her sleeping patterns. The sweet chai tea she liked to drink in the evenings, the book she'd accidentally left on the kitchen counter when I came down one morning.

The curve of her waist. The silky sheath of her hair.

I know her better than probably anyone currently in my life.

The same emotion flashes through her eyes again. It looks like hurt, but that makes no sense. Odds are I'm misreading her.

Wouldn't be the first time.

"Okay," she murmurs. "All right. Well, in that case, I guess we don't need my questions. Just one more thing... rings."

"Rings," I repeat. "Fuck, you're right. I'd overlooked that."

Her small, patient smile tells me she hadn't. "Yes. Well, not having any was fine before, but if we're to act married in public..."

"We need them," I say. "I'll fix it."

"You will?"

"Yes."

Cecilia nods. "Perfect. Well then, I only have one final question."

"What's that?"

"What's the dress code for tomorrow?"

I shrug. "I'll be in a suit."

"Shocker," she says. "Well, I'll go for a cocktail dress, then."

I think of her curves in a tight dress. I think of the way she'd looked when we'd gone out to dinner, with her eyes smoked and a neckline that was... well. I wrest my mind away from that image.

"Sounds good."

She nods again and pushes her phone away. "That's a wrap on this meeting, then. What time will we—"

Her phone rings. The loud signal cuts through the kitchen, echoing off the walls. She reads the name on the screen and then declines, sliding her phone into her pocket.

"I'm sorry," she says. "You were saying?"

"I wasn't talking. You were." My curiosity gets the better of me, mingling with the image of her in a tight outfit and loose hair. We'd agreed we didn't need to be celibate. She's as free to date as I am. "Who was that?"

"Just a friend."

"The woman who was one of our witnesses?"

"Yes," she says. "She's an artist, actually."

"So that's why you want me to patronize an art gallery."

She nods. "It's her first big show. Her stuff is amazing, but the New York art world is cutthroat, and there are fees just to exhibit."

Several things click into place at that. Cecilia didn't just marry me to quit her job. Didn't just want to fulfill her dream of starting her own business. She married me to make her friend's dream come true too.

In anyone else, it would be a weakness to care that much, to make business decisions based on sentiment.

But I'm not sure I can call the woman in front of me *weak* any longer.

She clears her throat. "I was thinking we'd go to the opening together."

"So I can buy some art, be seen, make some calls."

"Yes."

It's no different from what most people want. What every single one of the people who sent us wedding gifts wants. They wanted some of the St. Clair name associated with them, as if the sheen and the prestige of an old family could rub off. But it's not cheap and platinum-coated. It's gold through-and-through, and it doesn't stain.

"I'll do it." I rise from the table and put my plate into the sink. Her voice reaches me as I make my way to the hall.

"What do we say to people in a year?" she asks. "When they ask why we divorced?"

I look back at her, still seated cross-legged at my kitchen table. Miss Myers, and not a pencil skirt in sight.

"We tell them the truth," I say. "We wanted different things."

"That's not the truth. We'll want the exact same thing. To be divorced."

I roll my eyes, and she chuckles. "Myers."

"Sorry. Couldn't resist. Are you going to work now?"

"Yes."

"Do you work every evening?"

I frown. "Yes. What else is there to do?"

She smiles, like she had expected my answer. Like she feels sorry for me. I don't like it. I leave her and her questions by the table, retreating to the one place I've always felt at home. The place where I don't have to take care of deceased relatives' houses or sort out what ruse to put on with my assistant-turned-wife. The place where I'm in charge of all that happens.

My office. I pause with the door half-open, and then, knowing he'd disapprove, I shut it entirely.

9

CECILIA

My room has a few spectacular advantages. One is the Central Park view, which I still haven't gotten over. When I work at my desk, I sometimes get lost in it.

Another is the rain shower in the en-suite. There's just no denying that money buys quality, and nowhere is that clearer than in marble sinks and glorious water pressure.

But the full-length mirror in the closet is a game changer.

I turn around to get the full three-sixty look, examining every angle of the dress I'm wearing. It's black, fitted with three-quarter sleeves and a slit up my leg. Modest but sexy.

Perfect for mingling with four billionaires and their significant others, two of whom have been my boss.

Not like I'll be the odd one out or anything.

I'm not wearing any jewelry, and I hope that conveys understated elegance rather than I-didn't-have-anything-that-would-look-right-in-your-esteemed-company. Smokey dark eyes, no lipstick, blush and blowdried hair. If we were going out, Nadine would tell me I looked ready to tear men's hearts out. And that I needed to wear a shorter dress.

I glance at the high-tech alarm clock on my dresser. It's time for us to leave in a few minutes, and knowing Victor, he'll be ready. I slide into my nude pumps and head to my bedroom door.

I'm halfway down the hall when his bedroom door opens. Victor emerges in a black suit, a hand readjusting the cuff of his shirt. It fits him like a glove.

He gets them tailored. I know, because I've made the appointments.

Think what you will of him, he's impressive, all six-foot-two of him. He stops when he sees me.

I run a nervous hand over my dress. "Hello."

His gaze travels over my face, my neckline, down my body to my shoes. There's no mistaking the surprised admiration in his eyes. Seeing it is delicious.

"You look... well."

"Will it do?"

"Yes, it will."

"Well. Thank you."

He clears his throat and walks down the hall, reaching inside his suit jacket. His face is once more the collection of sharp lines I know so well.

"Rings," he says. There, in the palm of his hand, are two of them.

"Oh. Right." I'd sent him my ring size last night. He must have found a jeweler during the day.

I reach for the smaller of the two gold circles. My fingers brush over his palm as I take it. "This one is mine?"

"Yes."

I slide it on my ring finger and watch him do the same. His thick gold band fits perfectly, a contrast to the tan skin of his long fingers and broad hand.

"Does yours fit?" he asks.

I nod, curling my hand into a fist. The gold feels cold against my palm. "Sure does."

"Just one more." He reaches for his other pocket, and hand still inside it, he spins something around. Then he pulls out an engagement ring.

"Oh," I breathe. It's beautiful. A solitaire diamond on a gold band, surrounded by a ring of emeralds.

"As your engagement ring," he mutters. "See if it fits."

I slide it on my finger. It's tight over the knuckle, but once I've worked past the bump, the gorgeous ring slides into position next to the wedding band. It glitters beneath the spotlights.

"It fits," I say.

"Right. Well, we'll wear them for tonight."

This might be a business decision and a fake marriage, but it feels very real to look down at your hand and see rings there, to see your husband slide his on his own ring finger. "I'll give them back to you when we get home," I say. "I'd hate to lose one."

"They're insured."

"Right, well, I still wouldn't want to lose them."

"Let's get this over with."

My Prince Charming, I think, following him down the staircase. Bonnie is in the kitchen and she gives us both a smile as we pass. It widens as I meet her gaze, and she doesn't have to speak the words for me to hear them. *Good luck.*

Steven has the car ready for us outside. "Mr. St. Clair," he says, opening the door. "Mrs. St. Clair."

Victor's hand pauses on the hood of the car. The name hangs in the air between us. Mr. and Mrs. Is he about to protest?

But then he folds his tall length into the car and I follow, stretching out my legs. Knot my hands together to keep them from shaking.

I've done crazy and challenging things before. I've worked long hours, I've traveled with both Tristan and Victor for work, I've had no problem making last-minute phone calls demanding they get the last suite or a table at a fully booked restaurant.

I can do this.

I look over, only to see Victor's gaze resting on my hands. On the rings on my left finger. I can't decipher the expression on his face.

"Everything all right?"

He looks up, blue eyes meeting mine. They look dark in the dim lighting of the car. "There's something you should know about the guests tonight."

"There is?"

"Have you met my business partners? Apart from Conway."

I shake my head. The times I'd patched through their calls didn't count, nor the times I'd seen them walk through the Exciteur hallway to visit St. Clair.

"Well then. You won't have a problem with Carter. He talks more than is good for anyone, particularly himself."

"Oh. Right."

"But Winter is going blind."

I blink at him. "Winter? Anthony Winter?"

"Yes. It's noticeable now."

It wasn't something I'd picked up on, but I'd only seen him twice, and at a distance. "How sad," I say. "I'm so sorry."

Victor clears his throat but doesn't elaborate, so I keep my questions to myself and file it away under information to keep track of. Information to remember.

We arrive outside an Upper West Side apartment building flanking Central Park. It's the mirror opposite of Victor's, only across the park.

I make the observation and he snorts. "Conway is newer money," he says, as if that explains everything.

The nerves in my stomach are full-blown by the time we're in the elevator and feeling it rising slowly to the top. "Show-time," I whisper.

Victor doesn't respond, a stone-cold, confident statue next to me, the way he's always been. Impenetrable and as likely to ignore you as he is to lash out.

But then he reaches out between us and catches my hand

in his. The grip is warm and firm, large fingers closing around mine.

"Remember," he says, "that we're not strangers now."

My chest feels tight. "Yeah. I'll remember."

His thumb strokes in a slow arch over my wedding and engagement ring, tracing their solid shape over my ring finger.

And then the elevator pings and the doors slide open.

Victor escorts me into a modern apartment, decorated with beige and grey accents and smelling deliciously like Italian food. The first to greet us is a golden retriever, coat thick and tail wagging.

"Hi there!" I say, extending my free hand for him to sniff. "They have a dog?"

"No."

"Well then, what are you doing here?" I scratch his ear and he sits back on his haunches, doggy-grinning up at me.

"There you two are!" a familiar voice says. "I thought Summer's trusty guard dog heard something."

Tristan Conway is walking down the hallway. My former boss, here in his own home, wearing a shirt with the sleeves turned up and a pair of navy slacks. Salmon on rye bread. That was his favorite lunch, and he liked it twice a week, delivered to his desk. My free hand curls around the dog's fur.

"Conway," Victor says. "Thanks for the invitation."

I see the exact moment Tristan recognizes me. His eyes widen and drift down to my hand, resting in Victor's grip.

"Look at that," he says. "Miss Myers. Or I suppose it's Mrs. St. Clair now?"

I smile at him. "Nice to see you again, sir."

Victor's hand tightens around mine and Tristan smiles. "No need for formalities."

"You're right. Call me Cecilia, then, please."

"Cecilia," he repeats. "Well, I'll be honest with both of you. I'm surprised. Not just at the news."

"It was sudden," Victor says.

"Is it the happy couple?" A man strides down the hall. Tall and smiling with dark-auburn hair, he looks from me to Victor with twinkling eyes. "Hell, St. Clair, you couldn't give us a heads up? Let us congratulate you?"

"We preferred a private ceremony," Victor says. "This is my wife, Cecilia. Cecilia, this is Carter Kingsley."

I shake Carter's hand. "Nice to meet you."

"Oh, I assure you, the pleasure is all mine," he says. "I also have a million questions for you. How do you stand being around him?"

Victor snorts at my side and pulls his hand out of mine. "I need a drink if we're to face an inquisition."

"Not an inquisition," Carter says. "Well-meaning, friendly interest between business partners."

"You mean nosy," he fires back.

Tristan chuckles and cuts through the tension with the ease of a man who's done it many times before. "Come on in and have a drink. We put a bottle of the '07 Taittinger to chill so we could toast to your marriage. Cecilia, there are people here who are eager to meet you, and I can assure you, they won't be as nosy as Carter is."

"Oh, they will," Carter says. "They'll just be more tactful about it."

"As long as I'm allowed to plead the fifth on occasion, I'll answer as many questions as I can," I say.

Tristan leads me through the apartment and gives me a warm smile when I compliment him on the place. It should be weird, perhaps, walking side by side with him again after a year. But he's welcoming and kind and doesn't ask the question that I can see dancing in his eyes.

Why the hell had I married Victor?

He introduces me to his girlfriend Freddie, a short, dark-haired woman with incredible curves. She invites me to sit in-between her and Summer, Anthony Winter's blonde girlfriend, and owner of the friendly golden retriever who was roaming the living room in search of head rubs and scraps of food.

"He's a living, breathing vacuum cleaner," Summer says. "Let me know if he bothers you."

"Oh, not at all. I love dogs."

Freddie smiles. "So does Tristan's son, so we try to have Summer and Anthony over as often as possible. Beats having the can-I-please-get-a-dog conversation over and over again."

I chuckle. "I'm sure!"

Summer looks between the two of us, her giant smile infectious. "Changing the subject here, but... you've married St. Clair! We have to talk about it."

"Yes," I say. "It still feels very new."

"Congratulations! You're a newly-wed!" The sincerity in her voice makes me feel guilty.

"Thank you. It's been very overwhelming, to tell you the truth."

Freddie nods. "I can imagine. From what Tristan told me, it all happened rather quickly?"

Translation: give us the details.

So I do, telling them how we dated in secret and reached a point where we needed to make things official. He'd proposed, I'd accepted.

"It was a whirlwind," I admit. "But sometimes, when you know, you know."

My gaze lands on Victor as I speak. Standing in between all three of his business partners, his mouth a line, suit jacket still on. Holding himself apart, even here, amongst people he's known for years.

In the brief time since I agreed to marry him, I've seen glimpses of someone else. Someone who is capable of dry, teasing humor and sly comments, who answers questions, often reluctantly, but never dishonestly. Even when he knows what he's saying might be painful to hear.

"Yes," I say. "When you know you know."

Tristan uncorks a bottle of champagne and pours a glass

for everyone, hands clasping around the stems of crystal flutes.

"Let's have a toast to the happy couple," he says.

Freddie and Summer urge me up and I give a half-embarrassed smile, not fake in the least. I walk across the plush carpet to stand next to Victor. Not letting myself hesitate, I slide my arm beneath his and lean into his side.

Blue eyes meet mine. "A toast," he says, as if it's the worst thing in the world.

"It won't kill you," I whisper. "Look happy."

He smiles, a small but true smile that sends a shiver down my spine. His arm comes around my waist. "Bossy."

Tristan clears his throat and I look up to see them all standing in a circle, glasses raised to us. I sweep my eyes over them all: my former boss, Anthony Winter with his charming girlfriend by his side, the constantly grinning Carter, and Freddie with a golden retriever at her feet.

People I would never have been able to meet just a month ago, who wouldn't have exchanged more than a sentence or two with me while I was Victor's assistant. Who had lives and wealths and opportunities unimaginable.

Toasting to our fake union.

"To Mr. and Mrs. St. Clair," Tristan says.

"To Mr. And Mrs. St. Clair," the others echo, glasses held high. I keep my smile on my face and lean into Victor. For the first time, I'm grateful for his aloofness, for the relentless strength that keeps my own from flagging.

Summer's arms are tight around me. "Promise me," she says.

I laugh, running a hand over the silk of her dress. My head feels light with champagne and laughter. "I promise!"

"I have absolutely no one I can run with in this city, and if I don't run with anyone, I don't run at all."

"We'll do it," I say. "I'll text you next week with a time and a place."

"And you'll guillotine me if I don't show up." She lets go of me, a blinding smile on her face.

"I might not be quite so drastic, but yes. Can Ace come too?"

"He might slow us down," she says.

"How fast do you think we'll run?"

She laughs again, not stopping as Anthony wraps his arm around her waist. He looks straight at me. "It was very nice to meet you, Cecilia."

I think of the times I'd patched him through to Tristan. "Likewise. You're welcome to join our running club if you want."

Summer puts a hand on his arm. "Anthony doesn't run."

He nods. "I don't. Besides, if I tried, I have a feeling Summer and I would argue the entire way."

"We wouldn't," she protests.

"We would," he says. "You'll want to chat while we run, or stop for ice cream, or take a scenic route."

"You make me sound like a distracted squirrel."

"Aren't you, though?"

Their banter and obvious closeness sends a pang through my chest. It sharpens when Anthony presses a kiss to her temple.

"Are you ready?" Victor asks. He has my coat in hand and I take it from him, sliding my arms through the sleeves. The hallway tilts when I flip my hair back.

"Woah," I murmur.

In a move that mimics Anthony, Victor wraps his arm around my waist. That's the second time tonight.

"Thanks for having us tonight," I say to Tristan and Freddie. "For the champagne, for dinner... for everything."

"It was our pleasure," Tristan says. "See you around, St. Clair?"

Victor nods and presses the button for the elevator. His

arm falls from my waist as soon as the elevator doors close behind us. I take a deep breath. "We did it."

"Yes, we did."

"And we survived," I say.

"Did you think we wouldn't?"

"I thought it might be a close call. They didn't seem to question *why* we'd gotten married, either! At least not to our faces."

"It's probably all they're talking about now." He frowns, extending an arm to me. "How much did you have to drink?"

"Not a lot. Just what they offered."

"They offer all the time. You don't have to accept."

"Thanks, Dad," I mutter.

He rolls his eyes and drops his arm. "Right. You're not wobbly at all."

"It's my shoes," I say, walking after him through the lobby. "They look great, but they're not very steady."

Steven's waiting for us outside. Victor holds the car door open for me, an inscrutable expression on his face.

I unbuckle my strappy heels the second we're inside. "Ah. Relief."

He snorts, but he doesn't look away.

My head feels light. "Your friends are lovely."

"They're my business partners."

"You don't consider them friends?"

"Of a sort, I suppose. But we have shared investments, so I won't get too friendly."

I pull up a leg beneath me on the plush leather seat. "They don't seem to think that way."

"They have different values than me."

I raise an eyebrow and he turns to me fully, draping an arm behind the headrests. Something sparks in his eyes. "You take issue with that."

"No," I say. "It's just so you."

His voice deepens. "So me? Care to elaborate, Miss... Cecilia?"

"Well, that's an example of it, actually. It's been weeks, but you still find it difficult to call me Cecilia. You want to go for Miss Myers."

"It's a force of habit."

"It creates even more of a boundary between us, and that's something you like," I say. "Isn't that right? Because you and I are business partners."

"We are."

I'm on a roll, champagne and adrenaline making my words flow. "Do you know, that in the entire year I worked for you, I never once saw you laugh on the phone? Make a joke with an employee?"

"You kept track?"

I roll my eyes. "No, I didn't. But I can't remember a single instance. Your separation between church and state is absolute."

"As opposed to you, who prefers to mix them incessantly."

"I mix them?"

He raises an eyebrow. "Do you think I never noticed how much you and Eleanor's assistant talked? Some afternoons you chatted for hours."

"You heard us? Through the door?"

"Sometimes."

"Wow." Trying to sort through a year's worth of hushed conversations with Mason is difficult, but my brain attempts it. What incriminating things had I said about Victor?

He shifts closer, voice dropping. "Thinking of all the awful things I might have overheard?"

"Yes. I don't know if I should apologize."

"I didn't hear a thing. But if you think you should apologize, I'm willing to hear it."

"You vain man," I say. "Do you know how good of an assistant I was? I had *lists* of your favorite lunches, rotating them based on the day of the week and the mood you were in. I took pride in organizing your email inbox. It was labeled and color-coordinated and a work of art. I drafted the *best* memos and meeting notes for you."

Victor's lips curl, an expression I'm so unused to seeing that it stops me mid-brag. "I've noticed, now that Brad is here."

"He's doing a good job, isn't he?"

"Good enough. Probably thanks to your coaching."

The compliment is tiny, but it warms me. I'd wanted Conway's approval when I was his assistant. With St. Clair, I'd craved it, and every day he said nothing was a day I needed it more.

He's close, his aftershave a heady balm. In the dim light of the car, his blue eyes look almost black. "Cecilia."

"Yes?"

"They bought it. About you and me, and our marriage. Thank you for that."

"You're welcome."

He takes my hand in between both of his and with strong, sure fingers he slides my rings off my finger. He has to worry them around my knuckle, but then they're off, gleaming gold in his palm.

"Keep them safe for me," I murmur.

He puts them in his suit pocket. "Until next time."

My heart pounds. The champagne, I think.

Steven pulls the car to a stop outside our apartment building. Victor's the first to break eye contact and get out, but I follow suit, heart still racing.

He had always intimidated me. It hasn't changed.

Victor rests a hand on my low back and we walk through the lobby. There's no one here to see us, but his hand is there regardless, a warm weight through my dress.

He unlocks our front door and nods toward the staircase. "Get some sleep," he tells me. "You'll need it, because tomorrow, I'm going to tear your business idea to shreds."

The dry threat makes me smile. "Good. I don't want you to go easy on me."

"That's not my style."

"Oh, I know." I look at him standing alone in the hallway, hands in his pockets. He looks back at me until our gazes break.

The excitement of the evening makes it hard to sleep, despite my big, comfortable bed and the view of the dazzling city skyline outside my window. I tell myself I won't, but I listen for the sound of his footsteps coming up the stairs. The door to his bedroom shuts, and I imagine him in there, Victor St. Clair, running his hand through his hair.

Just before I fall asleep, I hear his footsteps again. This time down the staircase and out the front door. I hear it shut.

I lay awake for a long time, but I don't hear him return.

10

CECILIA

"It can't have gone that bad," Nadine says.

"How prone am I to exaggeration?"

"Look, you've worked on your business start-up for what, two years? And I've seen you slaving away at it on weekends. You've researched everything about this."

"The weekends I could, at any rate. But yeah. He warned me he'd tear it to shreds, and he did."

"Details," Nadine says. "I need them."

I reach for my glass of wine. It's served in a stemless glass, part of the hipster decor in this fancy bar. "He sat in his home office, looking just like he did at work, and I presented it to him like he was an investor and I was an entrepreneur."

"Which you are."

"Hopefully. But he's definitely a real investor." I shake my head, my cheeks heating up. "What he said makes sense. That I'm not ready yet to launch. That I need to make it clear what positions I want to hire and where, not to mention how I'll compensate them. My branding is muddled and if I'm looking to take in outside investors, I need to have a fully-functioning website up and running. A place where clients can purchase tasks or hours with us virtual assistants."

Nadine's eyes widen. "This," she says, "is why I chose a

career in the arts. Not a single word you just said makes sense."

I laugh, putting my hand on hers. "It's fun when you finally get it, I promise. It took me a long while."

She shakes her head. "No, you knew all about it in college. I remember. You'd sit in our dorm room with your bed littered by books. Like, you couldn't even sleep in it at night before you stacked them all up."

"Never stopped me from partying, though."

"Sure didn't. We could party all night long in those days."

"We're getting old," I say.

She nods. "I went out with a few buddies from the studio on Wednesday and I think I'm still hungover."

"That was three days ago."

"Yes," she says. "Exactly. Are you happy, though? With your husband's feedback?"

I groan. "Don't call him that."

"Your husband? Isn't what that he is?"

"Technically yes, as you very well know. But I don't think about him like that."

"My job is to tease you. It's in the job description of a best friend. Sorry, Cece."

I roll my eyes. "Fine. Yes, I was happy with his feedback, even if it made me doubt everything for an evening. But he knows what he's talking about, at least business-wise."

Nadine takes a sip of her rosemary gin and tonic, a staple of the trendy Soho bar we're at. It has trendy price tags too. "Is that this guy's secret? I haven't forgotten how much he made you work this past year, you know. Or how you cried on my couch two months in about how *impossible* he was to please. But you're still willing to take his advice."

"Gosh, I was really exaggerating back then."

"No, you were stressed and overworked. I'm friends with past you too, you know, not just present you."

"I guess I was. Thank you."

"Anytime. But can you explain it to me?"

I lean back in the chair, thinking of Victor. It's not hard to. He's everywhere in my life now, just as present as he was when I ran his schedule. "He has a driver who idolizes him and a housekeeper who's Wonder Woman. From what I can see, he barely interacts with either, but they're such class acts at their jobs."

"And he had you as his assistant," Nadine says. "What is it with this guy that has so many great people willing to work for him? From what I can tell, he's awful."

"He is. I'm not making any excuses for him. But... he invites excellence. You can't be anything but your best around him, you know? He wouldn't let you. And he works just as hard himself, Nadine. I've seen it up close. He'll drive the hardest bargains, and watching him do it is impressive. Even if it's scary sometimes."

Her smile tilts. "You sound like you're joining his little army of sycophants. I don't want you to become a Stepford wife."

I laugh. "Oh, there's no risk of that. Truthfully, I think I'm getting the best bargain out of this deal."

"Just make sure you do," she says, lowering her eyebrows and wiggling them. "I found someone I want you to meet."

"You did?"

"Yes. Jake, at the Francis Hunt Gallery. He's one of the curators and he's razor-sharp, but not in an I-color-coordinate-my-closet kind of way, you know?"

"Hey," I say. "I color-coordinate my closet."

She grins. "I know. I've lived with you. And you can't have two people like that in a relationship. What if your organizational systems clash? You'd argue forever!"

"No," I say. "Mine would win."

"Well, Jake would let you organize his closet. I can just tell. He isn't too artsy for your taste, either. A few years older than you. I don't know, Cecilia, but I think this guy could be the one."

"You say that about every guy you want to introduce me to."

"And have I ever been wrong?"

"Yes," I say. "Every single time."

She snorts. "Everyone's a possibility. But Jake is a certainty. Both you and your hubby are allowed to date other people, right?"

I groan. "Hubby?"

"Yes. Your better half, the yin to your yang, your happily-ever-after."

"St. Clair would have an aneurysm if he heard this conversation. But yes. We can date other people as long as it's kept discreet. Although," I say, reaching for the stem of my glass and twisting it between my fingers, "I don't know if that's changed since we went to dinner with his business partners."

"When you pretended to be happy newlyweds."

"Yes."

"Has the vibe between you changed in the past week?"

I shake my head. "We barely see each other. He works out in the morning, then he's at work the entire day while I work from home. He gets home past seven. We don't have dinner together. He doesn't watch TV or hang out in the kitchen. We're like ships passing in the night."

"The man is a workaholic."

"Textbook," I agree. "Although…"

"What?"

"In the past week, I've heard him disappear at night."

"Disappear."

I shift in the chair. "Yes. Leave the apartment. So I don't exactly think he's being celibate."

Nadine's eyes widen. "Oh. You think he's meeting someone at night?"

"Why else would a man that busy spend the nights somewhere else?" I ask, shrugging. It shouldn't bother me, and yet, the idea of Victor disappearing at night to another woman,

97

another apartment, feels like nails beneath my skin. Itchy and painful.

I know him. I used to run his schedule, his life, send emails in his name. He'd have a second apartment in our building or rent a hotel room close by. Anything for convenience and to save time.

"Maybe he goes for midnight walks," Nadine suggests, but her voice is doubtful.

I sigh. "Yeah. With all the free time he has. It's okay. I mean, I was under no illusions about our arrangement. He made it very clear in the beginning that we were both free to date."

"Which means you are free to meet Jake."

I roll my eyes. "So I can color-coordinate his closet."

"Yes, after you've made sweet, sweet love."

"Ugh. I hate it when you pull out that phrase."

She grins. "I know."

Her phone rings and I raise an eyebrow, watching as she digs through her purse. "Since when do you have your phone on sound?"

"I do when I might get important—oh." Her face changes in an instant, goes focused and predatory. "Hello?"

I sip from my drink and eavesdrop shamelessly.

"Yes," she says, nodding, as if the person on the other end can see her. "Of course. Yes. I understand."

"Understand what?" I stage-whisper.

She grins and shakes her head in my direction. "I'd be more than happy to. On the twenty-second? Yes. Yes, of course. I can have a completed series by then."

I stare at her in exaggerated surprise, my mouth open, and she grins at me again. "Yes. Thank you so much. Talk to you soon."

She hangs up and the next second she's out of her chair, reaching for me, shrieking. "Oh my God!"

"You got a date for your exhibition?"

"Yes! They've decided I'm a headliner! A headliner, Cecilia!"

"A headliner," I repeat, hugging her back.

"Someone dropped out and they just asked if I'd be willing to show sooner. If I'd be *willing, and I'd get a discount.*" She leans back, dark brown eyes meeting mine. "Of course I'm willing."

"This means you have the opening next month. The twenty-second."

"Yes." She wipes at her eyes. "I have so much to do. I have to complete my seven virtues series. In three weeks."

"If anyone can do it, it's you."

"I'll have to come up with the money a lot sooner, too. I hope you're as optimistic about that."

"Nadine," I say. "About that... I might have solved that little problem."

Her eyes narrow. "Have you married a second time?"

I snort. "No. The first time was enough."

"What do you mean?"

"I have the money for the exhibition. It was part of what I negotiated for."

She puts a hand on the table, as if she needs the support. "You... Cecilia. You're crazy."

"I'm determined," I say, "and you're more my sister than my best friend."

In the golden light of the bar, her eyes shimmer. "I can't accept that."

"Of course you can. You were the one who told me to marry St. Clair and skim some off the top, and this is me doing just that. I couldn't have done any of this without you. I'll be there on your opening day too, the proudest best friend there ever was."

She hugs me again, squeezing me tight, and speaks through a closed throat. "I don't know how to repay you."

"You don't have to," I murmur. "I love you, you know."

"I love you too," she whispers. "Getting your bosshole to help me too. You're a genius."

"If we rise, we're rising together."

She nods, leaning back to wipe her eyes. "I'm exhibiting."

"You're exhibiting," I repeat. It feels like ten years of work to get to this point, of seeing her experiment and find her voice, lose it again, rediscover a new direction.

My own throat feels a little tight. "You know what this means for tonight."

"We need to celebrate."

I nod, reaching for both of our glasses and pressing hers into her hand. "Bottoms up," I say. "To artists who cancel, and the artists who seize the opportunities they leave behind."

She raises her glass. "To friends who have each other's backs."

11

VICTOR

The computer screen in front of me fades in and out of view, my eyes struggling to focus. I lean back in my office chair and close them. The emails and memos can wait. They'll have to, because I don't have any more in me tonight. Running on empty.

It's past midnight and I should be in bed.

Had been, in fact, until the cold premonition that always signaled a bad night drove me out of it again. The best thing to do on such nights is to avoid my bed until I finally fall into it so exhausted I sleep like the dead. It keeps me from dreaming of them.

I run a hand through my hair. Where is she?

Cecilia hadn't mentioned where she'd be tonight and Bonnie hadn't known either. I'd called Steven, but he hadn't driven her anywhere. No notes left behind on the kitchen counter either.

Her schedule is usually predictable. Reliable. She's here when I get back home, chatting with Bonnie in low, cheerful tones in the kitchen or, in the last week, sitting on the couch in the living room with a book in hand. She always shuts her bedroom door by ten p.m.

And on her way up the stairs to go to bed, she always pauses at my half-open office door. "Goodnight," she says.

It had annoyed me at first, but she'd kept at it, professional and kind, like clockwork. I always say it back. "Goodnight." And then I listen to her soft steps heading upstairs, the sound of another person living in my apartment. Making it feel like a home.

But not tonight.

I push away from the desk and head into the kitchen. Maybe what I need is a cup of coffee. The clock on the microwave assaults me with a time that's far too late, showing twenty past one.

We have never discussed this. To keep or not to keep one another informed. But surely she should recognize that herself? Cecilia Myers, who is the paragon of organizational virtue and forethought. Who had run my life so smoothly I didn't know to miss her as my assistant until she left.

She might be in trouble.

Possible scenarios flash through my mind, of Cecilia lost in the city, her phone dead, her wallet a beacon to thieves. Cecilia in another man's apartment, in his arms, giving him all of her laughs. And then, my brain unable to stop, the image of her in a car wreck, her body bent and broken.

I wrest my mind away from that image.

Reach for my phone and find her number.

I drum my fingers along my kitchen counter as the signals go forth. One, two, three...

She answers on the fourth, but I don't hear her voice. I hear the pulsing of heady music. "Cecilia?"

"Victor?"

"Yes."

"Wait a minute!" The beat of tropical house blasts and her words are muffled by laughter and the shuffle of bodies.

She's at a nightclub. "Where are you?"

"What?"

"Where are you, Cecilia?"

"I'm at Ivory!"

I grit my teeth. "Are you coming home tonight?"

"Yes, of course I am. I'm just going—" The rest of her words are unintelligible, lost in the beat and laughter.

"How are you getting home?"

"Taxi. I can't hear you very well." Her voice is giggly. Like she'd been after Conway's dinner, only worse.

"I'll come pick you up."

"What?"

"I'll come and pick you up!"

Her voice turns into a squeak. "Now?"

"No. When you're ready to leave."

There's the sound of shuffling again, and then a door shuts. I hear a woman yelling about someone cutting in line. "Now I can hear you better," Cecilia says, her voice dropping. "Hi, Victor."

"Hello. Text me twenty minutes before you want to leave and I'll pick you up, okay?"

"Okay," she breathes. "That's very kind of you."

"I don't want you out in the city alone at night."

"I'm with friends."

"Still. Text me."

"Okay. I'll send you—" The call clicks off, and she's gone on the other end, lost in a bathroom stall at a club downtown.

I shouldn't have offered. Shouldn't have insisted. But here I am, pulling on my jacket and grabbing my car keys. I pass the hideous glass dick vase on my hallway table. She put it back after I threw it in the trash.

It sets my nerves on end. Teasing me. She's teasing me.

The elevator takes me down to the garage and the black Range Rover I use too rarely. Steven is more convenient day to day, skilled at parking and discreet.

The engine purrs to life under my hands.

She might not have texted yet, but I'm not going to sit at home and wait. Better to be in the city, to be moving. The streets of New York are filled with taxis and mopeds, delivering late-night food to drunkards and partygoers.

I weave through traffic with one hand on the wheel. Refuse to think about what I'm doing, the boundaries I'm crossing. Cecilia and I are not friends. Cecilia and I cannot become friends.

I pull up outside of the innocuous black facade of the club my GPS tells me is Ivory. The music is pulsing from inside, faint but noticeable, even through my car.

A cab driver gives me a dark look for occupying a spot, and I stare right back at him. He's the one who caves first.

It takes another ten minutes before my phone vibrates in my pocket.

Myers: I'm ready now. Thank you!

I wait a few minutes. Not nearly enough to make it plausible that I left when she texted, but I'm not willing to leave her waiting in the club.

St. Clair: I'm outside.

After I've sent it, my thumb hovers over her name on my phone. I don't do it. Having her name as Myers instead of Cecilia is good.

Distance is good.

But distance is an illusion, I realize, watching her step out of the club. She has an arm wrapped tightly around her friend, the dark-haired woman who'd served as our witness. The artist I'm to patron.

I lean across the empty passenger seat and lower the window. "Myers!"

Our eyes meet. Her dark hair is loose and curled around her face, a messy tendril falling across her cheek. She gives me a wide smile. Like I'm her favorite person ever.

"There he is!"

Her friend laughs and they walk, still entangled, to my car. Both of them.

I'm frowning as they help themselves into the backseat.

"Hi," Cecilia says.

"Hello," her friend says.

"Can we make a stop in Brooklyn first?"

Across the river, she means. Hell no. I open my mouth to say just that, looking at her through the rearview mirror. Cecilia's gazing right back at me. Her eyes are wide, and earnest, and… happy. The retort dies on my tongue.

"Okay," I hear myself say.

She smiles and I look away from the rearview mirror. I drive in silence toward the Brooklyn Bridge, thankful for the lack of traffic.

I'm Steven for the night, it seems.

"Thank you for this," her friend says from the backseat. Nadine? Is that her name? "I appreciate it."

I glance up to see her measured look, and give her a nod in return.

The two of them exchange murmured farewells in the backseat and hug firmly. Cecilia says something against Nadine's ear that leaves both of them laughing. I frown, knowing it's about me.

"Goodbye!" Nadine tells me. "Thank you again for everything!"

I nod, fingers drumming against the steering wheel. I'm just about to floor it when Cecilia surprises me by getting out as well.

She slides into the passenger seat beside me with a smile, fastening her seat belt. "Thank you. I wanted to ask you if you could drop off Nadine as well, but cell reception was really bad in there."

"Sure."

She tugs at the tight dress she's wearing, pulling it back down over smooth knees and thighs. "Aren't you cold?"

"A little," she says. "But I'm too happy to be cold."

I drum my fingers again, fighting with my own instinct, and losing. "I'll bite. Why?"

"Nadine is headlining an art exhibit next month!"

"You went out to celebrate."

"Yes. We had to, you know. Ivory isn't the best club in the city, but you always know you're in for a good time." She leans back in the seat, settling into the plush leather, and gives a happy little sigh. "Thank you for picking me up."

"You're welcome."

"Oh! You're driving!"

"Last time I checked, yes."

"But where's Steven?" She glances back, as if he's lurking in the backseat.

It makes my lips curl. "He has the night off. He's not hiding in the trunk, if that's what you're thinking."

"So you're driving." Her eyes look glazed and her full lips are smiling, as if they can't do anything else, as if she's locked in happiness for tonight.

"Still am, yes."

She chuckles and reaches down to take off her heels, just as she had after the Conway's dinner. "Dancing in these should be illegal."

I have nothing to say to that, so I don't. But I watch the length of her bare legs as she stretches them out.

"I didn't mean to.. well." She looks over at me, hesitation in her eyes. "Why did you call me? To see where I was?"

"You weren't home, it was late, and you usually are."

"I didn't know you wanted me to tell you when I'll be out."

I keep my eyes on the road. "Neither did I, to tell you the truth."

There's silence between us, punctuated by the sound of her turning in her seat. "You were up late, then?"

"I couldn't sleep."

"You're gone some nights, too."

I don't know what to say to that. It's not something I can put into words, and even if I did, I doubt she'd... no.

"I didn't know you noticed."

"I have," she says. "And I don't call you to ask where you're going."

"No, I suppose you don't."

She clears her throat, and there's something tight beneath the cheerfulness. "I appreciate the ride home. But I can be out for as long and as often as I'd like, just the same as you."

I can't argue with that. Nor can I admit to the feeling of unease when she wasn't home. "Noted. It was just out of the ordinary for you, and so I... checked in."

She relaxes against the seat, palms flat on her knees. I glance at her left hand and find it bare. Of course. The rings are with me, back in the safety box at home.

My mother's engagement ring had looked good on Cecilia's finger.

"Do you know," she says, "that we've been married almost two months now?"

"I did know that."

"Which means we only have ten months left."

"Looking forward to divorce?"

She laughs, running a hand through her messy dark hair. Gone are the low ponytails and tight buns. I approve of that. Long live the free, tumbling waves. I wonder what they'd feel like wrapped around my hand. "I'm just surprised at how smoothly it's gone," she says.

"Did you expect us to fight?"

She snorts. "No. But I expected more hiccups. We have less friction than we did when I worked for you."

"We had friction?"

"Yes. Maybe you didn't notice it."

I pull up to the garage in my apartment building, watching the steel door rise inch by inch. "We got a lot done."

"Yes, that's true. We certainly did. I don't think anyone who works for you can do anything else."

I park the car and walk around to open her door. But she's already stepped out, bare-footed, onto the concrete.

"Cecilia."

She laughs and bends to slide her heels back on, stretching out a hand to support herself. It lands on my arm, and I hold still. "You're a handful when you're drunk."

Her eyes fly to mine. "I'm not drunk, and I'm not a handful!"

"Sure you're not."

"I'm perfectly capable of walking in a straight line. I can recite the alphabet backwards and forwards—no! I'll do you one better!" She straightens, and to my amazement, she recites my social security number and my birthday. "Oh, and you're a Taurus," she says, "but you don't believe in astrology."

I stare at her. A million responses flit through my mind. I choose the safest one. "That does not prove you're sober."

"Come on, even you have to admit that was a little impressive."

"Sure."

She walks past me to the elevator, arms loose at her sides. "I shouldn't have asked. I know better than anyone that you have a no-praise policy."

"I don't have a no-praise policy."

"Ouch," she says. "That doesn't make me feel better."

I can't think of anything to say to her teasing, but then I don't have to, because the elevator doors open and she bounces out to open my front door. Her front door.

Our front door.

I should head straight upstairs, but nothing about this night has gone according to plan. So I follow her into the kitchen. She turns on lights as she goes and opens the fridge, surveying the contents.

I watch her. "What did you mean by that?"

She gives a low hum and takes out a packet. "Do you like this?"

"I can't see what it is."

"Hummus."

"No."

"I figured," she says, and digs through a box to find baby carrots. "I want to make sure I don't accidentally ruin Bonnie's planning by snacking on something she's set aside for you."

I lean against the kitchen counter. "Don't deflect. What did you mean?"

"Mean about what?" She bobs her head as she rips off the plastic lid, like she's still listening to music. The white lace edge of her bra peeks out of her neckline and it's suddenly all I can see.

Cecilia in her underwear. Cecilia in nothing at all.

Sleeping in the bedroom opposite mine every night.

She looks up at me, catching my eyes. A slow smile spreads across her lips.

I clear my throat. "My no-praise policy. That I don't have. You said *ouch*, afterwards."

She laughs, and the sound expands in the kitchen, fills it in ways it's never been full before. "If you say you don't have a no-praise policy, that means I've just never done anything praiseworthy. But as a stellar assistant—don't object—I know I did. I was great at my job."

I frown, watching her flow through my kitchen, opening drawers and finding utensils. She looks like she was the one who designed it. Like she cooks in here every day.

Maybe she does. I don't have any insight into how she spends her days when I'm away.

It suddenly strikes me as a crime.

"I praised you."

She raises an eyebrow at me. "When?"

I stare back at her and rack my brain. A workplace isn't helped by excessive praise. It doesn't increase morale or motivation, and too much devalues the entire operation. "We worked together every day. I don't know when."

Cecilia hums, a smile in the corner of her lips. "I can tell you how often. Never."

I frown, watching her as she dips a carrot into the hummus. Swirls it around. "So I don't believe in participation trophies," I say. "Every office I've headed has been successful."

She smiles, and it's a private smile, like I've made a joke only she understands the punchline to. "Of course they have."

"Of course? It took hard work and dedication."

"I know, I know. I'm not disputing that. You're the hardest-working person I've ever met." She tosses the compliment out like it's nothing. Like it's easy. Obvious. Self-evident.

I watch as she opens the fridge again. I didn't know the day would come when I missed Miss Myers' prim hairstyles, but I miss them now, watching the dark hair curl down her back. It's far too distracting.

"Here it is," she murmurs to herself and pulls out a glass bottle. She tries to twist the cap, but it won't open.

I'm moving before I decide to and knock her hands softly aside.

"Oh," she breathes, looking up at me.

It's a move from a bad high school movie. But I unscrew the lid for her and feel like I'm ten feet tall. "Here," I mutter.

Her voice is warm. "Thank you."

"What is this, anyway?"

"Kombucha. Want some?" Her hands brush mine as she takes the bottle back and the simple contact makes me mute. I watch as she takes out two glasses, and after she's gone through the trouble...

"You drink kombucha when you're drunk?"

"I'm not drunk," she says and pours a healthy amount into each glass. "This is restorative. It's healthy. And it means I'll feel absolutely terrific tomorrow."

"Why wouldn't you? If you're not drunk now?"

She narrows her eyes at me, but it's playful. "Do you want your kombucha or not?"

I don't. It doesn't look appetizing in the least, with little particles swirling around.

"I do," I say, and that's when I know I should go upstairs. Because she is nothing like the assistant I thought I had, nothing like the Miss Myers who answered my commands and never spoke back, who wore too-loose pencil skirts and had her hair in prim ponytails.

The woman before me is full of life and laughter, of interest and dreams, and for the first time in forever, it intrigues me rather than bothers me.

It reminds me of times in a kitchen like this. Times when homes were meant for laughter and life, instead of work and rest. When there was someone who dared tease me. Someone close enough to ever get the opportunity.

"Victor?" she asks. There's no hesitation in her voice. She says my name like she owns it, and not like she'd rather call me Mr. St. Clair and retreat back up her stairs like she thinks I bite.

"Yes?"

"Cheers to two months of marriage," she says and raises her glass of kombucha.

I look down at my own glass and it looks like dishwater. But I clink it to hers. "Only ten more to go," I say.

She smiles at me over the rim of her glass, and despite myself, I feel myself smiling back.

It dies as soon as I taste the drink. Cecilia bursts out laughing at my expression and she doesn't stop, folding herself double over my kitchen counter.

"Yes," I say. "Definitely drunk."

She laughs again. "I'm sorry. It's just... I'm sorry."

I pour the rest of my glass out in the sink. "It was probably bad luck to toast with something that disgusting."

"Your face," she says. "I've always been so careful to serve you things you enjoy."

"Things I enjoy?"

"Yes. You like lettuce on BLTs, but not in burgers. You prefer your steaks medium-rare. You hate creamers in coffee, and flavors even more. I once served you hazelnut coffee and never again."

Her smile is satisfied. I decide to unsettle it. "You might know my social security number," I say, "but that doesn't mean you really know me."

"It doesn't?" Cecilia shifts on the chair and it brings her closer, a whiff of perfume washing over me. Her green eyes are serious on mine. "I know who you hire, who you spend your time with. I know your taste in clothes and your tailoring sizes. I know that cutesy email farewells aggravate you. You don't like holidays. You *hate* when people use the word 'like' needlessly. I've seen the way your eyes twitch."

"My eyes do not twitch," I say. "But the word 'like' is pointless."

Her grin widens. "It didn't use to bother me, but now I think of you whenever I hear a person using it."

"So you know a lot," I say. "But not all."

She purses her lips. "I know your taste in women."

Ah. Interesting. "Do you?"

"Yes. I organized most of your dates, you know. Booked restaurants, put your calls through. You have a type."

Cecilia has never spoken to me like this. I doubt she would've just yesterday, and I doubt she will tomorrow, when the liquid courage has disappeared.

"And what do you think my type is, Cecilia?"

"Tall, slender, young," she says. "They often expect you to send a car to pick them up. By you, of course, they really mean me."

"Mmm."

"Do you know I had to prepare a list of excuses in my desk for when they ask to be patched through to you?"

"A list of excuses?"

"Yes. You know, you're in a meeting, you're on a phone

call, you're away on a business trip. You're finalizing an important contract or you have a meeting with the governor."

"I had a meeting with the governor?"

Her eyes laugh. "Yes. You've met the governor six times in the past year, at least as far as the women you've dated are concerned."

I shake my head. "Making things up, Miss Myers."

"You know, I'm surprised you didn't ask one of them to marry you. You could have had a real marriage. A semi-real one, at least."

I pull out the chair next to her. The motion puts our knees against one another beneath the table. "Why do you think I was dating so much?"

"Because you…" Her words run out, eyes widening. "That's what you were doing the past six months."

"Yes," I admit, and wonder if I'm offending her.

She bursts out laughing. "Sorry. I just can't imagine you going on dates with women, with the sole intention of… of…"

"Finding a wife," I say. "To fulfill a clause in my grandfather's will."

"Yes. It's so methodical. It's very you."

"Very me," I repeat, my gaze dropping to her lips. They're fuller than I'd noticed before, and when she worries the lower one between her teeth, small indents form. "You really do think you know me."

The last traces of humor disappear from her voice. "I know some things. There are a lot of things I still wonder about."

"I might not know your social security number, but that doesn't mean I don't know things about you, Cecilia Myers."

Her breath hitches. "You don't know much."

The kitchen holds danger, and I should leave. I don't. "I know you care deeply about your friends. So deeply you married me to help a friend's dream come true. I know you have no siblings or family close by the city. I know you want to stand on your own legs and launch your business, but that you're scared to, as well. I know you saw marrying me as an opportunity but also as an escape," I say. "I know clothes are a shield for you. You dressed modestly and frumpy in the office because you wanted to be taken seriously."

"I didn't dress frumpy."

My gaze travels down the neckline of her wrap dress. "You didn't dress like this."

She exhales softly. "No. Not in the office."

"I understand why." I wouldn't have been able to concentrate on work if she did. "To the best of my knowledge, you didn't really need this marriage or the money it provided. You wanted it. You wanted the opportunity, you're ambitious, you're determined. Which also means somewhere inside, even if you don't admit it to yourself, you didn't want to get rid of me that badly."

Her voice is low. "I wanted to do something wild."

It would be easy to lose myself in her gaze. The pull is there, telling me to stay, to drown. Victory pounds at my temples and sudden desire burns in my stomach. I could reach out, now. I could kiss her.

Cecilia swallows, her hand tightening around her glass. "You don't think badly of me for marrying you?"

What?

"No. Why would I?"

"Because I'm compensated for it."

"It's a business deal," I say. The words fortify my resolve, steady the pounding of need through my veins. "We both gain from it. If anything, I think well of you for it. You helped me." Business is what I understand the best, removing any vagueness or emotion. It's territory I understand. I stand. "Goodnight, Cecilia."

She watches me with dark eyes. "Goodnight, Victor. Thank you for tonight."

When I fall into bed this time, sleep welcomes me immediately, and I don't dream at all.

12

CECILIA

"Is that gnocchi?"

Bonnie nods and uncovers the plate of golden dumplings. "Tonight's dinner is gnocchi with ragu."

"I've been eating like a queen since I moved in here. This smells amazing."

She smiles, dropping them one by one into the boiling pot. "It's a passion of mine."

"Oh, and we can tell."

She looks over her shoulder. "We?"

"Yes. Well, I know Victor thinks the same thing."

Bonnie's pleased flush is clear on her cheeks, even when she turns back to the stove. I pull out a chair and have a seat at the kitchen table.

Today had been filled with headaches. I've been interviewing web creators for my start-up, and so far I didn't feel comfortable with a single one. They had to take my requirements and translate them into a functioning website for both the assistants I'd hire and the clients we'd have. Before this, I'd never realized how much work went into interviews.

The front door opens and familiar footsteps echo through the hallway. The route they take has changed in the past week, since the night he picked me up from the club.

The night we'd nearly kissed.

He doesn't head straight to his office. He heads toward the kitchen instead.

I smooth my hair back behind my ear and look over at Bonnie, but she has her back turned. Victor walks into the kitchen. He's taken off his suit jacket, and he's rolling up the sleeves of his shirt, inch by inch. "Hello," he says.

"Hi," I say. "Did you have a good day?"

He nods. "Brad didn't screw up quite as bad today."

A month ago, I would have thought he was serious. Perhaps he would have been, too. But the blue eyes that meet mine hold dry humor.

"Surprising," I say. "He didn't breathe in the wrong direction?"

"No. He didn't scald my coffee either."

"He's learning."

"He had a good tutor."

A pleased flush creeps up my cheeks. His thick, dark blond hair is mussed from where he's run his hand through it.

"You had to make big decisions today?"

He raises an eyebrow. "You heard?"

"I guessed."

"One of my business partners is negotiating with a media conglomerate about a takeover. It would be one of Acture's biggest purchases."

"Oh. That's really exciting."

He nods, but he's frowning. "Yes. Carter is eager to run point on this one, but we'll have to negotiate as a group. The media corporation doesn't want to sell."

"Family business?"

He waves a hand. "The major shareholders are all from one large, extended family. They're letting sentimentality cloud their judgment."

He says it like it's the gravest of errors, and I smile. "Do you have a lot of work tonight? We could have dinner, if not."

Victor's hand flattens on the marble counter. Silence stretches on, my offer hanging in the air. He could shut that door. He'd be right to.

"Sure," he says.

"Okay. Good." I flit up from my chair and get our glasses, a sudden bout of nerves flooding my system. "Doesn't the food smell delicious?"

"It does."

"It's almost done, too," Bonnie adds. She plates it for us and I grab a seat at the table opposite Victor. He keeps his eyes on his phone, but as I watch, he does the most extraordinary thing.

He turns it on silent and slides it into the pocket of his pants.

He sees me looking. "Anything wrong?"

I shake my head. "No."

The plates appear in front of us and Bonnie says bon appetit. "Thank you," I tell her, and I mean it. "This looks incredible."

She wipes her hands on her apron. "There's parmesan in the fridge and a bottle of red that would work great. Help yourselves."

"Thank you," Victor says.

Bonnie nods again and as she leaves the kitchen, I catch the curve of a smile on her lips. Wine in the fridge, huh?

Victor gets a bottle and uncorks it with a practiced move. The muscles in his forearms flex with each pull on the cork.

Damn shirtsleeves.

"Cecilia?"

"Yes?"

"How is your start-up coming along?"

It takes me a moment to gather my wits. But when I do, I launch into a description, and pray he's not deducting this from our monthly mentoring sessions.

"I've spoken to some personal assistants, actually. People I know through work or school. Several are interested in joining. It's flexible, you know? They can sign up to do as many hours as they'd like to in a given week."

He nods. "It's as flexible from the clients perspective as it is from the assistants. That's good, Myers."

"Thank you. The thing I'm struggling with at the moment is web design."

"Tell me."

Victor listens to my problems, drinking from his glass and digging into his food. He looks like he usually does at his business meetings, complete with the furrow in his brow.

He remarks positively on one change and critically on two points. After that, we fall silent, the only sound in the kitchen our cutlery against the plates.

I clear my throat. "My mother is coming to town in a month or two."

"Is she?"

"She doesn't know I'm married."

"Quite a change," Victor says. "Do you plan on telling her?"

"Yes. I don't think I can get around it."

"You could show her the contract. Might make it easier for her to understand."

I laugh. "Yes. And then she'd lose her mind."

"She wouldn't approve?"

"Of me turning marriage into a business arrangement? No. I doubt she would. Although she's... unconventional. She never chose marriage for herself, and I think she never really thought I would, either."

Victor's stopped eating, his gaze on mine. "Your mother never thought you would marry."

I shrug. "She'd say she raised me better than that."

His eyebrows rise. "Your mother sounds intriguing."

"She is. She's nothing like me, you know. She'll decide she's going to try fasting for a week, only to take a month-long culinary course the next. A husband would only have slowed her down, as she loves to say. 'Men for a season, sometimes for a reason, but never a lifetime,'" I quote.

Victor snorts. "And your father?"

"Not in the picture. Mom changed the story a lot when I was growing up. One week she'd say he was a traveling musician, and the next he was fleeing from the mob. Now that I'm older, I think she might not be quite sure who he is."

He shakes his head. "I did not expect this."

That makes me smile. "No, I can see that. I probably strike you as someone with a very proper background."

"Yes. Raised to be an assistant."

"God, I hope no one is raised to be an assistant."

He snorts, returning his gaze to his plate. "You hated it, then?"

"Hated what?"

"Your time working for me. You were counting down the days, Myers."

"I'm back to Myers again," I say. "That happens a lot when we talk about work."

"Force of habit. And don't deflect."

"I'm not," I say, though I am. The gnocchi is delicious, small pillows of heavenly goodness, and he eats them with methodical precision as he waits for my answer. "I didn't hate it all the time. There were days when I loved it."

"Oh?"

"Yes. I got to call a lot of powerful people on your behalf, not to mention say no to a bunch of Exciteur executives when they wanted your time."

"Gatekeeper," he says.

I nod. "You had the power, but I had access to the power."

His lip curves. "Sounds like you liked that."

"Sometimes, yes. Controlling your schedule and calendar, making sure everything was in order... I loved that part of it. I still love organizing. It's my passion."

He pushes his empty plate away. "So the part you didn't love was me."

"That's not what I'm saying, really."

Victor raises an eyebrow. "You told me, when I asked you to marry me, that you wanted to get away from me."

I shift in my chair. "I remember."

"So I was the part of your job you didn't like."

"Yes," I admit. "Not always. I learned a lot from you. But you weren't easy to please or to predict."

Even so, a certain part of me had been proud to be his assistant because of that very fact. *Look at me wrangle this beast.* I had access to the man who regularly bit his employees' heads off, and I hadn't been fired.

Seeing him in front of me now, shirtsleeves rolled up and dark blue eyes serious on mine, is like having double-vision. The image of him in his own home now, talking to me, superimposed over the image of him behind his desk telling me to *get it right the next time or else.* Same man. And yet.

The two are blurring, both softening around the edges, and I realize I'm not afraid of him anymore. I haven't been for quite some time.

"Noted," he says, as if I've spoken the realization aloud. "I know it's too late, but for what it's worth, you were excellent at your job. I hope you saw that reflected in your compensation."

Pride at his words makes my chest swell. Yes, he had compensated me handsomely, and I know I'm luckier than most with my savings account.

But he'd never said the words.

"Thank you," I say.

He nods again, like we're done with this topic, but doesn't rise from the table. Neither of us is eating anymore.

I reach for the wineglass. "Are you excited about tomorrow?"

"Tomorrow," he repeats. "Ah. Nadine's exhibition opens."

"Yes."

"I had Brad call a few art magazines and tell them about the gallery opening."

"You did?"

He crosses his arms over his chest, as if he's unsure of how to act. But he nods. "Yes. Should bring some more photographers there. They'll want to photograph us together."

"That's okay."

"We'll buy a few pieces for appearance's sake as well."

I grin. "Gosh, this is perfect. Thank you, Victor. For doing that."

"Yeah."

"I'm so excited for her," I say. "She's worked so hard to get to this moment, you know. The gallery is perfect for her and the owners have already hinted they want some of her pieces permanently exhibited." I laugh, then, remembering her words. "But even at something as momentous as this, her first gallery opening, she's still trying to set me up with someone."

Victor lowers his wineglass. "To set you up with someone."

"Yes. Apparently one of the curators is, and I'm quoting her, *a man I could organize a closet for.*"

"I have no idea what that means."

"Me neither," I say. "But it's Nadine for someone I'd match well with in a relationship."

"How would she know that?"

"She knows me very well. I don't think there's a man I've dated that she hasn't met."

Victor's voice is cool. "Do you only date men who are unable to keep their own closets in order?"

I shake my head. Why did I bring this up? "No. It's her version of a compatibility test, I suppose. She thinks I need to be with someone who balances out my organizational side."

"Ah," he says.

"It's not scientific. I kinda think she wants me to date someone who's like herself. Maybe it'd work out, you know. She is my best friend for a reason."

His lips are a thin line. "So you're going there tomorrow to flirt, as well as to support your friend. Sure you want me to come?"

"Of course I do. I have no intention of flirting with anyone."

"Except that your friend will encourage you to."

"I'm my own person," I say, and I mean it in more ways than one. Why is this silly little story a sticking point? He disappears several nights a week, going who knows where and doing who knows what.

With who knows who.

I'd snuck downstairs on one such night the past week, but he was nowhere to be found on the bottom floor. Gone.

We didn't promise one another celibacy, and he seems to be making full use of that liberty.

Victor rises from the kitchen table and puts his plate in the sink. It's an oddly domestic thing for him to do, but with his rolled-up sleeves and ruffled hair, he looks at home here in the kitchen. As elegant as one of his expensive kitchen appliances.

Bonnie's words come back to me. The St. Clair name is old. Moneyed. Historic. And he's the last one who carries it. It strikes me as tragic, suddenly, that he never pursues real relationships.

"You are your own person," he says, as if that settles everything. "Tomorrow evening. I'll meet you at the gallery."

"Sounds good."

"As there will be photographers there, I'd appreciate it if you didn't flirt in front of them."

I open my mouth to respond, but he's already disappearing down the hallway and out of view.

―――

When I come down the next morning, there's an envelope with my name on it waiting for me on the kitchen counter. Bonnie is nowhere to be seen and Victor had left the apartment over an hour earlier. I'd heard his bedroom door close and the telltale sound of his dress shoes against the hardwood floor.

Judging by the writing on the envelope, he'd left it here for me.

I open it. Two familiar rings lie at the bottom.

The message couldn't be clearer. For tonight.

I hold them in the palm of my hand, the heavy gold ring and the peculiar design of the engagement ring. It's gorgeous, the solitaire diamond reflecting under the kitchen lights, the ring of emeralds sparkling. It's not something I thought he would have picked out.

I slide them on and close my fist around them. He wants us to go tonight as a married couple. Him as the investor; me as the supportive friend.

Does this have anything to do with the careless comment I made last night about Nadine's friend Jake? The one she's so sure I'd hit it off with?

I smile down at the rings. Pretty they may be, but they're an illusion, and that's what Victor's keen to protect. Nothing more and nothing less.

And if he thinks he's the only one allowed to have his fun, I'll give him my opinion tonight, too. Because the contract goes both ways. I can date, as long as I'm discreet. Perhaps it's time to remind him of that.

A few hours later, and he's late and Nadine is busy, but I couldn't be happier. I'm surrounded by my best friend's art. It's professionally displayed on the walls and sets the sterile gallery ablaze with color, the abstract pieces flowing from one frame to the next.

The series with the seven virtues is my favorite. She'd been working on it for a year. Sometimes she'd worried whether it was old-fashioned to have the virtues represented. But we'd both agreed the world could use more of them, and she'd infused that into the paintings, with abstract concepts and colors matching each one.

I sip my glass of champagne and ogle Nadine without shame. She looks drop-dead gorgeous tonight, like she could take the stage and give an impromptu performance at any time. We'd been at her place yesterday to test out looks, and the fitted auburn jumpsuit she chose makes her look tall and graceful. The eccentric artiste and the polished young woman, rolled into one.

Ready to sell you a painting for a few thousand dollars right before she returns to her Brooklyn studio to paint her heart out.

She's wearing the gold hoop earrings I got her for her twenty-fifth birthday, and they catch the light as she talks to a visitor, her hands moving in a pattern that is so uniquely her.

If this is how parents feel when their children graduate, then I can understand why so many of them cry. I'm so proud, watching her own this space and this role. Nadine-at-sixteen would be overjoyed at this, having her biggest dream come true. I feel as proud for Nadine-at-sixteen as I do for Nadine-at-twenty-eight, standing there across the space.

"Gorgeous, right?" a voice says by my right.

I answer without taking my eyes off her. "Yes, she really is."

The man's laughter is deep and surprised. "Well, I was actually talking about the painting behind her. *Justice*. There's anger in it, too, can you see that?"

I chuckle and turn to the man beside me. He's a head taller than me, in a navy linen shirt and with a beard that looks artfully unkempt. "There is, yes. Perhaps justice is often accompanied by anger. Anger at the things that aren't so."

"Perhaps," he says. "The fantastic thing is that she managed to capture it in an abstract. I haven't met a painter quite like her, ever, I think."

"Nadine has always been talented at that. Making you feel things with her art."

He smiles, then, and his dark brown eyes are warm. "So you're the best friend. I suspected you were, but you also looked like you were contemplating a painting, and I didn't know if you were a prospective buyer."

"Best friend," I say and stick out my hand. "And prospective buyer."

He shakes it. "Supportive. I like that. I'm Jake."

"Cecilia," I say, my smile widening. So this is the messy closet-owner. "I heard you were instrumental in getting this gallery showing off the ground?"

He gives a half-smile. "I was there when Nadine pitched her art, yes. But I didn't do any heavy lifting, believe me. My colleagues were almost as enamored by the portfolio she showed us as I was."

My smile widens, watching as his eyes return to Nadine. There's true appreciation in them. I wonder if it's more than just for her art. Who should really organize his closet?

"She's always evolving, too." Pride laces my voice. "For as long as I've known her, she's been experimenting with different mediums and expressions."

"You two have been friends for a long while, right?"

"Yes. I think it's... fourteen years now. Yes. Fourteen years exactly next month. We were neighbors, once upon a time."

His smile widens. "Nothing like old friends."

"No, and you can't make new old friends," I say.

"An unfortunate truth." His gaze catches on something behind me. "Oh, someone's coming our way. I wonder if management sent someone new?"

I know who it is before I turn, based on that comment alone. And yes. There he is, striding through the gallery, dark suit tailored to his tall, strong form.

"He's with me," I say.

Victor puts his arm around me and presses a kiss to my temple. The simple, brief touch stuns me. He extends a hand toward Jake and speaks in clipped tones.

"Victor St. Clair. Cecilia's husband."

"A pleasure to meet you," Jake says, shaking his hand. His

gaze travels between us and then he takes a step back. "It was lovely talking to you, Cecilia."

"Likewise," I say. "I'm happy you were there that day when Nadine pitched her art."

His smile deepens. "So was I. I'll catch you later."

The moment he's out of earshot, I round on Victor. "What was that?"

"What was what?" he asks, his face a study in bored professionalism.

"You introduced yourself as my husband."

"Isn't that what I am?" He strolls toward one of the giant abstracts on the wall, one I'm familiar with. It's *Charity*.

"Yes, but not in *that* sense of the word."

"I don't know what you mean."

If my gaze could kill, that's what it would do. Have him drop dead right then and there in the art gallery. As it stands, it doesn't seem to harm a hair on his head. He just watches the blue swirls of *Charity* with his hands behind his back.

"Is this about last night? What I told you about the man Nadine wants to set me up with?"

"I think I'll put in an offer for this one," he says. "It would go well with the colors in the gym."

"Your home gym has no color."

"Exactly." He turns and strides on, and I'm forced to catch up with him. Still angry, because he might pretend otherwise, but we both know exactly why he'd come on as strong as he had.

He'd kissed me.

My temple, and only briefly, but still.

And it was not something we'd agreed upon beforehand.

"Victor," I say. "If you think I'll be happy to be—"

"Mr. St. Clair," a man interrupts. "And this, of course, has to be the new Mrs. St. Clair?"

"Yes," Victor says and there's his arm again, sliding around my waist with no thought to his self-preservation. "Good to see you here, Hadley."

"Likewise." The man gives me a hesitant smile. He's middle-aged, a camera in hand. "Mind if I take a picture of the two of you in front of the, uh, painting here?"

"Not at all," Victor says, turning to me. "Hadley works at the *Post*."

I put on my widest smile, because Victor or no Victor, we're doing this for Nadine. The camera flashes and I step away from him as soon as Hadley lowers it.

"What do you think of the art?" I ask Hadley. "Don't you just love the colors?"

That launches an hour of networking so intense, I have no chance to tell Victor off about his domineering. In my mind, all I can hear is the sound of his bedroom door, slamming at night, as he disappears out of his apartment.

But he has the nerve to kiss my temple, or to react like he did last night, when I mentioned flirting.

I give Nadine a massive hug when I see her. She thanks Victor in an earnest tone, but then she's gone again, swept away in the tide of visitors. Tonight is her time to shine, and everyone wants a piece of her.

We're alone in front of *Temperance* when I get my shot. "That wasn't fair, what you did back there. Or the way you reacted last night."

Victor turns flat, blue eyes my way. "Elaborate."

"We never agreed to be celibate or monogamous."

"I'm aware of that."

"Yes, I bet you are," I say. "But that cuts both ways, dear husband."

"I'm aware," he repeats, eyes narrowing. "But that doesn't mean you can flirt in a room full of people who belong to New York's art elite, many with cameras and here to report. Think of how that would look."

"I was having a conversation."

"With someone whose closet you're already planning to organize," Victor says, his voice dropping low with anger.

"Or was that not him? Are you still waiting to be set up with your Prince Charming?"

"I'm not being set up with anyone. It was a dumb suggestion and one I shouldn't have mentioned to you, clearly. But that's not the point."

"Then what is the point, Cecilia? Explain it to me."

I step closer, eyes darting to the couple by our side. I don't want to be overheard. "You spend several nights away every single week. I've told you I know about it before, and you didn't deny it. Why is it okay for you to be involved with someone but not for me? It's not as if a single conversation with someone here would make front-page news. Your fragile masculinity would remain intact, I'm sure."

Victor's voice is sharp. "What exactly do you think I do at night?"

"Do you want me to spell it out for you?"

"Yes, I think I do."

"If you get to have sex, I get to have sex," I say. The word *sex* feels like it echoes in the grand space. I glance around, but no one is looking at us.

"Sex," Victor says. His voice is midnight. "Myers, I haven't had sex since I married you. Which, if you recall, was several months ago."

He sounds like that's a painful revelation. "I recall. I was there."

"Good. So whatever you think you're accusing me of, I assure you, it's not that."

"Then where do you go at night?"

His jaw works, and then he turns away from me, looking out at the crowd. "As soon as we leave, I'll show you."

13

CECILIA

The drive is taut with silence. He'd taken the car himself, and looking at him from the corner of my eye, I wonder if the reason is to have something to do. A machine beneath his hands and a road to watch.

We haven't spoken since he got behind the wheel, taking us further and further out of the city. The skyscrapers turn to mid-rises that soon shrink into glorious suburbia.

The wide streets we drive through are tree-lined. I glimpse electronic gates and pools behind fences. Old Victorian houses and charmingly cracked pavement only enhance the wealth that hides behind these hedges.

I've never been to this area of Long Island.

I look out the window and speak for the first time since we left the gallery. "Are we going to visit a relative of yours? I might be overdressed."

Victor gives a harsh chuckle. "In a way, yes."

"Oh. You're sure I'm not overdressed?"

"You're not overdressed," he says. There's a brief pause. "I'm in a suit, Cecilia."

Funny, how in my head, that's what he always wears. Even in the comfort of his own home, I've only seen him in suits, heading to work or returning home from it.

He turns onto a smaller street. The pavement is smooth here, and giant oaks line it, their trunks too big to wrap my arms around. The car slows to a crawl outside a property and he turns onto its driveway. A giant wrought-iron gate swings open on electronic hinges.

The house is enormous.

That's my first impression. Enormous and Victorian and beautiful, with shutters and a wrap-around porch. Boxwood hedges line the building and give way to a stone staircase, slick with leaves. Behind the house I glimpse a lawn that stretches toward tall trees. No neighbors nearby.

"Wow. This house is…"

Victor parks the car. "It's a lot of things."

The air feels thick out here, smelling of fall and rain and nature. We walk toward the porch and scare a squirrel. It darts across the lawn.

"This is your grandfather's house?"

"Yes." He unlocks the front door, and just like that, everything makes sense. This is where he goes at night. This is where he grieves, even if he'd never call it that.

He won't look at me. I wonder if he's regretting this. That I'm here and witness to so much of *him*. But as I step into the wood-paneled entryway, his dry voice becomes that of a guide. Telling me about the property and the rooms.

I follow him through a sitting room with a giant fireplace, into a dining room with a table that's large enough to seat twelve. I drink everything in. The antlers mounted on the wall. The framed picture of a family tree that looks yellow with age. It's like a cabinet of curiosities, meticulously decorated and richly furnished.

"You married me to inherit this house," I say.

He's stopped by the bay windows in the sitting room. It would make for a great reading nook, I think, looking out over the backyard. Although I'm not sure if *backyard* is the right word. Property, perhaps, or estate. The lawn and gardens beyond look endless.

"Yes," he says.

"Was it a good bargain?"

Victor gives me a wry smile. "I haven't decided yet."

"Because of me, or because of the house?"

"Both," he says, and it feels like his gaze goes right through me. "Both."

I swallow. "Will you show me the rest?"

He nods. We walk through the kitchen, a guest bedroom, three baths. We finish our loop back in the entryway and the two grand staircases. The house is beautiful. It has character ingrained in every single floorboard.

"Do you want to see upstairs?"

"If you want to show me, yes."

He leads the way up the staircase and I let my hand slide along the worn railing.

"That was his room," Victor says, nodding down a hallway. I can just barely see a master bedroom.

"Oh."

"This," he says, pointing to an anonymous-looking guest bedroom, "was mine."

I know so little of his background, of his life, of his family. I know his parents are out of the picture. "You grew up in this house," I murmur.

Victor nods. "Since I was eight."

He pushes open a half-closed door and my eyes widen at the treasures beyond. It's a study, and it's glorious. Multi-paned windows look out on the property, letting the last daylight into a room that could have been made for Winston Churchill.

A wide, oak desk with a leather inlay sits in the middle. The floor is covered in a thick oriental rug. All around us are bookshelves. My eyes travel over the spines, over memorabilia and trophies and pictures.

"This was your grandfather's study? It looks beautiful. It could be the set of a movie."

Victor doesn't answer and I turn away from my perusal of

a small bronze statue of a dog. He's standing in front of a framed picture hanging by the side of the door. His hands are in his pockets, jaw tense.

Perhaps taking me here was an impulsive decision. Something to show me I was wrong when I accused him of sleeping around.

But this is not a place where he's comfortable.

"I'm sorry," I say.

"For what?"

"For the loss of your grandfather. I didn't tell you that, when he passed."

"You organized his funeral," Victor says. "You were there."

"In a way, I suppose." I step closer, my voice dropping. "Do you come here to feel close to him?"

Victor looks away from me. "No. Not consciously, at least."

"It's your house now. Are you planning on… changing anything?"

"Yes. I have to clean this place out. His things are everywhere. My parents' things are everywhere."

"Your parents died when you were eight?"

"Yes." He inclines his head toward the picture behind him, the one he'd been studying.

Two boys, one a head taller than the other, are standing in front of a smiling couple. The man has his arm around the woman's waist and his free hand on the small boy's shoulder. They're standing in front of this very house, I realize, but at the height of summer. The smaller boy's knees are scraped and his grin is wide.

It's Victor. The eyes are familiar, as is the thick mop of hair, much lighter back then. He's smiling at the camera like he's never known anything but joy.

"Oh."

Victor turns. "That was a long time ago."

"This is your brother?"

"Yes."

"What was his name?"

"Phillip." Victor rolls his neck, every line in his body tense. He's uncomfortable. Uncomfortable with me here. Uncomfortable in this space.

I step back from the picture. "Thank you."

"For what?"

"For showing me this."

He opens the door and I step out of his grandfather's office. Victor follows me, and halfway down the hall, his shoulders relax.

I catch his sleeve. "I'm sorry."

He halts, a tall, suit-clad shadow beside me in the dimly lit hallway. "You already said that."

I shake my head. "No, I accused you of something I had no proof of, and no way to back up. Not to mention something you're allowed to do under the terms of our marriage."

"Don't apologize," he says. "Or you'll force me to as well. For claiming you like that at your friend's gallery."

"You, apologize?"

"It would be a first." He puts steady fingers beneath my chin and tips my head up. "I'm not sneaking out at night. I'm here. Not having sex."

I can't think with him this close. "Good," I murmur. "I'm not interested in Jake."

"Good," he says. He's so close that the word ghosts across my lips, and then he descends, kissing me.

Not in a brief or tender way. Not really like it's our first kiss, either. He presses his lips to mine with strength and warmth, as businesslike as he does everything.

Maybe it's from the surprise, or from the long months without any physical contact from a man. Maybe it's the stress of the day.

But I kiss him back.

He groans into my mouth, hands sliding around my waist.

My body tightens, narrows, all sensations emanating from the spots where we touch. My back hits the wall.

I reach up to twine my arms around his neck, one of my hands finding its way into his thick hair.

I'm touching St. Clair.

His hands tighten around my hips, and it's like he's thinking the same thing I am, because he lifts his lips from mine. "Myers," he murmurs.

My whisper is breathless. "This made you think of work?"

"What?"

"You only call me Myers when we're talking about work."

I regret my words, because he lifts his head, a furrow in between his brows. "I can assure you, I wasn't thinking about work. At all."

"Neither was I," I say.

His lips curve and he reaches out to run a tendril of my hair between his fingers. He watches it for a moment before he tucks it behind my ear.

"Well," he says, stepping back from me. In the darkness, his eyes glitter. "Let's go home before we do something we regret."

14

VICTOR

It's a good thing I never knew how Cecilia Myers tasted.

If I had, I wouldn't have gotten a lick of work done with her outside my office every day, in demure clothes and ponytails and lips a man could devour.

The muscle strain in my arms makes me groan. I've loaded the weights too much today, and I know it, but the burn is good. It's necessary. It's accomplishment and achievement and if I'm not accomplishing and achieving, I'll lose momentum.

The thought makes me pause mid-bicep curl. Momentum was my grandfather's word. He used it relentlessly, describing everything from investments and exercise to studying. I sound like him.

Being in his house so often probably isn't helping. Walking around and daring myself to open drawers, to throw things away, to come to some fucking decision about the place. Right now it's a relic.

One I'd showed to Myers.

She'd dared me to with her accusation yesterday, thinking I was out sleeping with someone at night. Christ, I wish I was. I doubt I would've responded as strongly if that was the case.

But since my last foray into dating ended, a month prior to marrying Myers, I haven't slept with anybody.

I put the weights down with an exhale. I'd abused the gym instead. Worked more than ever. Taken every single meeting thrown my way, anything to get me away from Cecilia's questions and challenging eyes and the damnable tight leggings she wears around the apartment.

I'm attracted to my assistant-turned-wife.

It's a complication I can't afford, but judging from the taste of her kiss and the feel of her body against mine, it's one I'm going to repeat. Hell, it's the reason I'm working out in my home gym mid-morning.

It's the time she uses it.

I'd started noticing changes a week prior. The lighter weights in the rack were moved. Not much, but by an inch here and there. And when I fired up the treadmill, the incline wasn't at my usual setting.

Now I've stayed an hour longer than usual, and all for the chance to see her again. Not that I have a clue what I'll do when she's here. Ogle her in her workout tights, probably. I'm losing it.

I lift the hem of my T-shirt and use it to wipe the sweat off my forehead.

The door swings open and I hear a small intake of breath. I drop the hem of my T-shirt but it's too late, because Cecilia's eyes are locked on my chest.

She's seen the scar.

Well. If what my body burns for happens, she'd see the scar, anyway. Perhaps it was only a matter of when. But she'll have questions.

She always has questions.

"Hi," she says, a hand still on the door. "I didn't mean to interrupt."

"You're not interrupting. Come in."

She gives me a tentative smile. The memory is in her eyes,

the same thing I'm thinking of. Kissing her in the hallway last night.

She walks to the treadmill and yes, she's wearing her workout tights. The look of her ass in them makes my jaw clench.

"Everything okay?" she asks.

"Yes." I force my attention back to the weights. Grab one and lie down on the bench, ready for tricep lifts.

The air in the gym feels as weighted as the steel plate I'm holding, thick with possibility. Had she been lying awake last night too? Thinking about the two doors and a hallway that separated us?

I can only stand it for so long. I look over at her running on the treadmill, and I catch her watching me lift. Her cheeks color and her gaze darts down, landing on my chest. I have to divert her before she asks me about the scar.

There are a lot of things I want to do with Cecilia Myers before discussing the car accident.

"Have you heard from your friend?" I ask. "About yesterday?"

She nods, walking quickly on the treadmill. "Nadine's over the moon. I don't think she can really believe she sold as many paintings as she did, or how many journalists were there. I mean, neither can I!"

"Good."

"Thank you for that. I know you pulled some strings."

I shrug, which is a hard thing to do when you have a twenty-pound weight above your head. Making the calls had been painless, save some idle chitchat it had forced me to engage in.

Not much work at all, I think, watching the smile on her face.

Her voice lowers. "Thanks for last night as well."

I close my eyes against the tide of need rising inside me. She'd looked up at me with too much knowing, standing there in the hallway outside my grandfather's office. I'd had to kiss her to get away from it.

But now I can't get away from the memory.

"Anything to prove a point," I say.

Her voice turns teasing. "Right. All you wanted was to win."

"I don't like being accused of things I haven't done." I turn to her, meeting eyes that never looked at me this boldly before I married them. "Trust me, Cecilia. I'm *very* aware of all the things I haven't done since we got married."

The temperature in the gym rises another degree.

"Well," she murmurs. She runs a hand over her forehead and pulls her ponytail up higher. She's in a tank top, the smooth, strong lines of her arms on display. Then she jumps off the treadmill.

"Well?"

"I think I'll try this machine."

I sit up on the bench and watch her assault the shoulder press. She's shoving, not pulling. I put down my weight and cross the space to her. "Like this," I say, my hands atop hers.

This close, she smells like shampoo. Floral and warm and womanly. "Oh," she breathes.

"You pull like this… can you feel it between your shoulder blades?"

"Yes. Wow. I have no muscles."

"Building them will help you sit in front of the computer all day." I brush her ponytail aside and place my hand on her upper back, right between the wings of her shoulder blades. Hair curls along the delicate skin at her nape. "Right here."

"I didn't know that," she says.

I press a kiss to her neck. The skin is warm and fragrant beneath my mouth. "Now you do."

"Uh-huh."

I slide my hand down to her waist and continue my exploration of the long expanse of her neck. Dangerous, this. But my body is in control now, my stomach tightening with need.

"Victor," she murmurs.

"Yes."

She twists on the bench and I kiss her. Her lips are soft and pliable beneath mine. She tastes minty from toothpaste, fresh and warm and irresistible.

Her hands come up around my neck. I'm sweaty, but so is she, and we'd probably break a sweat in bed together anyway. Hell, if Myers is as feisty there as she had been negotiating our marriage, it's guaranteed.

I slip my tongue between her lips and she sighs, deepening the kiss in response. The sound goes straight through me and I feel my body responding, need sharp in my lower body.

I hadn't lied to her. It had been a long time.

I pull her into standing and she follows me fluidly, the length of her body pressed against mine. Finally, I think, and slide my hand down to cup her ass through her workout tights. The ass I only noticed a few months ago, but that has taunted me every single time she's worn these tights around the apartment.

"Victor," she says again, and I like it. Want her purring my name in all kinds of ways.

"Yes?"

"What are we doing here?"

"Does it matter?" I tug her tight against my body and let her feel just how much I need this. "We can do whatever we like."

"Mmm." Her lips return to mine and I wonder if we can do it right here, right now, and indulge in a different kind of exercise.

Then her hand slips down my neck and strokes the spot through my T-shirt where the diagonal scar starts. "I'm sorry about this," she murmurs against my lips.

"It was a long time ago." *And not something I want to talk about right now, not when I'm gripping your ass and your mouth is on mine.*

Happy place, right here.

"Will you tell me how it happened?"

I press another kiss to her lips before I lift my head. It hurts to pull my hands away from her, and I know I'll have to take a cold shower or use my right hand before I'll get any work done today. "I'm keeping you from your workout," I say.

Her swollen lips shift into a frown, and I turn, not wanting to see that I'd put it there. "Victor... I didn't mean to pry."

"It's okay."

"Come back," she whispers.

I sling my towel over my shoulder. The one I should have used to wipe my face instead of my T-shirt, and all this would have been avoided. "I should shower. Tomorrow evening, though."

"Tomorrow evening," she repeats.

I shut the gym door behind me and leave the heady smell of bodies and want. The rest of my apartment is in order, clean and fresh and quiet. It's like a balm across my feverish senses, even if it doesn't ease the aching length between my legs. What have I set in motion here?

15

CECILIA

My arm is through Victor's, and with every step we take, my body reminds me of that fact. He'd offered it casually, like we do this all the time. Like we're a couple. The scent of his cologne and his steady presence are as distracting as the grandeur of the opera house we're approaching.

Victor gives our name to the attendant by the vaulted entrance. "The St. Clairs," he says.

Tonight's another night to show a strong united front, to flaunt the success of our marriage. He'd warned me that one or more of his business partners might be here tonight.

That journalists, photographers, and New York's elite would be.

Which means for the purposes of tonight, we're very much in love.

"This place is gorgeous," I say. Light beams in from above, through the glass domed ceiling, making the limestone floor gleam.

"It took too long to construct," Victor says. "The architecture firm the city hired went over time by three months."

I lean closer. "I understand that must have been a major disappointment for you, considering that I worked for you for a year and not once did you have me schedule appointments to go to the theater or the opera."

He snorts. "I suppose I haven't gone as much lately."

"By lately, do you mean the past decade?"

"I might, yes. You're in a good mood tonight."

My fingers tighten on his arm. I am, and it has nothing to do with the opera. Excitement and anticipation is a heavy weight in my stomach. Against every one of my principles, I liked kissing him. The memory of his touch in the gym is powerful enough to make me shiver.

"I am in a good mood," I say. "Nadine came with me to shop for this dress. We had a great afternoon."

Victor looks down at me, dark blue eyes sweeping over my form. The dress is red and clings to my body. Nadine had called it a fuck-me dress, but the lite version. The one you can wear to a function... and ask a man to peel you out of afterwards.

Victor's voice is husky. "Good choice."

"Thank you. I like you in your tux."

He stops, eyes dropping to my lips. I tip my head back in welcome. The kiss is perfect. Warm and strong and filled with the promise of what's to come. He trails his lips to my ear afterwards, heedless of who's watching.

"It's a beautiful dress," he murmurs. "But it'll look even better on your bedroom floor."

A shiver runs over my skin. I catch sight of a few men in tuxedos watching us across the lobby and I laugh, breathless.

"Something funny, Myers?"

"I just realized that we won't have to work so hard to seem like a couple in love tonight." The second the words are out, I hear how they sound. "I mean, because of... well. Not that we're actually in love. You get what I mean."

Victor nods and pulls me along. His gaze is locked on the same group of men. "Indeed."

I want to press my hands against the warm flush in my

cheeks, but if he hasn't noticed how flustered my own words made me, I won't bring it to his attention.

Victor networks like he does all things. Intensely. Idle chitchat is brief and to the point, despite my efforts to string it out. I aim smiles at people to soften the bluntness of him.

"What was that?" he asks me as we step away from a couple. I'd asked the two of them where they honeymooned, because we never had a chance to go on one ourselves, and it had launched a refreshing ten-minute conversation about different Caribbean islands.

"That," I tell him, "was networking."

"Not any kind I do."

"No, I'm aware of that."

"What does that mean?"

"That you're prickly and to the point. And that works great in meetings—I've seen it work!—but not at events like this."

"You're criticizing me," he says.

I meet his gaze, and it's not fear that unfurls inside of me at the challenge in them. It's something else entirely, but it scares me just as much.

"I'm giving you advice. Not the same thing."

"You're talking semantics, now."

"Talking about shared interests outside of business is the most important part of networking. If we were a proper married couple, and if you really wanted them to remember you, we'd take their advice seriously. You'd call them in a few weeks' time and thank them for their input. You'd tell them we've booked a trip to one of the islands they suggested. Bermuda, say."

"Barbados," he says. "Better beaches, they said."

I smile. "Right. Barbados. When we'd eventually go on our delayed honeymoon, we'd email them a picture or send them a postcard."

"That's too much."

"No, it shows that we think they did us a favor. They feel

helpful and included. People like to help, Victor. They also love the chance to look knowledgeable in front of others."

His mouth is a frown. But it's his thinking frown. "A lot of work," he says.

I shrug. "Not necessarily. Just requires some forethought. And you'd really prefer we have our fake honeymoon in Barbados? I wouldn't have guessed you were a surfer."

Victor's eyes meet mine. "No?"

"I would have thought you didn't vacation at all."

"Not regularly, no."

"Surfing would not have been what I thought swayed you."

"You claim to know me," he says, "and yet sometimes I wonder if you do at all."

"Mmm. I know for a fact you don't know me."

"I'm starting to learn."

I don't think he's talking about my honeymoon preferences anymore. I run my fingers down his sleeve, finding a sliver of skin along his wrist. "What are we doing?"

"Whatever we want," he says, eyes darkening. "I told you that already."

It sounds so simple when he says it. It probably is, for him. I've spent a year watching him do as he pleases and take what he likes. And the world bows at his feet because of it.

What could be more convenient for him than sleeping with the woman he lives with? Who he's already married to?

But convenience cuts both ways. I'd once said I'd try to be more like him and his ilk. Going after what I want.

"Look," he says. I follow his gaze to a podium across the lobby. A small half-circle has formed around a well-dressed couple. He's tall and auburn-haired, in a suit. The dark-haired woman next to him is gorgeous, and despite barely reaching his shoulder, they look well-matched.

"Who are they?"

"The architects who designed this opera house."

"Really?"

"Yes."

"Are they a team, then? An architect duo?"

"They're a team, all right," Victor says. "They're married."

"Ooh," I breathe. "Imagine working that close and also coming home together at the end of the night."

"An absolute nightmare," Victor says.

I laugh. "You would think that."

"I'm not a team player. It's worked out."

"Businesswise, yes," I say, and ignore the look he shoots my way. I'd spent a year making observations about him and never once did I think I'd get the chance to share them with him. Doing it now is heady.

"That may be so," he says, "but could you do it, Cecilia? A fight at home would spread to your work, and that's intolerable."

"Not all couples fight that much."

"Married ones do."

"They do? We haven't had a single one."

His lips twist. "Not yet, anyway. But you and I are a different story."

"We are?"

"We're not a real couple. They," he says, inclining his head to the couple in the distance, "are."

"That's your take on relationships, then. They're bound to devolve into fighting?"

He looks away from me. The sharp line of his jaw above me looks like a pane of glass, distant and imposing. But he answers. "Yes. Small disagreements grow, turn to nagging, which turns to arguments. I don't have time for that."

"But the rewards are bigger, too," I say. "When you know someone well enough to get past a disagreement. It strengthens you."

He snorts. "Are you a psychologist, as well?"

I can't let this go, even if I'm just poking the bear. He leads the way beneath a large archway. "What was the longest relationship you've ever had?"

"I'm not lying on a couch in your office," he says.

"So you don't want to answer my question."

He turns me toward a set of stone stairs. I let my hand trail along the smooth wood railing as we ascend. The place still smells of new construction, the promise of memories yet to be made. It's beautiful.

"I'll answer your question if you answer it first," he says.

"Three and a half years."

He's silent as we walk along an empty hallway. I tighten my grip on his forearm. "Victor?"

"A year," he says. "Almost."

"Gabriella?"

He looks down at me. The question is in his eyes, but he swallows it, and shakes his head. "No. This was college."

I nod. I had been in charge of booking his weekly dates with his supermodel ex, and when they ended things right after he took over as CEO of Exciteur, I'd been the one to send her flowers, too.

"College was a long time ago."

"You're my wife," he says. "Not my therapist."

The gruff way it's said makes me laugh, and then I can't stop, the sound filling the empty hallway. "No relationships for you, then. Just marriages."

Victor shakes his head. It's not in anger, though. More like exasperation. "Yes, and only when they're business arrangements."

"Noted," I tease. It's his word.

"What I really don't like," he says, "is when a woman gets under your skin. When you can't get them out of your head."

"Oh."

Victor's voice drops. "It's worse when you're forced to be close to them."

"Like when you live across the hall from them?"

"Yes. When they walk around your apartment in tight pants."

Pleased surprise rolls through me. "How dare they," I murmur. "In their own home."

"The audacity," he says. His arm disappears beneath mine and a strong hand grips my fingers.

He pulls me into an empty cloakroom. Rack after rack has bare coat hangers on them. With no large audience, there's no staff and definitely no coats.

My voice is breathless. "If you're looking for a way out of talking about relationships, you won't find it here."

"Yes," he says, hands closing around my waist. "I will."

My lips are still smiling when he presses his against them, kissing me firmly.

It's a while until I speak again. "Oh. Effective."

His chuckle is dark. "The only way to shut you up."

I press my hands flat against his chest, strong beneath the fabric of his dinner jacket. He kisses me like he had in the gym, like he knows what he wants and has no qualms about taking it.

He kisses me like he negotiates. To win.

I've never felt wanted this way before, never wanted quite this much in return. It's heightened by the complicated tangle of emotions I feel for this man.

Respect, dislike, intrigue, awe. He's an enigma.

And right now, he's an enigma who's entirely focused on me.

His hands dig into my hips and I meet him in the same intensity, sliding my hands into his hair. The wall is hard against my back.

"Do you think this is why they designed so many cloak-rooms?" I whisper.

He laughs hoarsely, moving his lips to my neck. His beard tickles, sending goose bumps across my skin. "Yes," he says. "The architects are married."

"They needed somewhere to sneak off during constructions."

His hands slide down my body, over the soft fabric of the

dress, and it was worth every cent. Victor groans, his hand ghosting past the curve of my breast. A hard length digs into my hip. "Fuck, Myers. This wasn't part of the plan."

"Yeah," I say, locking my knees around his hips. "It wasn't part of mine either."

"And yet."

"And yet."

He kisses me again, more languorous this time, and with each passing second the heat in my stomach grows sharper. I want him.

"If it wasn't our first time," he says, "I'd take you here."

The words are like a bolt through me. Imagining him, imagining us... "Where anyone could walk by?"

He rests his head against my shoulder. "Fuck. But yes, I would."

I reach down and palm him through his pants. The hard length throbs against my hand and he groans into my neck, nothing like the Victor in perfect control of himself and his world.

It makes my head spin. "A shame it's our first time, then."

His hands dig into my waist, fingers an inch from the undersides of my breasts. "Yes."

I stroke him one last time through the fabric. Then I push him away and rearrange my dress. My lips feel swollen and when I look down, my nipples are visible through the fabric. "We should leave."

Victor is staring at me, eyes dark. "Yes. We should."

"Don't call Steven. I want us to walk home."

"Is this your way of getting back at me?" he asks. "For all the times I had you run my errands and handle my calls?"

"Maybe. Would you object if it was?"

In the darkness, and in his tux, Victor looks every bit as dangerous as he does at the negotiating table. The fire in his eyes speaks of battles to conquer.

"No," he says. "Bring it on."

16

CECILIA

Victor doesn't nod to the concierge in the lobby of our apartment building when we get home. He just keeps a hand on my lower back, steering me into the elevator.

He kisses me as soon as the doors close. I grip him tight, burning from the teasing, the taunting. The deliciousness of this man, usually leashed so tight, unwinding for me.

We make it into the hallway and the front door shuts hard behind us. We look at each other. His breath comes fast, wide chest rising and falling.

And I'm lost.

He reaches for me and I step into his arms, back into his kisses. I'd never known it could be like this.

"Victor," I murmur.

He gives a groan of acknowledgement but doesn't stop. His hands skim down my dress, finding the smooth curve of my thighs. "Hold on to me."

I grip his shoulders just in time. Victor lifts me up onto the hallway table. Something brushes past my hip and then glass hits the stone floor with a shatter.

"Oh, no. Our vase."

Victor sears my neck with kisses, stepping between my

legs. They split of their own accord, my knees rising to grip him tight against me. "Whoops."

I grin. "You're telling me that wasn't on purpose?"

"Of course not," he murmurs. "I keep removing it. You're the one who puts it back."

"It annoys you."

His fingers dig into my thigh. "You like annoying me?"

"Sometimes."

His lips return to mine, hot and strong. One of his hands smooths up my leg. "This dress is annoying me right now. I have to feel you."

"God, yes please."

"Where?" He cups one of my breasts through the fabric of my dress, and with unerring precision, brushes over a nipple. "Here?"

"Uh-huh."

"Or... here?" He finds the hem of my dress and lifts it up, up, up. I gasp at the touch of his hand on my inner thigh, my hands tightening on his shoulders.

"Victor..."

"Keep saying my name like that, Myers."

"Cecilia."

His lips catch mine and his hand cups me through my panties, warm against my heat. "Cecilia," he murmurs. "How about here?"

The confession is a whisper against his lips. "Yes."

He slides them to the side and I can't breathe, can't think, around the feeling of his fingers brushing my hot skin.

"Fuck," he mutters. "You're wet."

Yes, I think. *All for you, only for you*, but the words die on my tongue as he strokes. His fingers tease my folds and with a skill that shouldn't surprise me, he finds my clit.

My breath turns shaky against his lips. "That's right," he says. "Fast or slow?"

I can't believe we're doing this. But I tell him, my eyes closed and breathing fast. "Hard."

Another of his smiles against my lips and then the pressure increases on my clit. Heat radiates from that simple touch, and with each of his circles, it grows stronger.

I tighten my grip on his shoulders. Life support, that's what they are, as he takes me higher and higher.

His free hand joins the one he's using on me, and then I feel it, the sweet burn of his finger sliding into me.

"Oh my God."

"Do you know?" he asks. "How badly I want to be inside you?"

My fingers tighten around his lapels. I don't know, but if it's as badly as I want him inside me, he's burning too. The relentless movements of his hand feel like punishment. His fingers speed up and it's all I can do to hold on against the racing of my pulse.

I'm going to come if he continues.

"Victor, I…"

"I know," he says. "You hate me for this, but you love me for it too."

"Please."

He kisses me, tongue moving against mine. His thumb presses down on my swollen clit and I break apart. Pleasure sweeps my body and I squeeze my knees around his hips. He holds me through it, a finger still sliding in and out of me.

"That's it," he murmurs. "That's it."

I'm breathing hard when the high ends, hands tight around his neck. "Oh my God."

His fingers circle one last time before he slides my panties back into place. The fabric feels rough against my sensitive skin. "It's a good thing," he says, "that I didn't know how good you feel. I'd never have gotten anything done with you as my assistant."

My voice is breathless. "Yes. You'd have done me."

He chuckles and I reach for him, finding his lips again. He's hard against me. He had meant what he said. He needs to be inside me.

But I had meant what I said earlier too.

I want to tease him for what he'd done to me for a year.

So I slide off the console table on shaky legs and find my footing among the shattered glass. "Thank you."

"My pleasure."

"That was... enlightening."

His smirk turns into a full-blown smile, and it takes my breath away. "I'd use a lot of adjectives about what just happened, but *enlightening* isn't one of them."

"Yes. Well, I don't have a thesaurus on me."

"There's one in my office. You could accompany me there."

"In your office?" I raise an eyebrow, the aftereffects of my orgasm making me bold. "You would, wouldn't you?"

"Yes," he says. "As would you. My desk is big enough."

"But not tonight." I turn, though it hurts, and start heading toward the staircase. To where both of our bedrooms are, separated by a hallway and two doors without locks.

No distance at all.

"Cecilia," he calls.

"Yes?"

"I have a dinner tomorrow with business associates."

I put out a hand to lean against the wall. His eyes clock it, just as they do the flush in my cheeks. His lips curl into a half-smile.

"Oh," I say. "How exciting."

"Will you come with me?"

I swallow. "As your wife?"

"Yes."

"I will."

―――

"*Thirteen* paintings," Nadine says. "Do you realize how much money that is?"

"Yes," I say. "Well, almost. I saw what you sold them for."

"It's not beer-money. It's not even rent-money. It's rent-for-a-year-money!"

"Even with the commission the gallery is taking?"

"They're just taking ten percent! Jake told me they usually request thirty, but because it was such a last-minute booking, they're charging ten. "

"Jake said that," I say.

"Yes. He said he was happy to meet you, by the way. That it was clear you and I are great friends." Her voice turns bashful. "I have a confession to make."

"Out with it," I say. With my headphones in, I can talk to Nadine *and* survey my closet. Despite having the guest bedroom, it's big enough to house a small futon in the center.

"I think Jake might be interested in me."

I laugh. "Oh, do you?"

"Yes. I'm sorry."

"Don't be! I guessed that the second I met him."

"You did not."

"I did," I say. "The five minutes we spoke were all about how fantastic you are, and I didn't mind, because I love singing your praises. We were like two fangirls."

"Oh, stop it."

"It's true. So. Are you interested in him?"

"No. He's not my type."

I smile, grateful she's not here to see it, and reach out to grab a handful of dresses. "You know I love you, but you often see things in black-and-white."

"No I don't. I'm an artist. I see endless nuances of color."

"Sure you do. But not when it comes to men."

"He's perfect for *you*. He's too similar to me to work."

I think of Victor, and his precise way of speaking, the methodical movement of his hands. The ambition and the business sense and the discipline. "I don't know about that," I say. "I think attraction is more about finding someone who is complementary."

Nadine is quiet a beat, but when she speaks, her voice is heated. "Okay. Spill."

I laugh. "How did you know?"

"Your voice. Your words. Come on, you don't really want to know how I know, not as much as I want to know what you know."

"I have no idea what you just said."

"Spill!"

"All right, all right. So. Last night Victor and I attended the opening of New York's new opera house."

"Right. As you do."

"As you do," I say. "When you're married to a St. Clair. And well... some things happened."

Nadine is silent as the grave as I give her the whole seedy rundown of what took place, shortened to a few sentences. I make the scene on the console table in his hallway sound like a handshake, but by the time I'm done, my cheeks are still red. "Saying all that out loud... wow."

"So what now? What do you want?"

I look at my dresses. Most are boring, the ones I'd worn a million times at the office. One is... decidedly not.

"I think for him, last night was about control. Having it, specifically. For whatever reason, he always has to be in control."

"Sounds like someone else I know."

I snort. "I like things to be organized. I don't have to be in control."

"Right, I won't comment. Go on."

"Well, I want him to lose it." I run a hand over the silky fabric of the dress. "I'm going to try and seduce my husband, and I know just how to do it."

17

CECILIA

I wait until we're seated at the dinner table before I drop the bomb. Victor and I sit side-by-side, watching the two men approaching. Carter Kingsley talks to the media mogul he and Victor are here to woo. Me? I'm wooing my husband.

I lean in to murmur the words. "I'm not wearing any underwear."

Victor's jaw works. "Damn it, Myers."

"This dress is pretty short, too."

Flaming blue eyes bear into mine. "You're playing with fire."

"Am I? Or are you?"

He smiles, a barely there curl of his lips that sends heat through me. The first half of dinner is uneventful, except that Victor's arm is draped behind my chair. Every time his hand brushes my shoulder, left bare from the strapless dress, my attention zeroes in on the small point of contact.

I wouldn't have believed we'd be here six months ago. That I'd be sitting next to him at a fancy restaurant, and feeling less like a trophy wife, and more like a businesswoman.

Like someone who goes after what she wants. Someone

who doesn't care what her past, judgmental self would have thought about this arrangement.

"It's a pleasure to have you here," Carter says. He's shot me speculative looks all evening, and more than once, I've seen him note Victor's hand by my shoulder. "Married life seems to be treating you well."

Mr. Simmons, owner of a national media conglomerate, looks up from his steak. "I heard something about that. Congratulations, you two. Where did you go on your honeymoon?"

"Oh, we haven't, yet." I put a hand on Victor's chest, looking up at him. "Neither one of us has had a chance to get away from work. But we will."

"We're thinking Barbados," Victor says. His gaze flicks down to my hand and the two rings glinting in the light. Am I overdoing it? But then his lip curls. "Have you been, Simmons?"

Small talk. He's engaging in it, and the edge I'd noted in his voice earlier is gone now. We're halfway through a discussion of the merits of the Caribbean when something on my leg makes me pause, fork halfway to mouth.

Victor's hand beneath the table.

He slides my hem up, inch by inch, until his long fingers curl around my bare knee. "I heard you've branched into Spanish media as well," he says to the men across from us.

My brain tries to focus on Simmon's reply, but it's more occupied with his fingers tracing patterns on the inside of my thigh. Thank God for fancy restaurants and long, linen tablecloths.

Victor keeps his hand there, leaning back against his chair with smooth professionalism on his face, as the rest of us finish up our food. And little by little his thumb inches upwards.

Abort mission, I think. Because he still looks like the cool, calm sculpture of control, while I'm the one burning with need. Memories of his fingers between my legs yesterday combine with the public aspect of today, and if he reaches the spot between my legs, he'll feel just how much I want him.

I cover my mouth with a napkin and lean his way. "Victor…"

His thumb double-taps against my inner thigh. An acknowledgement, before it continues to smooth upwards.

"What about you?" Simmons asks me. "What did you do before you married St. Clair over here?"

The fingers pause, as if he wants to give me a chance to respond without distraction. I'm glad for it, launching into an explanation of my virtual assistant start-up. Simmons nods throughout.

At his side, Carter looks impressed. "This sounds brilliant," he says. "You'd essentially be selling the solving of tasks and letting clients pay through a subscription. Victor, are you considering investing?"

"Potentially," he responds, voice giving nothing away. "If she'd allow me, of course. It's not something we've discussed yet."

"It's early days still," I say.

Carter nods. "Of course, of course. But if he doesn't want a piece of it, I might." He gives a crooked, wolfish grin to Victor. "Don't scowl. I'm always on the lookout for good companies to shepherd, new entrepreneurs to mentor."

"I'm mentoring her," Victor says.

I clear my throat. "Thank you, Carter. At the moment I'm not considering outside investment, but if I reach that stage, I'll definitely bear it in mind."

Victor's hand tightens around my thigh at my words, and I close my legs in response.

A few seconds later I feel it. The soft, apologizing circle of his thumb. I open them again and his hand slides higher, only an inch away from where I need his fingers. One brush over my sensitive skin and I'd—

"Well, I have to get going," Simmons says. "This has been lovely, gentlemen. Acture Capital has a lot to recommend it."

Victor withdraws his hand. "The pleasure was ours."

"It was," Carter agrees. "I'll call you this week. We can draw up a mock contract for your lawyers to read through as well, and at your own time. We want you to feel comfortable with the decision, regardless of which way you're leaning."

I smile and say my goodbyes, and then we all three watch as Simmons walks out of the restaurant.

"I should call it a night too," Carter says, tossing his napkin on the table. "Unless you two are in the mood for clubbing?"

"We're not," Victor say.

"You go to clubs?" I ask.

Carter laughs. It's a wonder to see him go from business to off-duty in so short a time span. "No. Not in years. But if our lady here wants to…"

"My lady," Victor corrects him, and then shakes his head.

"Of course, your lady. And how the rest of us men weep at that. Cecilia, you look stunning tonight."

"Thank you."

He rises from the table and so do we, following him out into the cold New York air. Steven is waiting for us by the curb. The second we're in the car, Victor presses the button to roll up the partition. It seals us into the backseat.

Victor reaches for my hand. "Feel," he mutters, pressing it flat against his hard length. The outline is stark through his pants. "That's what your no-panties stunt did to me."

I feel lightheaded, power and desire rising like a wave inside me. "You liked that."

He kisses me, a hard press of his lips on mine. I run my nails along his hardness and he gives a low hiss. "Cecilia…"

"Yes? Can I get you another coffee? Reschedule a meeting? Book your date with a new woman?"

"You're punishing me," he says.

"You said you didn't object."

In the darkness of the backseat, his eyes look almost black. "Oh, I don't. But two can play this game."

His hand grips the hem of my dress and tugs it up forcefully, the other pushing my legs apart. The shocked silence that follows is sweeter than candy. "Fuck," he mutters. "You told the truth."

"You didn't believe me?"

"No. That's why I tried to find out beneath the table."

There's a hoarseness in his voice I wouldn't have believed it could hold, one that isn't polished or controlled or restrained. It's the Victor I saw in his grandfather's study, the Victor who dared me to follow him at Nadine's art show.

The Victor who *wants* with such burning intensity that all *I* want is let him consume me. I want to drive him to the edge.

And then I want to drive him straight over it.

His fingers stroke the seam between my legs, the same motion I'm raking along the length in his pants. "Two more minutes," he murmurs, "and I would have been doing this in the restaurant."

My breath catches. "You wouldn't have dared."

"You know I would have." His fingers part me, and then he bends down, putting his mouth right over my clit.

"Oh my God." I find the thick strands of his hair, gripping. "Yes. Right there."

There's brief chuckle against my sensitive skin and then his lips return, tongue manipulating my clit back and forth. With this angle, it's all he can do. But it's also more than enough.

"I was going to seduce you," I whisper.

Victor turns his head to look up at me, his beard scraping against my skin. "What do you think this is?"

"I succeeded?"

"You overperformed."

He returns to the task at hand and I have to bite my lip to keep from moaning. Twice in two days, Victor has focused more on my pleasure than his own. It's not what I would have expected. Perhaps it's because he has to be in control, but if this is what Victor in control is like, well…

Bring it on.

A large, impatient hand on my knee spreads me wider and I give up any pretense of stroking him through his pants. There's no room for concentration when he sucks my clit into his mouth. "Victor," I whisper. "Victor, I can't, not here."

He doesn't stop, and in the rising tide inside of me, my body says something different. It can, and it will. This is my husband. This is our car driving us home to our apartment. And it's my pleasure to take.

So I dig my fingers into his hair and focus on nothing but the sensation of his tongue, flicking back and forth. "Like that."

There's a hum against my clit as he agrees, and a few seconds later, the orgasm sweeps over me. I turn my head against the headrest to keep from moaning, fingers tightening in his hair. He doesn't stop licking me. Doesn't take his mouth away until my legs relax against the leather seat and my hand slides out of his hair, resting on the nape of his neck.

"That's right," he murmurs. "You can't tease me like that, Myers, if you can't take the consequences."

"Cecilia."

He presses a close-mouthed kiss to my sensitive clit. "Cecilia," he agrees, and pulls the hem of my dress down.

Dazed, I look out the window. "We're standing still."

"We have been for a few minutes."

"Oh. We're home."

"That we are," Victor says. He reaches down and rearranges himself, a frown on his lips. "Can't wait to get inside."

"Inside what, exactly?"

His eyes light up. "Inside who, I think." Victor knocks on the partition and raises his voice. "Night, Steven."

A muffled voice comes from the other side. "Night, Mr. and Mrs. St. Clair."

My cheeks burn. I'd forgotten him completely, but it seemed Victor hadn't. And he'd still done what he did. "Oh my God," I whisper to him, out on the sidewalk. "Steven just... he was there the whole time."

"He didn't hear or see a thing," Victor says. His arm wraps around my waist and I'm half-carried, half-escorted through our lobby. Good thing, too, because my legs feel weak.

"Let's give him a raise."

"Will it ease your embarrassment?"

"Yes."

Victor slams the button to the elevator. "Then consider it done. Now come here."

His kiss tastes like me and ignites the same fire he'd slaked just minutes earlier in the car. My body burns for his.

I'm the one who unlocks our apartment with the keycard tonight. Victor steps in behind me. Without letting myself hesitate, I push him against the closed front door. His eyes meet mine, but the flash of confusion turns to surprised approval when I drop to my knees.

"Myers..."

I undo his belt buckle and slide down his zipper. It's difficult to get it over the hard bulge beneath, but with heroic effort, I manage. I slide my fingers beneath the elastic of his boxer-briefs and tug them down. He springs out, hard and swollen and gleaming at the tip. "You don't think you're the only one allowed to tease?"

His eyes tell me he'd thought just that. They flutter closed as soon as I grip him, skin hot and firm to the touch.

"Christ," he mutters. I open my lips, closing them around his head, and then I swirl my tongue like he had done to me in the car.

The sweet expletives are gone, now. His hand finds my loose curls and he grips. "Fucking hell, Myers."

This is what I want. Him, unbound, and completely at my mercy. Victor St. Clair begging me for more.

Victor St. Clair needing me for a change.

I wrap my lips tight around his shaft and start to move,

careful to swirl my tongue at the end with every bob. I look up at him the entire time, and I don't think I've ever seen anything hotter than Victor like this, leaning against a wall and his face tight as if with pain.

He's so hard he's throbbing in my mouth, and it's all because of me.

I grip the base of him tightly and use my free hand to cup his twin weights. He tastes musky and delicious, and as I speed up, he groans above me. The sound sends a bolt of heat between my legs.

I can't wait until he's inside of me.

His hands tighten in my hair. "Myers, you need to stop."

I speed up.

"Myers," he says again. It's the voice he used in the office, calling me in from my desk, and I react to it on instinct. His hard length makes a sharp *pop* as I release it from my mouth and look up at him.

"Yes?"

"You've proven your point." His chest rises and falls rapidly, and the eyes that stare down at me are wild. "But I'll be inside you when I come tonight."

Oh Lord.

I nod, mute, and accept the hand he offers me.

We don't get further than the kitchen. He grips my hips and lifts me up onto the counter, the same one I've prepared breakfast on a dozen times or seen Bonnie bake bread on.

"Here," he says. "Now."

I reach for the buttons on his shirt and undo them, my fingers fumbling. "I need this off."

He helps me with an impatient growl, the shirt hanging off his frame. God, he's gorgeous, sculpted from a daily exercise regimen that prioritizes health and well-being. A wide, strong chest and the hint of a six-pack across a flat stomach, marred only by the long, jagged scar that sweeps across his torso. I run my hand over it, desire and curiosity at war within me.

The scar clearly doesn't bother him anymore, not as he tugs my dress down over my strapless bra. He undoes the clasp and my breasts spill out into his hands, nipples taut.

"Fuck, Myers. Fuck." He ducks his head to suck a nipple into his mouth, and my smile turns into a gasp. Sensitive, so sensitive, and I'm stimulated too far already.

I grip the hard length of him and tug him closer. He hisses out a breath, hands pushing the hem of my dress up. Fingers dig into my skin. "Condom?"

"I'm on birth control."

With that, he fits the blunt head against me and gives a single, deep thrust. Sensuous stretching and a fullness that reaches impossibly deep. My hands find purchase on his shoulders, my breath coming fast. He's big, and he's buried completely, and my entire body feels like a live wire.

"Finally," Victor murmurs as he starts to move.

It's all I can do to hold on, but I do that to the best of my ability, locking my legs around his hips and bracing a hand behind me on the kitchen counter. The sound of us fills the kitchen, amplified against the marble.

Concentration and pleasure-pain are stark on his face. "Look down," he tells me.

I do, and think I might orgasm from the sight alone, of him filling me with deep, measured strokes. I didn't know it could feel like this. That I could want like this.

"You feel unreal," he says, his voice like a benediction. "I'm not going to last for shit."

"Then don't."

He gives a hoarse half-laugh, and the sound goes straight through me, hits parts of me that are aching just as bad as the spot between my legs. He's out of control, and it's all for me.

Victor slides an arm around my waist to support me as he speeds up. The other hand strokes over the slick folds of me, spread around him, and presses down on the swollen nub up top.

I moan at the feeling. Too stimulated, I'm too stimulated, and he couldn't possibly—

But he does, and I do, my body breaking apart for a second time. I grip his shoulders and reach out, my mouth finding his bare shoulder. Teeth sink down.

Victor curses and speeds up, hips like pistons, my skin digging into the kitchen counter.

We'll have to sanitize it with bleach after.

His hands curl around my hips and fingers dig into my skin. "Fucking hell, Myers."

He comes with sharp, erratic thrusts that smart against my inner thighs. His chest rises and falls, the scar rippling with the heavy breaths. I dig my hands into his shoulders. Don't pull out, I think. Not yet.

But Victor does. He steps back, mouth soft and hair wild, and tucks himself back into his pants. The shirt still hangs off him and the chest is on glorious, glorious display. He looks like a god, a conqueror, a man thoroughly well-pleased.

I slide off the counter and wiggle my dress down past my hips, keeping my legs locked closed. The lack of panties is suddenly very apparent.

Victor runs his eyes over me, pleasure in his deep-blue eyes. "This might complicate things, but I don't think we'll let it. We've always worked well together."

"Uh," I say. "Yes, that's true."

He shakes his head. "You're my ideal woman, Cecilia. Business always comes first."

I reach for my bra. It's in the sink, and the flesh-colored satin is splattered with water drops. "Business first," I repeat.

He takes it as confirmation. "Thanks for an unreal night," he says, and then his familiar striding gait echoes down the hallway as he makes for the staircase.

Well. He lost control, but it didn't take him long to regain it.

18

VICTOR

It's been three days since the kitchen counter incident, but sleeping with Myers hadn't gotten the desire out of my system. It only increased it, to where my need for her feels like a fever beneath my skin.

The idea of prim Cecilia Myers, quiet assistant and organizational genius, wearing a dress without panties out to a dinner with business associates is... well.

Hot as fucking hell.

But the idea of Cecilia, with her wide smiles and teasing jokes, standing in the bedroom across from mine, and making the decision not to put on underwear so she could seduce me?

It makes me hard just to think about.

I reach beneath my desk and rearrange the ache. Three days since the kitchen is three days too long, as far as that part of my anatomy is concerned. It has a head of its own in more ways than one.

She'd tasted sweet in the car. If I close my eyes, I can still hear her muffled whimpers. I can see the bare treasure between her legs and taste it on my tongue.

The memories are doing nothing for my concentration or the pounding headache at my temples. Nothing to dull the ache in my pants, either, but I have no time to solve that issue.

Not now. Not when Myers and I have our meeting in fifteen minutes.

She arrives on the dot, punctual as always. We're at home, but with my office so similar to that of Exciteur, it's hard not to draw the parallels. The only difference is her slippers instead of heels.

"Hi," she says. Her hair is in a high ponytail and a flush creeps up her cheeks.

"Hello," I say. We haven't spoken much since we slept together, although *slept* is not the right word for the explosive kitchen counter fuck. She has her routine and I have mine.

I'm going to have to get more sex into it somehow.

"Are you okay? You look tired."

"I'm fine," I say.

She sits down on the chair opposite my desk, clutching a binder to her chest. "All right, then. I have a lot to share with you today."

"Go right ahead."

Cecilia launches into a refined elevator pitch, and I listen, humming occasionally. Her idea sounds like many of the hundreds of start-ups I've heard about over the years. Unease grows in my stomach when I realize she also sounds like many of the start-ups that fail within their first year.

She hands me an overview of costs and an expansion plan. "This is where I'm heading," she says. "The overhead is considerable, but with a quick enough expansion, I should hit my numbers."

I tap my pen against the paper. It's neat and orderly, like all the reports she prepared for me. In truth, the plan she's drawn up is impressive. She's thinking far ahead. She has her company's story brand nailed down. But.

"Your figures are too high."

She leans across the desk, and the neckline of the T-shirt she's wearing swings low. I can see the tops of smooth breasts.

Throbbing, aching pain.

"Have I miscalculated?"

"No, I'm sure you've done it correctly. But the figures are too high from a risk perspective."

Her wide, soft lips turn down at the corners. They'd been wrapped around my dick just three days ago. The image of her sinking to her knees, pressing me against the front door… taking command. Looking up at me. *Christ, St. Clair.*

"From a risk perspective," she repeats, voice turning hard. "I want to take risk. I've seen you, and your business partners, take risks all the time. It's always been rewarded."

I brush the back of my hand over my mouth to hide a smile. "Not always. I've made tons of deals that fell through."

Her eyes flicker up to mine. "You have?"

"Of course. I'm thirty-four, Myers. What do you think I did until I was twenty-five?"

"You made mistakes?" she asks. Her voice is so full of skepticism I want to laugh.

"Yes. You have to do things wrong to learn how to do them right. The sooner you make the mistake, the sooner you'll learn."

"Right."

I tap the paper in front of us. "With this overhead, so soon into starting the business, you have no room for error. No room for unexpected losses. One rough wind, and you fall. And there will be rough winds. There always are."

She blows out a breath. "If I cut this, I won't grow as fast."

"If you don't, you might not grow at all."

Cecilia snatches up the papers and sits back in her chair. She reads them over with a frown, looking like an angry kitten. But she'd asked for my advice and I gave it.

I run a hand through my hair. Not once had I cared if I offended the people I critiqued before. I'd given them hard truths and cold facts, letting the chips fall where they might. I'd certainly not been as measured as I am with her.

Fucking her has definitely messed with my head.

"Damn it," she says. "You're right. You can say I told

you so."

"There'd be little point in doing that."

She sighs, putting her papers down. "I'll start over with my calculations, then."

"Once you've changed them, send your plan to me and I'll take a look."

Her eyes look like they had when I glanced up at her in the car, my head between her legs. Shock at what I'm doing. "You mean for next month's meeting?"

"No, send them to me as soon as you're done."

"But you said…"

"I know what I said." I nod down to the papers, breaking eye contact. My head is killing me, and now my throat's started, too. It scratches when I speak. "But I have an interest in this company too. Send it to me."

"All right, I will. Thank you." She scoops up the papers and heads to the door, a look of deep concentration on her fair features.

A year with her walking in and out of my office, just like that, and I'd never truly noticed her before.

It strikes me as a gross oversight on my part.

Thirty minutes later Cecilia knocks on my half-open door again. She's holding a mug and wearing an apologetic smile. "Your voice sounded scratchy earlier. Do you think you're coming down with something?"

"I can't," I say. It's the truth. Too much work, and too many people depend on it being done. The steady stream of emails never ends. Brad is good, but he isn't Cecilia, and it shows.

Not to mention the conference in Boston next week with Exciteur. It will carve three days out of my normal work schedule.

"Still," she says, and sets the giant cup of tea down on my desk. A scent of honey wafts up from the hot water. "For your throat. And… thanks for agreeing to look at my numbers again this week."

"Yeah. Sure."

She's gone again, and I look at the mug for a long time. I can't remember the last time anyone did something for me. Something they weren't paid for and that I didn't ask them to do.

I drink the tea.

It's late in the afternoon by the time I leave my home office, mug in hand. It helped, but only temporarily, and now my throat feels like it's closing in on itself.

I haven't been sick in years.

I don't allow my body to be sick.

Which, of course, means it's doing it anyway. I wonder if this is punishment for mixing business and pleasure and giving in to Cecilia. Or maybe this is my body's way of punishing me for *not* giving in with Cecilia over the past three days.

I know which one my head wants it to be. Both of them.

Familiar voices drift from the kitchen and I stop in the hallway, listening to them chatter. Once, my apartment was always dead quiet. Not anymore.

Cecilia and Bonnie sound comfortable with one another, voices muted and soft. My mother and grandmother used to talk like that. My brother and I would sit at the kitchen table at Grandma's and listen to them chatter about everything and nothing as they cooked or baked.

They're all gone now, and in nine months' time, so will Cecilia be. My apartment will be quiet again.

I step into the kitchen. Cecilia's eyes brighten when she sees me, and the expression sets off an ache in my chest. But her expression quickly turns to concern. "Oh, you look awful."

"Hello to you too."

"You sound even worse." She steps around the kitchen island and puts a cool hand against my forehead. "You have a fever."

She makes it sound like something I've done on purpose.

"I'm fine, Cecilia."

"No, you're not."

"Don't fuss."

She steps back, eyes narrowing. I imagine it's the look she wore outside my office, warding off employees who wanted to speak to me for no particular reason. She was always good at that. My gatekeeper. "We're having soup for dinner," she says. "Should be good for your throat."

Bonnie speaks up from the stove. "Chowder and freshly baked bread."

"Christ, Bonnie," I say, sinking down on the kitchen chair. My head feels ready to explode. "You're worth every cent I pay you."

There's silence after my words, but I'm too tired to tell if it's stunned or disapproving. Too tired to care, too.

Then a warm bowl appears in front of me and a giant glass of water. A small hand, one I recognize intimately now, places an aspirin next to it. Tea and now this.

We eat in silence, Cecilia and I. Her usual attempts at chatter are gone, and I don't know whether I'm grateful or if I miss them.

After dinner, I make it halfway down the hall before her voice stops me. It has an unmistakable note of command in it.

"Where are you going?"

I reach out to steady myself against the wall. Consider lying, and then discard the idea. I'm the master in my own home. "To my office."

"You need to rest. Lie down."

"I can rest in the chair. It's ergonomic."

Cecilia snorts, and then she's there, in front of me. Her hand presses against my chest. "Please rest. At least lie down for a bit. Please."

Her eyes are impossibly close. Would she lie down with me?

There's no way I can deny that offer, even if my body is at war with itself. Desire against the disease.

"I've decided," I say. "I'm going to lie down for a bit."

Her lips quirk. "Great choice. How about your couch? I've never seen you use it."

"I use it."

"Well, you haven't in the past months."

"I didn't know you were keeping track."

This time, the smile on her face is unmistakable. She's laughing at me, but she doesn't say a word as we head back into the living room.

I stretch out on the gray couch. It had been one of the few things I'd told the interior designer: The couch had to be comfortable. None of that look-good-but-feel-awful bullshit. He'd delivered.

A sigh of relief. It feels good to be lying down, and the pillow beneath my head is... well. Maybe I should try sleeping down here for a change. Might be better on nights when the bed holds nothing but nightmares.

"Isn't this much nicer than working?"

I don't open my eyes. "Don't gloat."

There's the sound of footsteps, and then water being poured. I crack open an eyelid to see her returning with a clean towel in hand. She leans over my face.

"Hey, I don't—oh. Okay." The towel feels ice-cold against my forehead. It's delicious.

"I've put a big glass of water on the coffee table for you, too. Do you want anything else?"

"No." After a brief silence, I crack open another eyelid. "Thanks."

Cecilia smiles at me. "That was more than I ever got as your assistant."

"Kick a man while he's down, why don't you."

She laughs, and then her slipper-muffled footsteps recede along the hardwood floor. She's leaving.

"Hey," I say. "Where are you going?"

The steps stop. "You want company?"

I should say no. Shouldn't even have asked. I shift on

the couch, knowing that answering yes is showing weakness. It's definitely not a part of the business box, not even a part of the pleasure box where I'd placed her three nights ago.

"Yes," I say.

"All right. Let me just get something to drink."

A few minutes later she sinks down next to me on the giant couch and props her feet up on the coffee table. She has a large ice coffee in hand the color of caramel.

"That," I say, "looks disgusting."

"It's eighty-seven percent sugar, twelve percent milk, and one percent coffee. It's also one hundred percent delicious."

"Ugh."

"It's not your preferred single-shot Americano, that's for sure." She reaches for the remote control. It's in a basket on the living room table, together with the remote for my surround system. I haven't had music on in ages.

It has been a long time since I'd lived in my home, and not just used it to work, sleep and exercise in.

"Your TV is huge," she say. "Do you like watching things when you're sick? Or do you want me to be quiet?"

"You wouldn't be much company if you were quiet."

"You're even grumpier when you're sick. Can't say I'm surprised." Cool fingers rearrange the towel on my brow and briefly brush through my hair.

Oh. The faint touch of her fingers along my tight scalp felt like heaven. But her hand is gone, and I've already exposed myself too much tonight.

"I'm grumpy," I say, "because I have you relaxed and on my couch, but I don't have the energy to make full use of that."

The channel-scrolling stops. "You're talking about…"

"Yes. I'm talking about sex."

The channel-scrolling resumes. "You won't be sick forever."

"Thank the small mercies." I turn my head slightly. She's

stopped at a home renovation show. A couple from Texas redoing farmhouses.

"I love watching these shows," Cecilia says. "It combines all of my interests."

"You have an interest in old barns."

She laughs, and the sound doesn't grate against my headache. It's soothing. "No. But I like organization, renovation, fixing things up. I like seeing happy couples and their kids. I like... okay, I don't mind barns."

"Have you ever actually been inside of a barn?"

"Oh, yes. Many times."

I turn my head, ignoring the blinding headache. "You're serious."

"Dead serious. My mother went through a vegan phase. One of her best friends at the time had this place where you could pet rescued barnyard animals for spiritual healing."

My silence has to be enough, because she laughs. "Yeah. I know it's not something for you."

"Spiritual healing," I say.

She shrugs. "Or relaxation, I suppose. I have to give it to her, it's hard to feel stressed or angry when you're holding a lamb or petting a cow."

"There is so much about you that I could never have predicted."

"Happy I can still surprise you," she says. She stretches out an arm along the back of the couch, and I see her hand, dangling only inches away from my face. It would be so easy to have her run it through my hair.

And so complicated.

I close my eyes. "Tell me more about your mother."

"You're sure?"

No. "Yes."

She pulls her legs up beneath her on the couch, settling in. "She had me when she was twenty-one. She'd dropped out of college and was road tripping with a few friends at the time."

"Wow."

"Yes, not the ideal time to get pregnant." Cecilia's voice doesn't hold bitterness, though. Only fondness. "She's not normal. Not in the sense that you and I are normal. If we even are, because in truth, what is normal? She's special. Fearless, and obsessive. She'll go deep and far in one direction and inspire everyone she meets about it."

"Like veganism."

"Like veganism," she says, "or geology, or ocean conservation, or space exploration. It was tantric yoga once. She made me practice with her every morning and evening."

I make a choked sound and look up at her. She meets my gaze, and then she laughs, reaching out to slap me on the shoulder. "Tantric yoga is *not* the same as tantric sex!"

"Are you sure?"

"Very sure. God, Victor, no, she was not into that." Cecilia frowns. "Well, not that I know of. But maybe she was when I was at school. Ugh. I don't want to think about that."

"What's the difference?"

"Tantric yoga involves no sex at all. Just a lot of breathing, mindfulness, and praying to deities. This was at the same time she experimented with polytheism."

I rub a hand over my eyes. "Christ. I can't think of an upbringing less like my own."

Cecilia chuckles. "It was different than most of the kids at school, too. But thanks to her I am excellent at trivia. I know a lot about most things."

"Where'd you live?"

"We moved around a lot. The longest place we stayed in was Santa Fe."

"New Mexico," I mutter. "Figures."

"Be nice," she says, but there's only fondness in her tone. "She loves very freely, my mother, and has no boundaries. We often had her friends sleeping on the couch."

"I can't imagine you in that household. How did you become… you?"

"Someone had to be the adult."

"And that fell to you?"

"The first person I was ever personal assistant to was my mother. I organized our trips from the time I was twelve."

The image of a young Cecilia with a clipboard and a patient expression rises before my eyelids. Something tightens across my chest. Fondness.

I really am sick.

"Is that why you want to start your company? So you can be the personal assistant to a whole country?"

She laughs. "I suppose so, yes. Since the model is subscription and task-based, it's affordable. People in all walks of life will be able to buy some peace of mind from us. Helping people help themselves, in a way." Her fingers drum softly against her knee. "So my childhood was different from yours, then. I'm guessing your grandfather didn't bring you to any barns to pet cows for stress relief?"

I snort. "He would've had a fit if I suggested something like that."

"What recreational activities were acceptable for a young St. Clair?" Her tone holds fake grandiosity, but there's interest there, too.

I flip the cold towel over. It slips slightly and then her slim fingers are there, brief and wonderful. "Tennis, golf, sailing," I say. "Languages. We'd go to museums occasionally, especially if he knew the… the docent." I wave a hand. My skin feels flushed, too hot. Damn fever. "I came with him on most of his business trips. Travel was important for him."

"What did you do? When he was working on the trips?"

"I walked around whatever city we were in."

She rearranges herself on the couch behind me, and then something rests against my head. Definitely her thigh. This woman is killing me. "Tell me about it."

I sigh. My throat feels shot to hell, but I do it anyway, because she asked. "He went to Europe a lot, Asia on occasion. I walked across London when I was eleven. It's deceptively big. I had to ask someone to explain how the Tube worked so I could make it back to the hotel in time for dinner."

She makes an incredulous sound. "At eleven, I was getting up at six every morning so my mother could realign my chakras."

"Well, you seem very well-adjusted now."

"Thank you," she says. "I haven't had my aura read in years, though. I might be all out of whack. Do you miss him?"

"Who?" I already know, and she knows it too, but she presses on. She's brave. I knew that already, but she confirms it daily.

"Your grandfather."

"No." I reach for the buttons in my shirt. It feels as if my skin is boiling, as if the heat in here has ratcheted up ten degrees. "He wasn't... I don't know. It wasn't easy being his grandson."

"I can only imagine," she says.

I'm halfway down my chest when I remember the scar. She'll see, but she already has. She's already asked too, and damn it, I'm too hot. I undo the last button and take a deep breath. Still too warm.

"He had expectations, then."

"Doesn't every parent or guardian?" I ask. "His were just very well-articulated."

"Is that why you work so hard?"

"I'm sick," I mutter. "I'm not lying on a therapist's couch."

Her voice turns teasing, and then she lifts the damp towel off my forehead. Smooth fingers rub circles at my temples. "Yes," she says. "Your chakras are definitely off."

I sigh. She's good at what she's doing, spiritual nonsense aside. "Realign them for me."

"I really have no idea what I'm doing, you know."

"Never admit that."

"Right. Project confidence. Negotiate from your strengths. I've learned a lot, watching you do business."

I don't know what to respond to that, so I don't, sinking

into the feel of her taking care of me. It's weakness, and it's dangerous, and I should walk away. But I can't remember the last time something like this happened.

In the background, an excited couple squeals as their renovated house is revealed.

"He didn't want me anymore than I wanted him," I say.

Her fingers pause. "How do you mean?"

"He wasn't expecting an eight-year-old boy to raise, and I'd only known him as someone we saw once a month over dinner. But suddenly there was only the two of us."

Her fingers finally run through my hair. "He asked for custody, then? After your parents passed?"

"Demanded it, more like it," I say. "He wasn't going to let me go to my aunt in Florida. He didn't like her husband and he said I'd become a lost cause in that household. 'Charlotte lets her boys play too many video games, but there's still hope for you, boy.'"

Cecilia chuckles. "Was he like you?"

"No. He worked all the time. Didn't really have a lot of close friends, either. Just people he considered… worthwhile to have as acquaintances. He tried to raise me like I was my father, the son he'd lost. A chance to do it over again."

"Victor," she says. "That sounds like you."

I reach above my head and search blindly for her wrist. I find it and bring her hand back to my hair. "You've gotten a lot bolder since I married you."

"I'm not afraid of you anymore."

Her words are soft, matter-of-fact. But it takes me several seconds to process them. "You were afraid of me before."

"Of course I was," she says. Despite the seriousness of the topic, her voice is teasing. "You told me several times in the first couple of weeks how useless I was. Mason covered for me twice when I had to run into the bathroom."

"Run into the bathroom?"

"To cry," she says. "But you didn't break me."

I can't reconcile the emotions I had toward the assistant

back then, can't match them with the Cecilia I know now. But I can't deny the words she attributes to me. They sound like mine.

Shame tastes like ash on my tongue.

I'd made her cry. I hadn't even known her first name or cared enough to learn it, but I'd been able to make her cry all the same.

I am like him, only worse, because he worked for something. For the family legacy and the family name. I'm working to prove him right about me, but he isn't even here to see it.

"You're still alive under there?" Cecilia says, lifting the towel from my brow. "You have to let me know if you need an ambulance, you know."

"I'm sorry," I say. "I haven't said that before, I think. But I'm sorry for not treating you better when you were my assistant."

She's quiet. A hand smooths down my cheek, the softest touch, and it feels like forgiveness. We don't speak for a long time, not until my eyelids feel heavy and my skin cooler.

Cecilia changes channels until she finds a movie. It's one I've seen before, many years ago. A romantic comedy. She puts the remote down and rearranges behind me again. This time, she stretches out too, and her arm ends up draped over my chest. I glance down to see her hand tracing my scar. The ragged line is faint now, the only remaining evidence of the car crash.

I don't have the energy to protest, and her hand feels cool against my warm skin.

"A long time ago, this," she murmurs.

I close my eyes. "It's from a different life."

She sighs, a soft sound of relaxation. "Maybe you have many in you. That's what my mother would say."

Maybe I do, I think. And maybe this is the start of a new one.

19

CECILIA

I blink my eyes open to sunshine. I turn over in bed and search for the best pillow, the one with the perfect level of firmness, and pull the comforter up below my chin. Why is it sunny? I always draw the curtains.

I yawn and open my eyes, curled on my side, and look out at the view. I'll never tire of it. Central Park, the trees, the skyscrapers that line the other side. In one of those buildings lives Tristan Conway and his son, the apartment I was in with Victor over a month ago. When we toasted to our marriage.

Victor. We had been on the couch last night.

How did I get up here?

Either my memory has betrayed me, or I was asleep when he brought me upstairs. Did he lead me, half-asleep on my feet? Did he carry me?

I peek beneath the covers. I'm wearing the same clothes as yesterday, minus the cardigan and my slippers.

He put me to bed, then.

I groan, pulling the comforter over my head. He was sick and still he'd done that.

I'm in over my head.

He'd given me something last night I never thought I'd get. An apology and an insight into why he is the way he is.

I think of him traveling alone with his grandfather to cities all around the world, and then left to his own devices while meetings were being held. I think of a man who had no idea how to raise a grieving grandson, but stepped up to do his best. A son who lost everything and learned to play by his grandfather's rules.

I take a quick shower beneath the rainfall showerhead and wrap my fluffy purple robe around myself. I look in the mirror and see bright eyes, clean skin, and wet, towel-dried hair.

And then I plod out to the hallway in search of my sick, CEO husband.

He's not in his bedroom. The door is half-open and I peek inside, but it's empty, the bed made in exact precision.

He's not downstairs either. Not in his office, not in the gym, not on the balcony. I even check the two spare guest bedrooms. But nothing.

I grab my phone. The last text I'd sent had been the address to Nadine's gallery for the opening. It feels like ages ago.

We'd been two completely different people then.

Cecilia: Don't you dare tell me you're at work. With how sick you were last night, you should be in bed.

I don't expect a response, but the words need to be said. So I'm surprised when my phone chimes ten minutes later.

Victor: You know, you're considerably more bossy than I used to think.

It's easy to imagine the glint in his blue eyes when he wrote those words. He's flirting back with me.

Cecilia: You're deflecting. And thank you. Seeing as how I'm now my own boss, I take that as a compliment.

Victor: You should. Yes, I'm at work. I had a number of meetings that couldn't be changed and I felt better this morning.

Thirty seconds later, my phone chimes again, and this time I chuckle.

Victor: I also don't know why I'm justifying my actions to you. If you're your own boss, then so am I. Get to work changing those numbers, Myers.

Cecilia: You sound like you need to pet a cow.

Victor: I can think of much better ways to relieve stress.

My stomach clenches at the innocent string of words. I imagine them in his voice, the dark, low tone that brokers no discussion. The way he'd spoken to me in the backseat of our car.

Cecilia: A shame you didn't choose to work from home, then. I took a shower before I went looking for you... and I'm only in my robe.

Victor: Great. Now I'm hard, and I have a meeting with Japanese investors in five minutes.

Heat blooms inside. Imagining him, tall and imposing and in a suit, sitting in his office. I've seen him like that hundreds of times. Every day I worked for him.

But the mental image of him reaching beneath his desk and readjusting himself because of me...

I do something I've never done before.

I shimmy my bathrobe down my shoulders and tighten the tie around my waist. My modest cleavage looks tantalizing in the camera on my phone. No nipples, just the tops of my breasts and the dip of my cleavage disappearing down into my robe.

I take a picture and hit send, heart pounding.

Victor: Fuck.

Moments later, an image of his own appears. The imprint of his hard length against his gray suit trousers, his hand pulling them taut. Every single inch of him is visible through the Italian fabric.

It makes my stomach clench. I know those inches. I need those inches.

Cecilia: Someone's feeling better.

Victor: Someone better still be in that robe when I get home.

Cecilia: Can't make any promises... so you'd better come home soon.

He doesn't respond to that, probably heading into a meeting with investors with me on his mind. It makes me feel powerful. Wanted.

Funny, how the one area where we have absolutely no problem communicating in is the physical one. The desire I feel from him obliterates all the usual hiccups I've faced with men in the past. There's no room to think about my insecurities with him, and it's intoxicating.

Despite my text, I change out of my robe pretty quickly. Bonnie always arrives midday and I have no intention of walking around half-naked with someone else in the house.

No, I do what I always do, which is work. My desk in my bedroom with the incredible view has become my home.

I run with Summer in Central Park around lunchtime and then eat a quick meal at the kitchen island. I don't shower afterwards, my head filled with new ideas, and return to my computer. His words made sense.

I need to be more conservative with my numbers, and now I know how to swing it. I'm deep into my calculations when I hear footsteps coming up the stairs.

They're not Bonnie's careful strides.

I push back from the desk. That's all I have time to do before my door is pushed open. I shriek as Victor crosses the distance between us, eyes focused, hair messy.

"You're not in your robe," he says, hands closing around my waist. "But you'll do."

He lifts me up and moves us to the bed. My laugh turns into a gasp. "What a compliment."

"I can do compliments." His hand smooths over my thigh. "Your legs and ass look fucking unreal in these tights. I've never seen a woman wear things like this before."

"Yoga pants?"

"Yes." He kisses me, hungry and wanton, and I spread my legs to accept his weight on top of me. Against my thigh, I can feel how hard he is.

He's still in the gray suit.

"How was your meeting?"

"Torture. All I could think about were these." His hands find the hem of my T-shirt and slide it up. He grabs the elastic of my sports bra and tugs it, baring me for his gaze.

He bends to a nipple and I sigh, putting my hand in his hair. "Well," I murmur. "You seem to be much better than last night."

He gives a thrust against me, as if disputing that. I chuckle and reach down to palm him through his pants. "In some ways, I mean."

"I am much better," he says, his five-o'clock shadow scratching my skin as he kisses down my stomach. He hooks his fingers into my yoga pants and panties and tugs them down. "Lift your hips."

I do, and then I'm once again naked before him, but this time it's full daylight. Any qualms that rise to the surface are gone at the hunger in his eyes, the appreciation as they sweep over me.

It makes me bold, ignites my body in ways that make it burn.

This time, I ride him.

His eyes flash at first and then turn molten, gaze settling between my legs. Watching as I take him inside.

Like he's done before, he focuses on me. There's no artifice to it and no pressure. Not once has he told me to come. He just circles my clit with his finger, eyes hooded.

"You look unbelievable," he says, eyes shifting to my breasts. And I believe him.

I come first, beneath the steady movement of his thumb and the deep movement of him inside of me. Hands bracing on his chest, I speed up through my orgasm, body shuddering.

I open my eyes to his pleasure-pained expression. He'd held off, but judging by the sheen on his forehead, it cost him. I kiss him. He lifts his hips and then I'm the one holding on, face buried against his neck, as he fucks me with piston-strength. Thrusts turn erratic and he growls into my ear as he explodes, emptying himself inside me.

I've never heard a hotter sound than Victor St. Clair losing control.

His chest rises beneath mine, strong arms wrapped around my back. I close my eyes and breathe in the scent of him, soap and shampoo and the briefest hint of aftershave.

"Who are you?" he mutters into my hair. "Accompanying me to dinner without your panties. Sending me nudes at work."

I chuckle. His eyes are molten and sated, the furrow gone from between his brow.

"I'm not sure," I say. "But it seems to be working on you."

"That's an understatement."

I kiss him again, my lips soft now, and settle beside him

on the bed. His arm is beneath my head and his wide chest rises with his labored breathing. He stares up at the ceiling.

"Good thing you didn't put no physical relations into our contract," I say. "Or we would both be in breach."

"This," he says, "was not something I anticipated."

"Neither did I."

He runs his free hand through his hair. I doubt he's the kind of man who cuddles. I shouldn't press, and yet... I can't let this opportunity go. I turn on my side and put my head on his shoulder.

Victor doesn't react either way, just looks up at the ceiling. His Adam's apple moves beneath his stubble as he swallows.

"Thank you for carrying me upstairs last night," I say.

It takes him a while to reply. "Steven uses the gym some mornings," he says. "Couldn't let him see my wife like that."

The words 'my wife' feel like they rattle around in my head, in my chest, taking root.

"I have to leave for a conference next weekend," he says. "It's Exciteur's big—"

"Conference. I remember. In Boston."

"Right. You know about it."

"I organized Mr. Conway's flights there last time, and I did yours as well."

"Come with me," Victor says. He raises his left hand and strokes it over my back. "I'll have a suite. You can work during the days. We can have dinner at night. Do this."

I bury my head against his shoulder. The part of me that he's just teased into orgasm wants to say yes to that. Three days at a hotel with him, with this, with one giant bed and bathtub and shower.

But I don't want to accompany him just to be available for sex. He has his job and I have mine... and sex can't just be a perk. Another part of our deal.

It doesn't have to mean a lot, but it has to mean something.

20

CECILIA

"Let me get this straight," Nadine says on the other end of the phone. "You've slept together multiple times now. He has apologized for how he treated you as his assistant, which he should have done a long time ago, by the way, and invited you along as his sex toy at a conference."

"Christ."

"That's the gist of it, right? And now you're cooking him his favorite dinner." Disapproval is faint in her voice, but it's there.

"It's a strategic move," I say. "I'm going to tell him to sit down for dinner when he comes home, and then I'll do what he responds well to. I'll negotiate."

She groans. "I do not understand the two of you and your weird fascination with playing office."

"I never played office," I say. "It was my actual job."

"Remember our Introduction to Philosophy class? You made a study guide from your notes and printed copies for every single one of our classmates."

"You illustrated the front page," I fire back.

She laughs. "Fine, fine. So you're going to renegotiate with St. Clair. Renegotiate what, exactly? Your marriage?"

I reach for the giant pepper shaker Bonnie keeps on the

kitchen counter and add a hefty dose to the tomato sauce. "Not our marriage, really. But what we are."

"You're going to ask him to define the relationship."

"I couldn't define it myself." I lean over the stove and breathe in the scent of pasta pomodoro. "But I want to make it clear that it can't just be sex. Despite cooking for him tonight, I'm not going to be his convenient wife who got him his grandfather's house and is always around when he wants to have sex. It has to be separate from the deal."

"Hell to the yes," she says. "How are your feelings?"

It takes me a moment to admit it. "I'm getting attached."

"Of course you are. You wouldn't be you if you weren't." She pauses, and in the silence, I can hear all the things she isn't saying.

"I know," I say. "I'll be careful."

"You're too good for him. Don't let all his money and power and suits intimidate you."

"I won't," I say. "So, you and Jake are finally going on a real date?"

"Yes... and don't laugh, but I'm actually nervous about this one."

"That's a good sign! You never are. Tell me what you're wearing?"

We're deep into a discussion on hairstyles when I hear the front door open. "Sorry, I have to go, he's home!"

"Good luck!"

I tuck my headphones into the pocket of my yoga pants and turn around, leaning against the counter. His footsteps echo on the hardwood floor.

Victor stops in the entryway, eyes moving from me to the empty kitchen. No Bonnie. "Hi."

"Hello."

A slow curve to his lips. "You're alone."

"I am. I decided to cook dinner for us."

He puts down his briefcase and undoes the button of his suit jacket. "Any particular reason?"

"Not really," I say. "Want something to drink?"

His eyes search mine, but then he nods. "Yes. I'll get it for us. Wine?"

"Sure."

He passes by me, and then, as if he catches himself, he stops to press a kiss to my temple. The affectionate touch sends heat to my cheeks.

"I looked at the numbers you sent me today," he says, opening a wine bottle.

"Oh? What did you think?"

"Much better. The lower overhead will handle slower, but more sustainable growth." He sits down at the kitchen table, eyes on me. "You're ready to put the plan into motion."

Excited nerves flutter through my stomach. "I think so too."

"Carter offered, and I wouldn't be doing my job as mentor if I didn't bring it up again," Victor says. He looks down at his glass of wine, jaw working. "If you put a proposal together I can forward it to Carter. He's on the lookout for more start-ups to invest in."

"Do you think that would be a good idea?"

"Investment would get you off the ground faster. He has a network and connections you could use."

"I sense a *but* here somewhere."

His eyes meet mine. "But I'd rather it was me investing."

My heart is pounding in my chest. "If I let you, though, we'd only be mixing business and pleasure even more than we already have."

"I'm aware of that," he says, voice dry. "It's a bad idea."

I turn off the stove and keep my eyes on the food I'm plating. "As bad as the two of us sleeping together?"

"No," he admits. "That's probably worse."

His honesty makes me smile. For better or for worse, Victor always gives it to you straight. I put down our plates and accept the glass of wine he hands me in exchange. "Thanks."

"No, thank you. Did Bonnie prepare this?"

"I made it from scratch." His housekeeper hadn't objected at all when I said I wanted to cook dinner for the two of us. She'd smiled, actually, in a way that was a tad too knowing.

"It's good," he says. "Your mother taught you to cook, too? Between all the tantric sex and cow-petting?"

"Tantric yoga," I correct him, and he gives me a crooked smile. "But yes, she did. For a while we lived in a commune with a big kitchen garden and there was always fresh produce."

He shakes his head. "A commune."

"It was great, for a time. There were always other kids to play with."

"Do you think your mom is the reason you agreed to marry me?"

I look up at him in surprise, and steady blue eyes gaze back at me. I consider the question. "I do, actually. Not directly. But she was never afraid to think big or differently. She always said that the most important thing was a person's integrity. That going to bed at night wasn't difficult as long as you had that. She also told me the sky was the limit." I look down at my food, thinking about her. About the things I haven't told her. "She's adventure itself. And if I start this company, if I pursue my own dream, I will have had an adventure in my life. An attempt at one, anyway."

Victor's silence is complete. I don't look at him, embarrassed at my own outpouring of words.

"Are you afraid to tell her about our marriage?"

"Yes, a bit."

"If you explain it to her in those terms, I don't think you have anything to be afraid of," he says. "You've been true to yourself throughout this whole thing. And if it's an adventure you want, well…"

I smile, looking up at him. "Marrying my boss is definitely an adventure."

"Happy to oblige," he says.

I bite my lip, considering my words. "Actually, speaking of integrity and mixing business-and-pleasure... I don't just want to be here for you when you want sex."

His eyes burn with sudden focus. "All right," he says. "What do you want? If you're asking for a relationship, Cecilia, I—"

"Oh, I'm not. Not at all. Don't worry. I know our marriage is a business deal and I respect that. What I'm saying is that I want a friendship too. I want *this*, what we're doing, to be equal. We're equals."

"I'm aware," he says. "I've never seen you as someone who just caters to me."

I snort. "Right."

"Fine. I no longer see you as that."

"Good, that's honest."

"I'm always honest with you."

I nod. "I'll do the same with you."

But the words don't soften the expression on his face. His eyes narrow instead. "What brought this conversation on? Was it something I said or did?"

"Not per se. Just... I'm not going to come with you to a conference just to be in the hotel room when you come back from work, just to satisfy you."

His voice turns dark. "Don't I satisfy you in return? Last night, you came not once, not twice, but—"

"Yes, you do. A lot." My cheeks are on fire. It's one thing to do it, another to talk about it casually over dinner. "I have no complaints in that department."

"No complaints," he mutters. "After she just promised me honesty."

"Fine. The sex is amazing. Better than I've ever had. If I had known it would be this good between us, I would have jumped you a lot sooner."

A smile breaks across Victor's face. It's pleased and masculine and it transforms his stern features entirely, as if a spotlight has just illuminated them. "Best you've had, huh?"

I rub my neck. "I didn't think this conversation would go in this direction."

"First she makes me dinner, then she compliments me in bed. Fuck, Myers. This place has gotten a lot better since you moved in."

It's not on par with what I'd told him, but... the words make my chest tighten. "Oh."

"Don't tell me you're in those tights again?"

I stick a leg out beneath the table. "Whoops."

He groans, eyes dancing. "You're killing me."

"But do you see what I mean? I don't want to feel like I'm just a convenient booty call, just because I also happen to live here. I want this to be completely separate from our contract and our agreement."

"It is completely separate," he says. "This has nothing to do with your compensation, with mentoring, with my grandfather's house. Was that what you're worried about?"

"A little bit, yes."

"Don't be. They're not related." He pushes his empty plate away and reaches up to undo the top buttons of his shirt. I catch a hint of dark blond chest hair and have to look away. "I was going to suggest dessert, but I've changed my mind. Taken your words into consideration."

"Oh."

"Do you have work to do?"

"I always have work to do," I say. "I'm starting my own company."

"That you are. All right. Let's work in the living room for an hour, and then you choose a movie for us."

"Choose a movie?"

His voice turns gruff. "Yes. Isn't that a suitable friendship thing to do? And then I can finally fuck you on the couch. I still haven't forgiven my body for being too sick for it last time."

"Yes," I say. "That does sound like a suitably friendship

thing to do. You might regret giving me free rein of movie choice, though."

My eyes feel like glue. Heavy and weighed down with tiredness, and my bed is like a cloud of cotton. The room is still dark, and the alarm clock by my bed reads two-fourteen a.m.

No reason for me to be awake.

I turn over and snuggle into the pillow, relaxing back into sleep. I'm nearly there when I'm jolted awake by a sound. The same one that must have broken through my sleep earlier.

It sounds like someone yelling.

I throw the covers back and grab my phone from the nightstand. Is someone in the apartment?

I pad across my bedroom floor and press my ear to the door, but all is silent. Not a peep. The scream had been close by, too. I crack the door open. Everything is dark.

Then a muffled sound echoes in the hallway. It's coming from Victor's bedroom. I walk closer on bare feet and stop right outside his closed door. On my phone, I dial 911 and keep my finger over the call button.

My heart feels like it's about to burst out of my chest, a thousand possibilities racing through my head. Is there someone in there with him? Is everything all right?

I turn the handle and push his door open.

Victor's large bedroom is cast in shadows. The king-sized bed stands in the middle, and only one figure is outlined on it, covered by a single thin sheet around his hips.

He hasn't drawn the drapes and there's enough light from the city behind to see his pained expression. He turns over, another low, agonized sound escaping his lips.

He's having a nightmare.

I'm locked in indecision on the doorstep. The one thing I can rule out is calling 911. But from what I know of Victor, he would not appreciate me seeing him like this, not to mention waking him up.

Weakness, I've found, is one of the many things he hates.

I turn to leave. But then he gives a hoarse scream, this time into his pillow, and it twists my heart. I have to wake him up.

I leave my phone on the floor and hurry across the soft carpet. Dressed only in the oversized T-shirt I always wear to bed, I crawl onto his California king.

"Victor," I murmur. "Victor, I think you should wake up."

He stirs, twisting onto his back. His eyes rove beneath his eyelids. I put a hand on his chest and find it clammy to the touch.

"Victor," I say.

"No," he mutters, legs moving beneath the sheet. His knee hits my shin with agonizing strength. "No!"

I grip his shoulders and shake him. "You have to wake up. It's not real, it's only a dream."

His body stills and I soften my hands, moving them up to his cheek. His hair is damp where it sticks to his sweaty forehead. "Victor, you're okay."

His eyes open and blink. They take a moment to focus before settling on mine. "Cecilia," he says. His voice is hoarse.

"Yes, it's me. You're okay, you know."

He looks down at my hands on his chest. I'm about to lift them when he moves, pulling me against his chest. Through the thin fabric of my T-shirt I can feel the pounding of his heart. It mirrors mine.

"What are you doing in here?"

"You were having a nightmare. I... I heard you."

"You heard me," he says. "All the way into your bedroom?"

"Yes." I don't want him to retreat, though, so I turn and kiss his neck. His pulse thunders beneath my lips.

"I'm fine," he says. His hand smooths up my back, and finding the hem of my T-shirt, slips inside of it. It's warm as it strokes up my spine. "I'm fine."

"Do you want to talk about it?"

He kicks off the sheets and shifts my hips against his, to where I learn that Victor St. Clair sleeps naked. "No."

I lift my head and kiss him. The racing of my heart turns into something else, and trapped against my stomach, he grows long and hard. He doesn't want to talk about it, all right. His free hand curves up my thigh to the elastic of my panties and tugs them down.

He turns me onto my back and I arch mine, letting him peel the T-shirt off. A strong hand tugs at my nipple. The raw need he's exuding has me more than ready, and he discovers the same thing, fingers teasing between my legs.

We don't speak as he fits himself against me and pushes inside. I lock my legs around his hips, arms around his neck, and hold him as he speeds toward release. It doesn't take long. He collapses on top of me with a groan and I close my eyes, gripping him tight in every possible way.

His weight feels delicious and even sweaty he smells good, of man and soap and Victor. He kisses the spot right beneath my ear, pressing his lips to my skin for so long that it feels like an apology for the frenzied, hurried sex. *Sorry.*

I run my hand up his muscled back. *Forgiven.*

I don't return to my own bed that night, instead remaining curled up in his arms, and we both drift off to sleep.

21

VICTOR

"I can't believe it," she says. "I mean, I know we haven't signed anything yet, but still. I can't believe it!"

"You'd better start."

"But I mean—oh, thank you so much, Steven. Have a great evening."

My driver tips his head in Cecilia's direction, a faint smile on his lips. "You too, ma'am."

"Goodnight," I tell him. He nods and closes the car door behind us. I wrap my arm around Cecilia's waist. She's wearing heels, and even if they aren't that high, the leaves on the sidewalk can be treacherous.

She leans into my touch. "I know you'd rather it be you, but... I hope you understand why I have to accept Carter's offer."

"I understand," I say, and I mean it. While I'd rather it be me she's coming to for money as well as guidance, she wants to stand on her own legs. Keep what distance she can between us. Her company will last longer than a year... and our marriage won't.

The happiness in her voice is enchanting.

"He said you pitched to him," I say. Unwelcome jealousy

burns in my chest. It has no place here. It's me she's going home to. Hell, it's my rings she's wearing on her finger.

She nods. "I did, right after dinner. Rather unprofessional, perhaps, at a party."

"It was just a quiet dinner at Tristan's. Business makes sense."

"Carter said my start-up sounded exactly like the thing he's been looking for."

I press the button for the elevator, my arm still around her waist. "Carter's good at what he does." I can hear the obvious reluctance in my voice.

"I have a business! I have an investor! Oh, I can't believe this is happening. I'll soon have a launch date. Within a few months, I might have clients. Can you believe this?" She shakes her head, dark curls flying. Her eyes are lined with elegant sweeps of makeup, but it doesn't take away from her natural beauty. It just makes her more striking.

I tip her head back and kiss smiling lips. She tastes sweet, like white wine and elation.

"Sorry," she says. "I've been bragging."

Stupid, endearing humbleness. I grab her hand and lead her into our apartment, straight to the hidden wine cooler in the kitchen.

"Bragging," I say, opening the door. Bottles of champagne stare back at me. "Do you remember where you put the saber we got as a wedding gift?"

"The one I was brandishing as a weapon when you got home?"

"The very one."

"I'll get it." A few minutes later she meets me back in the kitchen. I have three bottles tucked beneath my arm. They should be cold enough.

Her eyes widen. "Wow. Are we having a party?"

"We're celebrating you scoring your first investor, and we're doing it the way I know best."

"By drinking a lot of expensive champagne?"

"By using the saber you're holding. Come on. Let's do this on the balcony."

"Outside?" But she's smiling, leading the way through the living room. Two champagne glasses dangle from her left hand. "I've never sabered champagne before."

"I've done it enough times for the both of us. Come on, I'll teach you."

"You will?"

"Yes." I open the door to the balcony and we step out in the fall air.

She pulls her jacket tight around herself, the wind playing with curls around her face. The evening air is cold, but I feel warm, watching her looking with open curiosity at me untwisting the screw caps of the champagne bottles. "How do you do it?"

It's been too long since I've done this. Too long since someone looked at me like that, with openness and ownership.

"Peel away the foil like this, exposing the neck… unscrew the cage. Remember to keep your thumb on top of the cork. Now, hand me the saber."

She does, apprehension in her eyes. It makes me grin. New York with its glittering high rises as the backdrop and a beautiful woman looking at me. I feel fourteen again, showing off in front of a girl.

"Then you run your finger along the neck. See the seam in the glass here? You need to slide the saber along the seam, toward the head, and strike at where the cork is. The spot where the two seams meet is the weakest. Pressure on that point will make the glass crack clean and the cork will fly."

"Are you sure this is safe?"

"Yes," I say. It mostly is, anyway. "I've done this hundreds of times."

"So that's why you got it as a wedding gift."

I shrug. "Yeah. It was probably from one of the guys I went to boarding school with."

"Boarding school? I didn't know you went to boarding school."

"Yes, I was at Andover for a time. It was better for both my grandfather and me. We did this a lot, there. You can even do it with a kitchen knife, or if you've an appetite for risk, a credit card."

"Wow."

The wind whips at my clothes and lifts her hair from her face. "Ready?"

Her eyes widen. "You're going to do it out there?"

"Yes." I angle the bottle at forty-five degrees out toward the dark city beyond. It's been years. But I slide the saber along the neck once, twice, tighten my grip, and then strike.

The glass breaks clean and the cork shoots out into the cold New York air and into the darkened park.

"Oh my God!"

I laugh and pour out an inch of champagne onto the deck. It had been a clean hit, but the practice is ingrained into me. Removes any glass splinters.

"Can I try?"

"Of course. Why do you think I brought several bottles?" I hand her the saber with a flourish. "You just got your first investor, Cecilia. Brag as much as you like. This night belongs to you."

A smile lights up her face. It reaches deep inside of me, twists. Too much. She sees too much, but I don't want her to stop looking.

It takes several tries, and a bit of coaxing, but then she manages. A single swipe of the saber in her grip and the cork shoots out over the railing.

"Oh!"

"You did it."

"Holy shit! That was such a rush!"

"You picked it up fast."

"Liar," she says, grinning. "It took me a dozen tries."

"I couldn't do it at all my first month at Andover."

"I still can't believe you did this at boarding school. What kind of place was that, really? I'm imagining you in a school uniform, harassing teachers."

I chuckle. "It was an interesting environment, that's for sure."

"Is that Victor for 'I hated it'?"

"I didn't hate it," I say. "At times, sure. But it was good for me to get away from living with my grandfather for a few years."

"So you could drink champagne and smoke in the dorms."

"Pretty much." I wrap an arm around her shoulders and open the door. "Come on. You're getting cold."

"No, I'm not. I have champagne to warm me."

"Then why were you shivering?"

She stifles a yawn with the back of her hand. "You need to stop winning arguments."

"That's the way I am," I say. "And you, Cecilia, need to stop apologizing for bragging, or for your success, or for taking what you want."

She sets her glass down and wraps her arms around my neck. I smooth my hands along her hips. She hasn't said a word about the nightmare she'd woken me up from the other night. Nor did she comment when I got her from her own bed last night either, pulling her toward my bedroom. Sleeping next to her hadn't been difficult. It hadn't felt like a burden... and I hadn't been waiting for her to fall asleep so I could head downstairs to my office.

I'd fallen asleep with the scent of her hair on my shoulder and the weight of her on my arm, and dreamt absolutely nothing.

"So," she says. "Are we still going to the house tonight?"

"I'm planning to. But if you feel tired, stay home."

She shakes her head. "I'm coming. It's my opportunity to learn more about you."

I snort. "Right. The Spanish Inquisition. If you ask too many questions I'll banish you to the first floor."

"That's okay. I'm sure there will be interesting artifacts to uncover. Childhood trophies... your baby pictures."

"If you're looking for anything sentimental, you'll be disappointed. But come on, let's go."

She hums along to the song on the radio as I drive us out to the house. The familiar route takes us out of the city and into the suburban paradise.

I'll sort through papers tonight. That's the goal, anyway, even if I know Cecilia might be a distraction. But she'd said she wanted to do more friendship things, whatever that meant. Not relationship-things, though. I'd thought that was what she'd been asking for, and had opened my mouth to agree when she'd cut me off with a staunch denial.

Which was just as good.

Relationships invariably soured, grew full of expectations and whininess and women saying one thing while meaning something different.

I look at Cecilia. She has her legs crossed, fingers playing with the hem of her skirt, as she sings along to the radio. Somehow I doubt she would be like that. She's always been honest and straight with me. The trouble, because there's always trouble, might be less this time. Might be something we could work through together.

Might even be worth it.

An hour later, she sits in my grandfather's study with me, cross-legged on the floor. A giant binder of photographs is open on her lap.

I've glanced at her several times already. It feels raw, exposing, to have her see the albums I never knew he kept. Half of me wants nothing more than to snatch them away.

But that would be admitting they mean something.

I return to the neatly kept ledgers of expenses on his desk instead. He has dozens of these, records dating back decades.

There are things here he expected me to pick up after he died. Things I've neglected to.

Including the yearly expenses he paid for cemetery upkeep. I look at the receipt until the letters blur. Of course he paid for that. And with him dead, the responsibility falls to me. How had I not realized that before?

Are my parents' graves overgrown now? Devoid of flowers?

"Oh," Cecilia says. "You were adorable."

I tear my gaze away, focusing on her. She's wearing a soft smile. "I can't believe you actually found baby pictures."

"This goes in the keep pile." She closes the leather-bound album with a snap and stacks it on top of the others in the corner.

I close the ledger I'm reading. Gravesite maintenance. Things I've never thought about, not since I moved away from this house. I can't even remember the last time I was there, and for the first time in years, guilt punches me in the gut.

"Hey," she says. "Are you okay?"

"Yeah. I'm fine."

"It must be hard, being here. Surrounded by all his stuff."

I brace my hand against the desk. His desk. Suddenly, my hands look foreign to me. A grown man's hands on a desk I remember so vividly from childhood. I'd been sent here to do my homework on occasion. He'd sit in the armchair and watch with a book in his hand.

I'd considered it punishment, then. Now I wonder if it wasn't his attempt at getting us to spend time together.

"He sat here so often, even after he retired. Work was such a big part of who he was."

Her eyes soften. "Part of his self-image."

"Yes," I say. I stroke the leather inlay with a single finger. "He loved trivia and quizzes. It was the only game we played, him and I. There should be an old Trivial Pursuit box around here somewhere."

"Trivia, huh?"

"Yeah. The questions got outdated eventually, and we'd end up in arguments about whether or not to accept the answer on the card or the actual truth. You know, Moscow is the capital of the Soviet Union. That sort of thing."

"Did it get heated?"

"Yes. Stupidly so. We were both pretty stubborn."

She smiles. "You, stubborn?"

"Hard to believe, is it?"

"Incomprehensible."

I look at the neat rows of books surrounding us, gaze wandering. "On the anniversary of my parents' and brother's death, he'd order pizza. We never had takeout pizza otherwise. I think he assumed greasy pizza was the best way to take a nine-year-old boy's mind off of their deaths."

"What kind of pizza did you get?"

"Always pepperoni for him, and I chose something different every time. We'd eat it in the backyard." I reach for his letter opener and look down at the engraved handle. *R. St. Clair.* "He always made sure he was home that week. No business trips or meetings."

Even the last few years, we'd had dinner together on that day. We'd skipped the pizza. Our conversations hadn't been lively or deep. They'd been what they always had been. Businesslike and demanding and, running like a current beneath the surface, our shared loss.

"That was thoughtful of him," she says. "Do you miss him?"

"You've asked me that before."

"I know. But sometimes questions have different answers."

I brace my hands against the desk, the gold of my wedding band hard against the oak. A grown man's hands indeed, like my father's.

"Yes," I say. "He was the last piece, you know?

Connecting me back to my family. The last source of information about my mother and father."

"He was your father's father?"

"Yes."

She rises from the floor in a smooth movement. Dark curls fall down her back, tickling the edge of her tank top. She walks to the wall and the framed picture that hangs there.

She plucks it off the wall, and my heart feels like it's standing still in my chest. "These are your parents?"

"Yeah."

She turns toward me, frame gripped tightly. There's a smile on her lips. "You look like your dad a bit, but you have your mother's smile. Not that you use it often enough."

I swallow. "Right."

"You look similar to your big brother too. I've always loved that about siblings. The same features but tossed together in a different order. How much older was Phillip?"

"Three years."

"Did you look up to him?"

A memory breaks through, and I chuckle. "Yes. I followed him around everywhere when I was a kid. Every single interest he had, I picked up a week later, without fail."

Cecilia smiles down at the picture, and then back up at me. "I have a feeling you were even more stubborn as a kid."

"I've been told I was, yes."

She walks around the desk, picture frame still in her grip. "Are they part of your nightmares? The time you lost them?"

I can't get air into my lungs. They work, uselessly, against the tide of shame that rises up inside me. It had been too much to hope that she'd never bring them up.

In all the years I lived in this house, my grandfather had mentioned my nightmares exactly once, and then only to tell me to keep it down. They got rarer and rarer with the years, but fatigue or stress brought them out in full force. Or, it seemed, lusting painfully after Cecilia.

She puts the frame down on the desk and steps behind my

chair, hands landing on my shoulders. "I'm sorry," she says. "We can pretend I never asked."

Her palms against my chest restarts my breathing. I look down at the frame, at the familiar image of all of us happy and blissfully unaware.

"Yes, they're what I dream about."

Her hand traces the scar through my shirt. It doesn't surprise me that she's put it together. What surprises me are my own words, slow and pained. "It was a car accident. A drunk driver. We were driving home from dinner in this very house, actually."

"Oh."

I grip her wrist and tug her around, pushing back from the desk. She settles onto my lap with a sigh. I fit my hands to her hips, pressing her tight against my chest. Something to hold on to.

"Dad and Phillip died right away. They were on the left side of the car, where the other car hit."

She tightens her grip on my shoulders, and I see them in front of me, my brother and my father. Stuck next to me in the crushed car, not breathing, not...

I clear my throat. "A piece of metal went straight into my chest. Not deep, but wide. The rescue team had to cut me out of the car."

"Oh, Victor."

I say the next part because it belongs to the story, because it's important, because it's her memory. But I hate every single word. "Mom spoke to me in the car, when it was just the two of us and the silence, before the sirens came. Told me to hold on. We both made it to the hospital in ambulances, but I was the only one who left. Turns out a giant piece of metal in your chest isn't as bad as a head injury and internal bleeding."

The memories of those long, painful days in the hospital are ones I've never managed to suppress. Lying in a hospital bed, body half-broken, and being told that Mom had gone. I hadn't even seen her. They'd wheeled her into surgery, and then she was no more, and I was given Jell-O and pitying glances and the crushing sense of being absolutely and completely alone in the world.

Never again would I feel that powerless. Grandpa saw that desire in me, helped me mold myself into someone who took control. Someone who wasn't at the mercy of fate.

Cecilia leans back in my hands, shimmering green eyes meeting mine. Her voice is shaky. "I'm so sorry, Victor."

I close my eyes. I don't want to see her pity, I don't want to hear it. Women I've dated in the past have always looked at the scar like that. At first, it seems to make them want me more, for some reason I've never understood. But then they want an explanation, and the explanation leads to pity.

And I've already had so much fucking pity. My entire life was full of it back then, in the months and years after. Every single time someone at school asked an innocent question about my parents and I had to say the words. *They're dead.*

"Don't," I say. "Don't feel sorry for me. I don't want it."

With the uncanny way of knowing she has, she shakes her head. "It's not pity. It's compassion."

My thumb moves in a sweep over her hip, and I can't think of a single thing to say. She doesn't say anything either, just kisses me, and that's good. That I know how to do.

I lift my head a while later. My throat and chest both feel uncomfortably tight, and it's not from her glorious weight on my lap. I reach for her left hand and hold it between our chests, running my thumb over her wedding rings.

"Oh," she murmurs. "I forgot to give them back to you earlier."

I separate her engagement ring from her wedding ring, pressing my thumb down on the emerald-encircled diamond. "This was my mother's engagement ring."

"It was?"

"Yes."

Her voice is quiet. "Thank you for letting me wear it."

"It's been in a safe for over twenty years," I say, eyes on the rock. "And it's just a ring."

"It's not just a ring." She starts to worry it off her finger, sliding first the engagement ring off and then the wedding band. Her ring finger looks bare without them. She puts them in my palm, warm from her skin.

I look at them for a long time, but then I slide them back on her finger. "I'd rather they be with you than in my safe."

"You want me to wear them?" she asks. "All the time?"

I keep my eyes on the rings. "If you don't mind."

Her hand closes, rings on. "I don't mind."

22

CECILIA

"So this is a code red situation," Nadine says.

"It's code black. Code... midnight. Whatever's worse than red."

"You're definitely overreacting."

"Am I really, though? I talk to her on the phone every single week and I haven't mentioned this. She's not going to be happy."

Nadine cocks her head. She's done her hair in braids and they're a waterfall down her shoulder. She looks comfortable in Victor's living room, curled up in one of the armchairs. "Your mother never reacts the way you'd expect. I bet she's going to congratulate you and ask when the grandchild is due."

"She is the living embodiment of 'screw the establishment.' She never got married herself."

"She did marry Jeff."

"Not legally. The ceremony was ancient Mayan."

Nadine grins. "I remember. Your job was to invoke the fire element."

I'd accidentally dropped the match and it had lit the hem of my mother's dress on fire. She'd laughed and Jeff had stomped it out, and their friend Harry, fulfilling the role of shaman, said it signified a fiery union to come.

And it had been, all two long years of it.

"You did an excellent job on wind," I say.

Nadine grins. "Thank you."

"She's coming on Friday. Usually she stays with me, but this year she's staying with her friend Gwen. Thank God for that. I think she'd have a heart attack if she came into this apartment."

Nadine looks around, a smile on her lips. "It is rather... austere."

"I'll tell her over dinner. It's the only way."

"Will you introduce her to St. Clair?"

I twist the rings on my left hand. "I want to. But I don't know if it'll spook him. My mom is nothing like the kind of people he's used to. I mean, our childhoods couldn't have been more different."

Nadine shrugs. "It could be a test. If he cares about you, he'll do it without hesitation."

"That might apply to normal men. I'm not sure if it applies to him."

She tuts. "He's a normal man, Cece. I don't want to hear you giving him special allowances just because he's rich and powerful."

"I'm not doing that."

"Good." She looks like she has more to say, but the sound of the front door opening stops both of us. Bonnie's in the kitchen preparing. Steven never comes into the apartment unannounced. Which means Victor's home early.

Nadine smiles. "This should be interesting."

Victor stops in the living room, gaze moving between the two of us. "Hello."

"Welcome home," I say. My cheeks feel warm and I don't know what to do with my hands. His eyes glitter, meeting mine. Seeing all of it and more.

"I didn't know you were coming over, Nadine," he says. "Would you like to stay and have dinner with us?"

She glances at me before responding. "I'd love to, but I'm afraid I can't. I'm going to a new exhibition opening in Noho."

"The Tavaso Gallery?" he asks, shrugging out of his suit jacket.

"Yes. Do you know it?"

He nods. "They called about investing, a year or so back. I passed at the time, but I might reconsider. The place looks good."

"It does. They're opening an exhibition on the theme of Ruins tonight. The lineup is impressive."

"Well, the next time we see each other, you'll have to let me know what you thought," he says.

"Sure, happy to."

I clear my throat. "One of the paintings Victor bought from you hangs in the lobby of Exciteur now. It has a large sign next to it with your name."

Nadine's voice turns high. "It does?"

"Yes," I say. Victor had taken a picture of it one day and sent it to me. No comment along with it, no explanation. Fulfilling his side of the bargain, and yet... it had made butterflies explode inside.

"Wow," she says. "Thank you, Victor."

He nods, working on the sleeves of his shirt, rolling them up inch by inch. "*Temperance* is a good fit. Come by and see it some day."

"I will." Nadine looks at the both of us, a stunned expression on her face. "I'm not sure when I'll get used to the idea of my paintings actually being out there in the world. I'm not sure if I ever will. It still feels surreal."

"You will," I say. "Because it won't stop happening."

Victor hums in agreement. "Own it. You worked to get to this point, and if people didn't want your art, they wouldn't buy it."

We say goodbye to Nadine and she shoots me a mouthed *oh my god!* in the hallway. I grin and mouth *good luck!* back. She's going to the Tavaso with Jake for their second date.

Victor is talking to Bonnie in the kitchen when I return. He's seated at the table, long legs stretched out in front of him, uncorking a bottle. "Wine?"

"Yes, please. Although we can't have it every night. We're becoming alcoholics."

He waves a large hand, his wedding band catching the light. Wearing it every day, the twin to mine.

"We rarely have more than one glass each."

I sit down opposite him. "You're persuasive."

"I know," he says, lips quirking. "Hi."

"Hi," I say. "We already said hello."

"Yes, but you had guests."

"Well. Hello, then."

He glances at Bonnie. What would he do if she wasn't here? Pull me across the table and kiss me hello? Lines are blurring, and yet I couldn't be happier.

Bonnie serves us salmon, broccoli and wild rice, a dinner that's so healthy it's practically fighting our cholesterol with every bite. It's also delicious, with a sour cream sauce and rye bread.

We're halfway through dinner before I ask the question. "I have something coming up this weekend that I need your advice on."

"Not Carter's investment, right? It's too soon."

"No, not that. This is family related. My mother is coming to town."

"Ah. Yes, you mentioned that a while back. Have you told her?"

"Not about our marriage, no. Not that I quit my job either. I've been… avoiding it."

He puts his fork down, eyes focused on mine. "Do you want to share it with her?"

"Yes. We've always shared everything. I know her

reaction might be negative, but I couldn't live with myself if I kept this lie of omission up for an entire year."

"Then you should tell her," he says. "Do you want me to be there?"

"You would meet her?"

"If you want me to, yes."

"If I want you to," I murmur. "Well, how about we have dinner together on Saturday night? That gives me Friday to… explain things to her."

"Sure. I'll clear my schedule."

"Oh. Are you busy that night?"

He shakes his head. "A function I've been trying to get out of."

"Thank you. I know you don't really do things like this."

Victor raises an eyebrow. "Meet people's mothers?"

"Well, yes. It wasn't part of our contract."

"We've done a lot of things that weren't a part of the contract."

My cheeks heat up, but I don't look away from his gaze. On my left hand, my rings feel warm. "I don't think either of us could have anticipated this."

"No," he says. "I certainly didn't. I didn't know I was attracted to you when I suggested marriage."

"Ouch."

He chuckles, light dancing in his eyes. "I was blind back then. But trust me, that's a good thing. I wouldn't have made the suggestion if I had been."

"Because it complicates things."

"Because it might, yes."

We look at each other for a long moment. Questions rise in my throat, but I swallow them down. Not yet. Not now.

Victor cuts into his salmon. "How do you think she'll react?"

"Impossible to predict. I know she'll be mad I didn't tell her about it sooner. We've been married four months now."

"Four months next Tuesday," he says. "I'll play along with whatever scenario you want, Cecilia. Just let me know."

I clear my throat. "I think I'll go with the truth."

"Noted," he says, jaw working. "I can't imagine your hippie mom will like that very much. Nor me, for having coerced you into this arrangement."

"You didn't coerce me. If I remember correctly, I negotiated pretty fiercely for myself."

A smile ghosts past his lips. "You did. So well, actually, that I had an oh shit moment afterwards."

"What?"

"You were hot when you negotiated," he says. "I stopped being blind."

"Oh, really? That's good to know."

"Are you going to argue with me at every turn now?"

I grin. "I just might, if you enjoy it."

His lips tug, but only briefly, features returning to seriousness. I've seen him focused and intense many times before. Negotiating business deals, dealing with lawyers, facing opponents across a table, on stage at conferences.

But being the subject of it takes my breath away.

"You'll tell her the truth, then. That means I'll have some things to answer for on Saturday."

I shake my head. "I'll tell her to go easy on you."

"Don't. I can take it."

Yes, I think. *But you shouldn't have to.* Meeting family was nowhere in the job description, but we're in new territory here.

"Thank you. For agreeing."

He nods, returning to the food. His hair isn't mussed today. It had been a day free from frustrations.

"You have to let me know if I can return the favor," I say. "Any distant relatives you need to explain your sudden nuptials to?"

"Only the ones who would have benefitted from us not getting married."

"Oh. I didn't think about that. Are they upset?"

He shrugs. "I haven't spoken to them since the will was read."

"Real close, huh?"

"Not at all."

"I'm guessing they didn't send any wedding gifts."

He gives a half-grin. "You'd know better than me. You were the one who sent out all the thank-you notes, after all."

"Right. Did you see that the champagne saber was engraved with our wedding date? Some people really put thought into it."

"Or their assistants did," he says. "You sent a lot of gifts on my behalf."

"Oh, I sure did. I don't think you realized it, but white lilies with pink peonies was the standard bouquet you sent to the women you dated. Very thoughtful of you."

He looks down at his food. "Right. Was that based on your preferences?"

"Yes. I never told you, but I sent it to myself once, on my birthday. You paid."

His eyes widen, and then he laughs. It warms the kitchen and sets his eyes alight. "Fuck, Myers. I can't say I disapprove. You earned them."

"Yes, I rather think I did."

"Have you figured out who gave us the glass dick, by the way?"

I chuckle. "The one you deliberately broke?"

"Wasn't deliberate. If you remember, I was very focused on something else at the time."

"Oh, I remember," I say. "Carter gave it to us."

Victor snorts. "Of course. The asshole. He knew exactly what he was doing."

"Think it was a sign?"

"Yes." He pushes back from the table and takes my empty plate with him to the sink. It's as rare a display of domesticity as the laughter he'd let out earlier. "That he thinks I'm a dick."

"Is that your role in your foursome?"

"Our foursome," he mutters. He returns to the table and leans over me, mouth hovering inches from mine. "Yes. With my business partners, I'm generally the one with the most practical business sense."

"You mean you're the most ruthless."

"The world is like that," he says. "The strong and the weak. The takers and the taken. My grandfather made that very clear. I've always known which category I want to fall into."

"I think you're succeeding."

He kisses me, long and searching. "We can't have a foursome," he murmurs. "Will a twosome work?"

"What did you have in mind?"

"A bath."

"For both of us?"

"Yes. The tub in my bathroom is huge, but I've never used it. I imagine we could put it to interesting use."

Over his shoulder, my eyes clock Bonnie. She enters the kitchen, but seeing us, she turns on her heel. Giving us privacy.

I slide my hands up his neck. "You're sure your office isn't more attractive?"

"Compared to you? Absolutely not."

His tub is big enough for two, even if we're a snug fit with his tall frame. I lean against his chest in the water and close my eyes at the rising pleasure. His fingers have become expert, teasing between my legs, one hand on my soapy breast. His hard length is trapped between our bodies, digging deliciously into my back.

He puts his mouth by my ear. "Good idea?"

I give a shaky laugh, but it cuts off as he slips a finger inside. "Yes. Very."

"You're not too sore from yesterday?"

"A bit. The warm water is helping. Was that your plan?" I turn around to catch his eyes. They're fixed on my breasts, rising above the water's surface.

The sex we'd had last night had been rough and hard and I'd loved every single moment of it. It had also left my inner thighs sore this morning.

"It occurred to me, yes." He adds another finger and my body stretches to fit him, aching in the sweetest of ways. "Think you can take me in the water?"

I lean my head against his shoulder and close my eyes. His thumb has started to circle my clit and it's hard to think around the rising tide of pleasure.

"Yes," I whisper.

His chuckle is dark in my ear, but he makes me orgasm first, taking his time to warm me up. And when we shift in the bath, and he pushes inside of me, we both groan at the sensation.

It's soft and quiet, a stark contrast to last night.

Afterwards, we're silent and slow. Each movement feels heavy and I don't want to speak, don't want to break the magic.

We lie on our usual sides of his king-size bed. The room is cast in shadows, but they're soft, comforting ones. I close my eyes at the sated tiredness in my body. He'll be the death of me, this man. I can't wait to see where it leads.

"Cecilia," he says.

I turn on my side to face him. His profile is clear against the faint light of the city, the high forehead and the straight nose. "Yes?"

"I haven't had someone like you in my life for a very long time," he says. "I'm not always going to know how to handle it."

In my chest, my heart does a double take. "I'm aware."

"I'm going to fuck up, Myers. Probably a lot."

"I know that, too."

The words hang in the air. *Be patient with me.*

I reach out and find his arm, curling my hand around it. A wrong word from me could shatter this olive branch, the weakness, the honesty. So I give him an out.

"When you do, I'll order myself flowers from you again."

He chuckles. "Good. Plan for that."

I fold myself against his side. After a moment, he turns, and a heavy arm wraps itself around my waist. I bury my face against his chest, the tickle of his chest hair, and breathe in his scent. He might be the most complicated, infuriating man I've ever known. He's also the most hard-working, layered, dedicated one.

We might not be a real married couple, but I'm hopelessly in love with my husband.

23

VICTOR

I'm sitting at my desk on Saturday when the phone rings. Thank God, I think. I'm looking into grave upkeep for my parents, brother and grandfather, not trusting Brad with it, and a distraction is welcome.

Especially this one, I think, seeing the name on my screen. "Hello, Mrs. St. Clair."

"Oh," she says. Taken aback by the name? It's hers, after all. "Hello, Mr. St. Clair."

"How did the day go?"

"Good. She's in the restroom now."

"How did she handle the big reveal?"

"You know what? Much better than I thought."

"Of course," I say. "If she's all that you've described her as, she's the queen of original ideas."

"Oh, I reminded her of that. You're coming to dinner, right?"

"Of course I am. I made the reservation."

"Thank you so much, Victor. Would you mind printing my business plan from my computer and bringing it along? Mom wants to see it. I think it'll help, you know. With explaining exactly *why* I decided to enter the archaic institution of matrimony."

"Her words?"

"Yes."

I head toward the stairs. "Password on your computer?"

"Promise me you won't laugh."

"I promise."

"Chocolate."

I don't laugh. I'm grinning, though. "Of course it is."

"It's on my desktop. See you soon, then," she says. "Mr. St. Clair."

"Looking forward to it, Mrs. St. Clair."

The line clicks off, but my grin doesn't fade. A fool, that's what she's turning me into. Not a single part of my orderly, contained world is the same with her in it. But I don't miss it.

Her bedroom is filled with her, despite the furniture being the same as mine. Clothes draped over a bed she no longer sleeps in. A desk with neat papers and a closed laptop.

I open it up. Her screensaver is a beach on some faraway tropical island. It makes me think of our joke about honeymooning in Barbados. Did it have a kernel of truth in it?

I can take a week off work if it means seeing Cecilia in bikinis, laughing on the beach, teasing me in a pool.

I type "chocolate" and the tropical island dissolves into her desktop. It's filled with neat folders, organized and color-coordinated. Best assistant I'd ever had. Should have appreciated her more when I had her.

Even if I prefer the way I have her now.

My eyes flick from folder and file to the next one. They stop on top of a widget on the desktop. It's a timer. A stopwatch, to be exact.

It's set for months, weeks and days. Seven months, twenty-two days, fifteen minutes, fifty-six seconds. Above it in tiny letters are seven words. *Until I get rid of St. Clair!*

I watch the timer for a long time. The seconds add up. Fifty-seven, fifty-eight, fifty-nine. Another minute shaved off her sentence.

She's counting the days until our marriage ends.

When I finally print her business plan and staple it, I don't have the mind to appreciate the neat front page. All I can see is the timer.

She'd pitched her business to Carter, because she wanted his investment, not mine. She's committed to not making our marriage messier, because she's always planned on ending it. Following our contract.

Like I was, once.

Like I should always be.

Business and pleasure don't mix. How many times had I heard that? How many times had my grandfather told me that?

Never hire your friends. Never work with your family.

He hadn't mentioned girlfriends, probably because he never assumed I'd be that stupid. Well. Watch me now, Richard. You shouldn't have died.

I dress for dinner. Dinner with Cecilia's mother, which was something she'd asked me to do. Introducing me to her mother feels off now. Not as a step forward, but as damage control.

Shame is like a beat beneath my breastbone, hiding a more painful emotion. I'd been so poor of a boss to her that she, still, couldn't think of me as anything more serious than a business partner or a playmate in bed.

Steven doesn't say hello when I get in the car. Perhaps he's learned to tell my moods by now. Or perhaps he doesn't dare because I'm that fucking intolerable as a boss.

I tug at the sleeves of my shirt. Fucking dinner with my fucking wife who can't wait to fucking get rid of me. Everybody leaves. Everybody has always left. Why would she be any different?

Traffic makes me late, and the blackness of my mood turns sulfur. It's oil beneath my skin. Tar-black and sticky.

I need to shake it off or I won't be able to play my part.

"St. Clair," I tell the hostess at the restaurant. "My wife should already be here."

She shines up. "Oh, yes. We gave you a great table in the back. Follow me."

I walk through the crowded Upper East Side restaurant. I shouldn't have booked something like this. The white tablecloths and candles scream pretentious, money, expectations. Everything her mother is not. Another strike for me.

They're seated at a round table in the back of the restaurant.

Marguerite Myers looks like her daughter, only two decades older. They're the spitting image of one another. One polished and dark-haired, the other wild and with hair streaked with gray at the temples, but both sharing the same wide smile.

The expression on her face makes me guess she's not holding a grudge about our marriage. No wonder. Cecilia has probably told her she's going to be rid of me soon enough. Only seven months and twenty-two days left.

Cecilia sees me and a private smile lights up her face. It's not fair of her. "You made it!"

"Traffic made me late." I press a kiss to her cheek. It's hot and flushed beneath my lips. "I'm sorry."

"Not a problem at all. Victor, this is my mother, Marguerite. Mom, meet Victor."

She stands. The table had made her look taller, but now I'm looking down at a woman a head and a half shorter than me. Green eyes run me over before she extends her hand.

"He's tall," she says.

I shake her hand. "Nice to meet you."

She flips my hand over and grips it in both of hers, studying my palm for a few seconds. "Good grip."

"Thank you."

"Mom."

She releases my hand and sits back down. "Good hands are important, Cece."

"I know they are."

Well, I didn't.

Marguerite locks her eyes on mine. She's going to be the one in control of this conversation, I think. Not me and not Cecilia. "I wanted to meet the man my daughter married as part of a business transaction," she says.

I nod. "I'm sure I would have wanted the same."

Her eyes narrow. "You're also the one my daughter spent a year working for, on evenings and weekends. Fetching your dry-cleaning and ordering your lunches."

Cecilia's voice is fierce. "Mom, that's not all I did. You know I learned a lot from my years at Exciteur. I attended conferences, I traveled."

"I know. But I also know that the man right here made your life very difficult for a long time. It's a good thing that he learns that."

"He knows," Cecilia says. She sounds embarrassed.

My hands are white-knuckled in my lap. "I'm aware, Miss Myers. Cecilia did excellent work for me and I didn't appreciate her enough. I like to think she gained valuable experience, though, and learned things to apply to her own business. But that's only a hope. I've apologized to her for the times I stepped out of line."

"I did learn a lot," Cecilia says. "You're talking like he took advantage of me with this marriage. Like I said, it's a mutually beneficial agreement. It has a start and end date. We signed a contract, Mom."

"Contract," her mother says. The word is infused with dislike. "Contracts can be broken."

I brace my hands against the table. The stakes are high, and beneath my feet, I can feel the thin tightrope I'm treading. "Not by me, they won't," I say. "The contract Cecilia and I signed was checked by three separate lawyers. It protects her as much as it does me."

Marguerite waves a hand like that was never the real issue. "Why my daughter? Why did you offer this deal to her?"

We haven't ordered food yet. I glance toward the waiter,

but he's nowhere to be seen.

Get me a drink. Please.

"Mom, he doesn't have to justify himself," Cecilia says. "He has been nothing but professional through this entire process."

"And that was why you didn't tell me for months? Cece, you have so much light inside you. I don't want you to waste it with someone who can't appreciate it."

Cecilia's cheeks are on fire, but her eyebrows are drawn in the same determination mirrored on her mother's face. One has diamond studs in her ears and the other has feathers dangling, but they're the same, these two. Different sides to the same coin. It's a marvelous thing to watch.

"I'm not wasting myself. Victor and I aren't—it's not like that. I'm also an adult, capable of making my own decisions."

I clear my throat. "To tell you the truth, I offered the deal to Cecilia because she was the best person for it. I knew her as someone loyal, competent, intelligent and looking for a new job. In the months since, she's proven me right a hundred times over. She's all that and more."

Marguerite's gaze meets mine. I don't look away. Let her see how true every single one of those words were.

"Well," Marguerite says. "You know, honey, that it's not the transaction itself I'm disapproving of. Marriage is an archaic institution. If you two have managed to reinvent the wheel and both gain from it, more power to you. I just don't want to see you being exploited by this young man here."

"I'm not," Cecilia says. Her voice is firm. "Please trust me when I say I'm not."

I focus on Marguerite. "I understand your concern, and I'm sure I would feel the same in your position. Ask whatever you'd like tonight. I'll answer."

It's risky as hell, giving someone that power. But Cecilia had asked me to do this. So do this I will.

Cecilia looks at me with warm eyes. Like she's glad I'm here. Like she hears more than just the words I'm saying.

I look down at the menu.

We order eventually. Marguerite and Cecilia decide to share dishes, something it seems they do often at restaurants. They chatter about options, and in my mind, all I can see is the timer.

Until I get rid of St. Clair.

Halfway through the meal, Marguerite clears her throat. "You clearly have an arrangement that works. I felt myself slipping into the territory of judgement earlier, and those are not the fields I like to wander."

"Mom," Cecilia murmurs.

"It's a metaphor. Look, Victor, St. Clair, whatever you like to go by. If what you and my daughter have told me is true, then I'm happy for you. You're both gaining from the experience. Perhaps gaining understanding and sympathy for the other, as well? But I'm getting ahead of myself."

"Thank you, Miss Myers," I say.

"Call me Marguerite. Miss Myers is my daughter. Or I guess she's Mrs. St. Clair now?"

Cecilia shakes her head. "I didn't change my name."

No, she never had. Her name wasn't really Mrs. St. Clair, as much as I might tease her about it. Why would she change it legally, when we only have seven months and twenty-two days left.

"I'll just tell the two of you one more thing. You should get out of the city for a bit. Both of you. You're too pale, Victor." She shakes her head again, reaching for her glass of red. "Working all the time isn't balanced."

"We have to work," Cecilia says.

"No one has to. It's a decision." She shrugs, looking between the two of us with glittering eyes. "Maybe this little fake marriage of yours will even become real by the end?"

Cecilia gives a pained laugh and shoots me a look out of the corner of her eye. I look out at the other guests and pretend not to see. If she wants me to laugh with her at the preposterousness of the idea, I can't.

Not anymore.

We're quiet in the car on the way home. Cecilia has the air of someone about to speak, but whatever she's working up to doesn't emerge.

It isn't until we're back home that it does. Her voice is soft. "I'm sorry about that. I know it wasn't easy for you."

"It was fine."

"No, she... she implied a lot of things, and assumed others."

"She's protective. I'm glad your mother is like that."

Cecilia nods, eyes searching mine. "Okay. Thanks for dinner, and thank you for doing that. I know you had other plans tonight."

I shake my head. "A function. Like I said, I didn't want to go to it anyway."

"No, instead you got to play twenty questions." She smiles, looking at me. Waiting for me to reciprocate.

"Yeah. Survived it, though. It's late. I should go to bed."

"Oh, yes. Me too. It's been a long weekend, and tomorrow I'm going with Mom to her friend's pottery class."

"Right. Well, I'll see you for dinner tomorrow, then."

She braces her hands against the kitchen counter, and for a moment, the expression on her face is lost. "Yes, of course. Goodnight."

I take the stairs in two and close the door to my bedroom. My breathing comes heavy. My bedroom feels empty and alien without her in it. I want her here, but not if she's waiting to get rid of me. Not until I know she's really forgiven me for how I behaved during our year together at work. Her mother's words ring in my ear. The assumption that I've exploited and used her. Cecilia's own confession that I'd made her cry at work.

This is why I don't get involved. This is why I've always kept up boundaries. Because someone ends up getting hurt if you don't.

I'd just never thought that person would be me.

24

CECILIA

Victor hasn't been himself for the past week.

He comes back late from the office, sometimes way past dinner, and goes straight to his computer. We don't sleep in the same bed anymore, despite me trying to twice. I'd wrapped my arms around his neck and kissed him desperately, passionately. He'd kissed me back for a long moment and then lowered my arms from around his neck.

"Victor?"

He'd run a thumb over my lower lip, eyes on the movement rather than meeting mine. "We'll talk more this weekend."

"This weekend?"

"Yes. Will you let me take you out to dinner?"

"On a date?"

"Yes."

"I'd like that, yes."

"Good," he'd said, and we'd said good night right there, in the long impersonal hallway between our two bedrooms. It had been the only time this week where we'd had an actual conversation.

In some ways, he's every bit the Victor I once knew. The one who came home and went straight to his office, who hated unnecessary small talk, who avoided emotional intimacy.

And I can only think of one reason why that's happened.

It had started when we came home from dinner with my mother. The distance. I'd been replaying some of Mom's words in my head in the days since, especially her thoughtless suggestion that this might become more than a fake marriage.

Victor had looked away from me when she said that, obviously pained by the suggestion. Pained because he couldn't fathom it, or pained because he suspected it was what I now wanted?

I know he's easy to spook, and still, I'd insisted on that damn dinner. I'd hoped it would settle my mom's nerves and in some naive, foolish way, I wanted them to meet. Two of the people who meant the most to me. The only one missing was Nadine, but we hadn't needed any more fuel to that fire.

It had managed to scorch us all on its own.

My phone rings and I put my headphones in before I answer. "Hi, Mom. Did you make it home okay?"

"Sure did! Had a lovely flight, too. The clouds were gorgeous. Aiyana was waiting for me at the airport and we're on our way now."

"To the flower festival?"

"Yes. She's exhibiting and I'll help."

"You'll have to send me some pictures of all the flowers."

"I will. Hey, say hi to Aiyana."

I raise my voice. "Hi Aiyana!"

A cheerful voice, slightly echoey, from the other end. "Hi, Cece baby!"

"Good luck with your exhibition!"

"Thanks, honey!"

Mom's voice returns to the phone. "I've been thinking a lot since we said goodbye."

"Oh?"

"I don't think I made it clear just how happy I am that you

finally made the decision to tell me about your marriage. I understand why you were hesitant. It's not like I've ever spoken positively about marriage."

I run my fingers along the marbling on the kitchen counter. "No, nor about secrecy, New York's corporate scene, rich people, men in suits, inheritances in general…"

"Hey now," she says. "I've always said that suits have a certain appeal. They're just an outdated custom."

"Not to mention you think they kill originality."

"No man was blessed with life only to dress forever in gray or black," she says. "But honey, that wasn't the point. I wanted you to know that I appreciated your honesty. Your path and my path aren't the same, but they are perpendicular, for as long as I'm treading mine. And I'm so grateful I get to see the beautiful, strong, ambitious woman you've become."

My throat feels tight. "Thanks, Mom."

"Victor was… interesting. He has the conflicted power of a man who knows himself and his abilities well, but hasn't fully incorporated his shadow self. He still fights his weaknesses, when he should be embracing them."

"He won't let me heal his chakras," I say, half-joking, half-serious. "I tried once."

Mom hmms in thought on the other end. "A man like him wouldn't. But there's healing to be done in other ways, sweetie. He'll find it in time, and you can't do it for him. Just remember to keep your channels of communication open."

I sigh. "Yes. I will."

Mom once drew a chart of the channels she considered a part of communication, and you'd be surprised how many non-verbal ones she included. This week, we haven't been using much of any channel, Victor and I.

"I love you," I say. "You know, I don't know if I've ever thanked you for giving me a childhood unlike any of my friends'. I know I wasn't always grateful when I was younger. But I am, Mom. We were a team, you and I, and we saw so many things, and did them all together. You were always there for me."

There's a beat of stunned silence on the other end, and then Mom sniffles. Her voice is warm. "Honey, I love you too. I know the life we lived wasn't always easy for you. You're cut more from your grandparents' cloth than mine, you know."

"Yes, I know."

"But the years I raised you were the best ones in my life. Always."

"Thank you," I whisper. I'm going to cry if we don't end this. Perhaps she thinks the same, because she gives a strangled half-laugh, and I join in.

"Well. Aren't we a pair of criers today?" she says.

The conversation stays with me as I cook my lunch and eat it in silence. She had always been there. No boarding schools, no cold silences. Listening to every thought I had.

My phone chimes again. I'm expecting a picture of bohemian flower arrangements, and knowing Aiyana, perhaps with white lotuses in the center to represent the female sex. That's not what I get.

Nadine has sent me a selfie. Her braids are a mess and her eyes are smudgy with mascara. Her smile is also huge, a comforter pulled up to her neck. She's in bed.

She's written five words. *So I did a thing.*

I type back.

Cecilia: Did you just wake up? I'm so jealous of the life of artists.

Nadine: I did. And think, Cece. Is this my comforter???

Cecilia: Oh my god. You're at Jake's!!! You're in his bed!

Nadine: Yeeees.

Cecilia: What! Judging from your smile I should say congrats, so congrats! How was it?

Nadine: Unreal. Can we have brunch next week, please please please? I have so much to tell you.

Cecilia: Clearly! And yes!

Nadine: I thought he was too similar to me, but he's not. He's amazing. He understands my art and we have these long debates about Cubism and the future of mixed media and it's so hot? Who knew? Also I saw his closet and it wasn't messy at all.

I laugh. She's infatuated, and I couldn't be happier. Not when he's as enamored by her.

Cecilia: People can surprise you. I'm happy for you. Get your ass up and make him some abstract art eggs.

Nadine: How's your hubby? Falling for him yet?

Cecilia: I'm very much afraid the answer is no… but only because I've already fallen.

There's no response, so I guess Jake woke up. I smile at the picture of her grinning from ear to ear on my phone. I can't think of anyone who deserves love more than her, after years of working so hard and dating only weirdos.

I recognize her smile… because that's me, too.

I can't figure out when it started, what moment things shifted inside me, but when I look back it feels like it was always there. A thrumming in my body when I'd see him striding down the hallway at work. Pride when he'd negotiated and strong-armed, and I'd be the one to come in with his memos. It had been buried deep at times, fleeting and ephemeral. But it had been there.

Now I've seen the other sides to him, the ones he keeps hidden. The tortured side, the caring, the confident. The silly and the surprisingly sentimental. The one that holds me tight at night and breathes in the scent of my hair like it's more valuable to him than air.

I want this to be a real marriage. I want it so much my heart aches with it. Is that so crazy? After everything we've done together?

The front door rings. I startle from my desk and wait a moment, but then it rings again. Bonnie isn't in.

I run down the stairs in my slippers and answer. "Hello?"

"Hello, ma'am. We have a delivery in the lobby for Mr. St. Clair that requires a signature. Is he available?"

"I'm afraid he's at work. Where's the delivery from?"

"A law firm, ma'am."

"I can sign for him." My voice snaps into professionalism. How many times had I done this for him when I was his assistant? "You're welcome to send the courier up."

The concierge breathes a sigh of relief. "Excellent, Mrs. St. Clair. She will be outside your door in a minute. Would you like a longer delay?"

I look down at my yoga pants. "No, that's okay. Thank you."

The courier is hesitant outside of our door, but I shake away her concerns. "I'm Victor's wife," I say. "I'll make sure they get to him."

"All right, ma'am," she says. The manila envelope she's clutching is thin.

I sign my name with a flourish on the paper and smile at her. "Thank you. We appreciate it."

"Of course, ma'am. Have a good day."

"You too, miss."

The door shuts behind her and I stand in the hallway, envelope in hand. I flip it over. It's from his lawyers, Irving and Hardmann. I've seen dozens of these envelopes before.

They always contain important documents for his various business acquisitions, investments, hirings.

It had been express-delivered here, which means it must be urgent. Had they sent it to the wrong address? It's only two p.m. and Victor won't be home for hours yet.

The decision is split-second. I've opened his mail a hundred times before. I've sorted and organized it for him, I've scanned it for him when he's been on business trips. This is no different.

I open the seal with careful fingers and pull out the document inside.

The headline is in bold, black font, and falls like a scythe.

Petition for Divorce.

Below, already printed in fine font, are our names.

Victor St. Clair and Cecilia Myers.

25

CECILIA

I follow the hostess in a numb daze. Around us, people sit at long oak tables, talk mingling into a low-level chatter. Paper lanterns hang from beams in the ceiling. It's cozy.

I can't appreciate any of it.

Victor walks behind me. His presence is solid, real, ever-present... and yet I can't look at him. I had resealed the document and put it on his desk. He asked about it when he came home. "On your desk," I'd said.

"Thank you," he'd replied, face a mask. As if the document inside isn't premature, isn't an end to us.

My heart feels twice its normal size, beating so hard it might break out of my chest. He brought his briefcase tonight. Did he bring the papers? Is that why he wants to have dinner?

He's going to talk about our divorce. About how this has gotten too complicated, too messy. We mixed business and pleasure and we shouldn't have. The end is coming.

And there's not a thing I can do to stop it.

"Is this okay?" the waitress asks with a bright smile. It dims slightly when she glances from me to Victor.

I guess he doesn't look happy either.

His voice is low. "Yes. Thank you."

"Of course. I'll be back soon to take your order, or if you prefer, you can order through an app on your phone. The info is in the menu."

She leaves us, and we sit down, silence reigning supreme. I force some cheer into my voice. "This is an interesting place. Not your usual restaurant?"

"Thought I'd branch out. Was that okay?"

"Yes, yeah, absolutely." I look down at the menu and fight the knot in my throat. Of course I'd end up here. It's a surprise to absolutely no one, least of all myself, and the sense of *I should have known better* is crushing.

"If you don't like what they have, we can leave," he says. "I'm not set on Asian fusion."

"No, we'll stay. This looks good. Look," I say, tossing out the first thing I see. "They have BBQ pork buns. I like those."

"All right."

We order through the app on my phone, and I'm grateful for it, for the practical discussion and something to do with my hands. But it doesn't last, and as soon as the order goes out, we both fall silent.

He looks still as a statue, gazing out at the fully packed restaurant. Not at me or the silent pleading in my eyes. As impenetrable as he ever was.

"You've been busy this week," I say.

"Work is gearing up," he says.

"Oh? Anything in particular?"

"Exciteur is purchasing a small Canadian consulting firm. It's failing, and by taking over their operation and clients, we'll expand our reach."

I force a smile. "A venture capitalist, serving as a CEO, turning back to venture capitalism?"

He snorts. "I guess, yes. It's a good opportunity."

"I'm sure it is. Did you negotiate it?"

"No, Eleanor did a good job with it. I was only needed at the final stage."

I can imagine how he'd done it, too. Broad shoulders and

sharp tones, commanding the room. Not taking no for an answer. Laying out his arguments in a pattern so ruthlessly logical you could only agree.

Victor runs a hand through his hair. "Did you have a good day?"

Panic crawls up my spine. No distance tonight, not like he's been for the past days. All focus. I have Victor St. Clair in front of me, and he's preparing himself for a negotiation.

"Yes. A good week, even. Got my business plan sent to my new accountant. I hired the one you recommended a while back. And I have a meeting set up with Carter next month."

Victor gives a single nod, eyes intent on mine. "Good. That's good."

"Yeah. Nadine, actually, she finally got together with Jake? You know the man she thought would be good for me?" I say, and seeing his jaw tense, my words tumble out with the weight of bricks. "You know I never thought that. I wasn't interested in him then. Anyway, point being, she's happy. Which makes me happy too."

"Right. That's good too."

"Yes," I say. "So all is good. I'm having a good week."

Don't destroy it, I think. Please.

He clears his throat. "Cecilia, I want to talk to you about something, and to tell you the truth, I'm not sure where to start. It's not the kind of conversation I'm used to having." He runs a hand through his hair, the telltale sign of frustration. And I can't let him get the words out.

"Look, I've been thinking too," I say. "About us and what we're doing means for our contract. You know, about how it complicates things? But I want you to know that I have a lot of respect for what you're doing with your grandfather's house. I'm not going to jeopardize that. So while mixing business and pleasure isn't good, I think—"

"No, let me go first. Please."

It's the *please* that leaves me silent. I nod, mouth still open.

He turns to his briefcase. Here it comes, doom in an envelope, and horror rises within me at the sight of the familiar manila color. Victor pulls out the piece of paper like he's comfortable with it. Like it won't bite him.

I don't want it anywhere near me.

His jaw works once as he reads it over. "This is for you," he says. "If you want it."

He puts the paper down on the table. Petition for divorce. And at the bottom, his signature. The hard press of the V and the flourish on St. Clair.

He's already signed it.

The words vanish in a haze of tears. I bury my face in my hands, but he's seen it.

"Cecilia?"

"It was my mom, right? It got too much for you last weekend?"

"Don't cry, Myers. Please."

"My husband wants to divorce me. I think it's appropriate."

He gives a low groan. "I don't understand people," he mutters. "No, it wasn't your mom. She's a tough negotiator."

"You think so?"

"Yes."

"Then why?"

Victor braces both forearms against the table, blue eyes boring into mine. "Cecilia, don't cry. Please. Look, I know I've been intolerable. I was a horrible boss, I'm tough to deal with, I have a short temper. I'm sorry for all of that. For making you cry at work. For making you cry right now. If you only knew how much that's killed me, to think about. I know it's all my fault."

I shake my head, but I can't find any words.

He doesn't need them. "I saw the timer on your computer. You're counting down the days until you're out of this marriage, until you get rid of me. I don't want to shackle you to me for a day longer than you want to be. This," he says, touching the divorce papers on the table, "is an offer to you.

No strings attached. I'll still mentor you if you want. The money is still yours, Nadine will continue to get as much press as I can throw her way."

"You're offering me a divorce... if I want it?"

His jaw tightens. "Yes. I've signed it. You can do whatever you like with it. Sign it now. Sign it in six months. But after you divorce me, I want to ask one thing."

"Yes?"

"Will you let me take you out on a date? Properly, as you deserve. Not as equals, because you're much better than me, but I think I can change," he says. "It just won't be overnight."

I shake my head. It's slow at first, but soon becomes so strong my hair whips at my neck.

His eyes look pained. "No? You wouldn't go out with me afterwards."

"No, I don't want to divorce you. I don't want this piece of paper."

"You don't?"

"No. Not at all. Victor, I... God, the stupid timer on my computer. I'd forgotten about that. I'm so sorry you saw it. It was something I had when I worked as your assistant. Because I heard you say to Tristan that you doubted I'd last a year."

A flush creeps up his cheeks. "I don't know how to apologize to you for all the shit I've pulled. I could spend a lifetime trying to make it up to you, and it wouldn't be enough."

I grab his hand with mine. It's stiff beneath my fingers, but then he flips it over, fingers twining with mine. "You're a different man now than you were back then. You're letting me see a different side of you."

"I can't relate to the person I was then. To have you right under my nose and not recognize the treasure. I'm sorry, Cecilia."

"I forgive you. You know that, right? The timer was such a

silly thing. I reset it when we married, and then forgot all about it."

"You don't want to get rid of me?"

"No, and don't you dare try to get rid of me either. I'm not going anywhere."

His eyes search mine, and I look back at him, letting him see just how serious I am. A smile starts on his lips. It spreads, transforming his face. "Really?"

"Yes. Really."

"Well, then. I like that."

I laugh. "I like that too. But Victor… a divorce. Wouldn't you lose the house if we're not married for a full year?"

He nods. "Yes."

"But it's your grandfather's house. It was where your father grew up, where you grew up. You couldn't—"

"It's just a house," he says, and there's steel in his tone. "It's the past. I'm looking at my future right now."

My tears well again. His eyes turn alarmed, the hand beneath mine tensing. "Cecilia?"

"These are happy tears. Victor. I really thought you were going to divorce me. I saw the papers yesterday."

"You saw them?"

"I always opened your mail when I was your assistant. The envelope was from Irving and Hardmann, and I thought it might be urgent. I'm sorry."

"Was that why you were so nervous tonight?"

"You noticed?"

"Yes. I've learned to read you pretty well."

"You have," I say, tightening my fingers around his. "God, Victor, what are we going to do? Stay married? Are we truly married?"

His lips curl into a smile. The sight sends an ache through my chest. "Yes, we are. Although I'm going to take my wife out on a lot of dates. More than most husbands."

"More than most husbands, huh?"

Victor slides his chair next to mine, ignoring the disapproving looks of the people sitting behind us. He puts his arm around me. I grip his hand, resting on my shoulder, and feel the cold metal of his wedding band against my palm.

"If we're going to be married," he says, "we're going to be the best married couple ever."

I laugh. "You're too competitive for your own good."

He kisses me, right there in the restaurant. I feel light enough to float away at the touch. A proper marriage. A proper relationship. Dates. My husband.

Love is a beautiful ache in my chest, and the words dance on my tongue. I swallow them for now and give him a wide smile. Not yet. Not now. They'll be my secret for a while.

"I don't have to be competitive anymore," he says. "I won you."

My grin widens. "Flatterer."

"I'm learning."

"But I have to tell you," I say, tapping my fingers along his jaw. "If you ever have your assistant send me flowers, I'm going to refuse them by the door."

"White lilies with pink peonies," he says. "I remember, and I'll get them for you myself. I promise."

26

CECILIA

"He shouldn't be emailing you this much," Victor says. "You're on vacation."

I look over my shoulder at my grumpy husband. He's lying in the shade, a dog-eared biography beside him on the wide lounge chair. Despite the privacy of our backyard and private pool, he's wearing swim trunks.

Not me. I'd packed cute bikinis I hadn't used yet.

"He's not on vacation," I say. "You know Carter is helping me set this up. I can't afford to be picky about when I answer an email."

Victor's look tells me I should be pickier. I smile and finish off the quick email, sending it off. I close the laptop and shove it back in the shade.

I turn to him. "That's not what's really bothering you, is it?"

His eyes run over my body with naked appreciation, stopping at my breasts. My skin is picking up a tan in record-speed here in Barbados.

"No, that's not what's bothering me," he murmurs.

I push him back on the lounge chair. He leans back with a grin and grips my hips, settling me cross-legged over him.

"A private pool was an excellent decision," he says.

"It was," I say. "But you're still annoyed that Carter's investing, despite it being your idea."

He focuses on my skin instead of my face, fingers painting patterns over my stomach and hips, occasionally brushing across the underside of my breasts. He's getting a tan too, the sun has started to bleach his dark blond hair, and he hasn't shaved in days.

He looks glorious.

"Victor?"

"Yes," he says. "Fine. I'd rather it was me investing. Call it illogical or just plain sexist, I don't know."

"You did invest," I say. "You invested in me. Our agreement gave me what I needed to start the business, not to mention giving me the time I needed. You're the initial investor."

His lips curve, eyes on the nipple he's teasing between his fingers. "I like that."

"Besides, if this is some weird jealousy thing, you know Carter isn't my type. He's too easy to talk to. I like men who make you work for it."

His fingers clamp down on my nipple and I gasp, swatting his bare chest. "Hey."

He laughs and closes his lips around my nipple in a sensual apology. I grip his broad shoulders and press a kiss to his damp hair. "Do you know something?"

A *humm* sends shivers along my chest.

"You don't know how to relax. We've been here for four days so far, and you're either working, catching up on reading for work, or making love to me."

He speaks against the skin between my breasts. "You ranked them in the wrong order."

"Oh, did I?"

"Yes. Do you know, you once called me the hardest-working person you'd ever met."

I chuckle. "Did I?"

"I remember. It was quite the compliment, you know."

"Of course you'd think that was the highest compliment."

"Well," he says, kissing his way across my breast. "I used to think it was. But working isn't my favorite thing anymore."

"Mmm." I close my eyes at the feeling of his lips on my nipple. "But no work tonight, on the dinner cruise. For either of us."

"None," he says. "Which means we should make good use of the time we have now."

His hands slide down to grip my ass and he rocks me forward, over the growing hardness in his trunks. I laugh. "God, you have a one-track mind."

"I'm on my honeymoon with my wife."

A thrill runs through me. It hasn't stopped, whenever he says the words. *My wife.* "When you put it that way…"

His beard scrapes against my neck, a kiss pressed to my skin. My pulse thunders beneath it. "Thank you for this trip," I say. "For taking the time off."

It had been his idea, and I'd been as shocked as everyone around us that he was going on vacation. But he'd reminded me that it was my mom who'd told us we should go.

"I have to make my mother-in-law happy," he'd said, and I'd gotten the feeling it was only partially a joke. "We didn't start out on the right foot."

Victor kisses the hollow in my throat. "You're welcome, but that's the third time you've thanked me. Do you think spending time alone with you on a tropical island is hard? It might be the easiest thing I've ever done."

I run my fingers through his hair, scraping my nails over his scalp. He hums in pleasure, like a large golden cat. I can't resist. I rock my hips along his erection. "Something sure is hard."

He groans, eyes downcast. "God, I love you without clothes. So beautiful."

I revel in his words, his hands, the feel of him. Our bodies had understood one another long before Victor and I did. I'm not concerned about walking around naked in front of him in bright daylight, wearing only the two rings on my left hand. Comfortable intimacy is like a web between us.

Victor kisses me, slow and languorous. There's no rush here. We're not hiding from our feelings, and we're not hiding from each other. I brush hair back from his forehead. "Victor."

He trails a line of kisses along my collarbone. "Yes?"

"I love you."

His lips pause. Against my chest, I feel the sudden pounding of his heart.

I hug him closer. "I'm not asking for anything, or demanding it back. I just really wanted to tell you. Even if—"

His lips crush against mine. The languorous kisses are gone, replaced by a hunger that sets my heart racing. He tugs at my ponytail and my curls spill over my back, tickling my bare skin.

Then his fingers are between my legs, stroking and circling. "Victor, I—"

"I have to be inside you."

His words set off my own need and I tug at his swim trunks. He lifts his hips and then he's free, hot and hard in my hand. I duck my head to suck him into my mouth and he lets out a deep groan. I can't resist, not when he's like this, a trip wire hovering at the edge.

Victor doesn't let me enjoy him for long. He flips me over on the lounge chair and we both sigh at the sweet, blessed relief of his entrance. It feels like I'm welcoming him home.

He braces himself on his elbows, kissing me as he starts to move. They're deep, earth-shattering kisses, mirroring the slow, steady roll of his hips. Every hard thrust of his pelvis against mine sets my pleasure off.

"Cecilia," he murmurs. "God, I..."

"I know," I say, wrapping my legs around him. "I know."

I orgasm before him, the bastard, as he angles his entry just the way I need. Brushing against my clit with every hard slam.

When he gets close, I hold him tight and whisper the words in his ear again. "I love you."

He finishes with a force that takes my breath away, his groan in my ear. We lie there for a long time, still connected, our breathing coming fast.

He finally rises up on an elbow and sated, blue eyes meet mine. "Say it again."

"Say what?"

"You know what."

"I love you."

His eyes shutter for a moment, like he's taking a hit. But they're clear as the sky above when he opens them again. "I love you too, Cecilia."

"You do?"

He kisses me in reply and I hold him tight, taking all he's offering and tucking it safely inside my heart, knowing he's doing the same in return.

Victor turns on his side and pulls me close. "So much," he says. "More than I know what to do with. You know that, right? I have no idea how to handle it. I'm completely powerless with you." His hand finds my thigh, notching it over his hip. "I hate you for that sometimes."

I stroke his lip with my finger. "I know. It's scary. Trusting another person this fully."

"It's terrifying."

"But it's worth it. You know, I can't imagine my life without you now."

"I can," he says. "And I want to avoid it at every cost."

I smile, wandering my fingers up his cheekbone to his forehead. His eyes close. His eyelashes are dark at the roots and blond at the tips. "Was that why your grandfather wanted you to marry, do you think? So you'd have someone in your life when he passed?"

Victor's breathing catches. It's brief, but it's there. "I've never thought of it like that."

"Why did you think he required it?"

"Because it was my job to carry on the St. Clair name. He said that often enough while he lived. That if I didn't put the hours in, the family would die with me." Victor clears his throat, eyes drifting to my temple. His fingers trail one of my curls. "I think he wanted me to carry on my father's legacy. Grandpa never really got over the loss of his son, I think."

"I can't even imagine that."

"But maybe he didn't want me to be alone, either," he says. "I like the idea of that."

"He loved you," I say. "I know you never spoke about it, the two of you, and from what you've told me, he was far from perfect. But he loved you."

Victor closes his eyes again, leaning into my touch. It takes a long time before he replies. "Yes. I think he did."

I stroke his hair, enjoying the warmth of the Caribbean sun and the gentle breeze sweeping across our sweaty skin.

But eventually, my curiosity wins out. "So?"

"So what?"

"Are you interested in carrying on the St. Clair last name?"

Victor's lips tug. "I don't know. My wife never took the St. Clair last name. There's no guarantee she'll agree to give it to my children."

I lift up on an elbow. "Your children?"

"Yes. Our children."

"So you are interested in having kids."

His gaze drops to my collarbone, and he reaches out, tracing it with a long finger. "Not any time soon, and I don't know how good of a father I'd be."

"You'd be amazing."

He snorts. "You don't genuinely believe that."

"Yes, I do. I'm not saying it wouldn't take some work. It would for me too. I don't know the first thing about being a mother."

"But is it something you want?"

I smile at him, his beautiful strong face and clear blue

eyes, the furrow between his brows. Loyal and skilled and dedicated. "I do," I say. "But not anytime soon."

He closes his eyes, hand curling around my hip. "Well. That's good, then. Even if it's mildly annoying to give my grandfather the last laugh. He always loved being right."

"Like his grandson?"

Victor's hand tightens on my hip. "Watch it, Myers."

I laugh. Happiness makes my chest feel like a bubble, floating high.

His voice is lazy. "You know, if you change your name, I won't be able to call you Myers anymore."

"You'll still be able to."

"Technically yes, but it wouldn't be accurate."

"Well, if you started calling me St. Clair, wouldn't that be confusing for you?"

"Mmm. I think I'll manage." He shifts me closer on the wide lounge chair, a tanned leg resting by mine. "You know, we only have two months left until our one-year anniversary."

"You're right. One year since our wedding in the courthouse. The one you wanted scheduled at lunchtime to avoid traffic."

"Christ. I clearly had my priorities right." His gaze turns teasing, mercurial, the Victor I love best. The side only I'm allowed to see. He walks his hands up the curve of my waist. "I've decided to do things right."

"Oh? That sounds ominous."

"I've looked into vow renewal ceremonies."

"You have? That's... interesting."

"It is. Some even look like real weddings. White dress, catering, the works."

"Catering, huh."

"Tons of it. Well, it looked exciting. Something my wife deserves. So I think, when the time is right, I'll ask her if she'd want to renew her vows with me."

I bite my lip, holding his face between my hands. "When the time is right?"

"Yes," he says. "When she'll say yes. I think I might even go down on one knee. But then again, perhaps she'll find that corny."

My heart is stuttering in my chest and I speak the next words against his lips. "No. She wouldn't."

EPILOGUE
VICTOR

The numbers on my computer screen bleed in front of my eyes, my mind drifting. It's been doing that a lot lately. The work doesn't hold my attention the way it once did, and try as I may, I can't seem to find my way back to it.

The only business I like working on these days is Cecilia's, and half the time, she doesn't want my opinions. The thought makes me smile.

The autumn's late sunlight streams in through the bay windows, tinted orange from the shifting leaves on the great trees. I look around my office, memories interposing on one another, a kaleidoscope of the past and present and future. Seeing my father and grandfather in here, arguing about trusts and investments. Myself, twelve and sullen, giving my grandfather the silent treatment. He'd been sitting in the chair I'm in. Or Cecilia and me in this room, newly married and unsure of one another, sorting through documents that tore my heart to shreds.

A small hand curls around the half-open door and pushes it open. Philippa's ponytails are half-askew, her brown eyes curious. "Daddy?"

"I'm in here."

"Whatcha doing?"

"Working. Did you just wake up from your nap?"

She shakes her head, but the imprint from her pillow marking her cheek give her away. I push back from the chair and open my arms. Philippa runs on legs that have too much energy to ever walk. I swing her up and put her on my knee.

Her little body is sturdy, and getting heavier by each passing month. The marvel of her hasn't stopped knocking the breath out of my chest. How can a person be so tiny and still be a fully formed human being? When they'd placed her in my arms at the hospital, she'd been so small. Minuscule and infinitely precious, her head fitting in the palm of my hand.

Impossible. Incredible.

"Whatcha working on?"

"Numbers, lots and lots of numbers."

She screws her face up and I laugh, pressing down on her button nose. Philippa has so many of her mother's features, including the beautiful eyes, but her hair, as Cecilia likes to remind me, is all mine. As light blonde as mine had been at her age.

"I know you don't understand it, honey."

"Boring," she says. "Daddy, let's go outside."

"You want to play?"

"Yes."

"Isn't it snack time?"

She shakes her head, eyes glittering. We both know it is.

I lift her up and walk out of the office, and Philippa sits content on my hip, happy to be carried. Cecilia keeps telling her that she needs to walk more, and that her mother is too far gone to carry her, but she knows she can still demand rides from her dad.

"Outside, outside, outside!" she sing-songs.

"Your playhouse?"

"Yes."

"Where's Bonnie, then? And Mommy?"

"I don't know," she says, eyes blinking at me. For a two-

and-a-half-year-old, she's remarkably clever. Too clever for her mother and me on frequent occasion.

"Oh, really? I'm going to guess Bonnie put you down for a nap, and after you woke up, you were to go straight to the kitchen for snack time. But you went to my office instead. Hmm?"

She giggles, leaning back in my arms. A sticky hand presses against my mouth. "No!"

"No?" I mumble. "I don't believe you."

"Shhh, Daddy!"

"Mmhm. Right."

We walk through the living room, past the French doors that open up to the backyard. Philippa makes a sound of protest.

"Nope," I say. "We're informing your mother about your little escape first, before we play."

I find my wife in the dining room. She's pacing in front of the reading nook she'd created, her headphones in and hands at the small of her back.

"No," she says. "I don't think that's a good option. Can you get another appraisal? Thank you."

I hoist Philippa up and we stand in the doorway, watching Cecilia pace.

"Mommy's working," my daughter whispers.

I nod. "She'll be done soon."

Cecilia spots us and gives us a wide smile. Then she looks down at her belly, back up to me, and rolls her eyes. Ah. So our son is doing backflips again. I'd tell him to be nicer to his mom if I he could understand me.

"Look," Philippa says. "Look, look."

She's pointing at Cecilia's feet. She's in slippers, but they're not matching. One is her gray, fluffy slipper and the other is too large and leather. She's wearing one of mine and one of her own.

I chuckle, and Philippa laughs along, her toddler laughter filling the dining room. Cecilia turns to look at us with warm eyes. Her free hand is smoothing over her rounded belly, and I watch the movement. My beautiful wife. "That's good. Thanks for getting back to me. I'll talk to you tomorrow."

She pulls out her headphones. "Sarah?" I ask.

Cecilia nods, pushing hair back from her forehead. She looks flushed. "It's about the West Coast expansion."

"She's good. I'm glad you have her on board."

"So am I. But what do we have here? Did you wake up from your nap, honey?"

Philippa squirms in my arms and I set her down. She's moving before she hits the floor. "Yes! And Bonnie wasn't there! So I went to Daddy!"

"We're going outside to play," I say.

Cecilia runs a hand over our daughter's fair hair. "Oh, are you? Do you have time for that?"

"I do."

"Good. But that means there's a certain little girl here who has to have her afternoon snack."

Philippa looks up at her mom, hopefulness etched on her face. "Can I have a Pop-Tart?"

"No."

"Ice cream?"

"No. There are apple slices and peanut butter for you in the kitchen. Go on. The faster you eat, the sooner Daddy will take you outside."

Philippa looks at me, as if to confirm this. I give her a serious nod. "On my honor."

She doesn't understand that, but she reads my nod well enough, and scampers off to the kitchen. Through the open doorway I hear the sound of Bonnie's voice and Philippa's questions. It wouldn't surprise me if she's angling for a Pop-Tart or ice cream again.

I close the distance to my wife and wrap an arm around her waist. "How are you feeling?"

"Swollen. Like a toad. I feel ready to burst at any moment."

"With over a month left." I rub my hand over the small of her back and she sighs in pleasure. Her lips part and I kiss her rosy cheek. "How's our son doing?"

"*Your* son is alternating between kicking me in the ribs or the bladder. Or both. I swear, sometimes he's doing the splits in there."

"He'll be athletic, then."

She leans her head against my shoulder and I breathe in her hair, the familiar shampoo, the smell of her. "Athletic," she murmurs. "When did you become such an optimist?"

When my wife is carrying twenty-five extra pounds of baby, I think, but I keep that thought to myself. Seeing Cecilia pregnant and giving birth had been one of the most humbling experiences of my life. It put everything into perspective. I wasn't close to the strongest person in this relationship, and seeing her bring Philippa into the world had confirmed it.

"I'm just very grateful for you, and all that you've given me," I say.

She snorts into my shirt. "Charmer."

"Always." I bend closer to her ear. "You know as well as I do what we can do to make this baby come faster."

She shivers in my arms. I look down and yes, her nipples are at the ready. Her breasts are getting heavy again. I do my best to tend to them when they're aching.

"Victor," she says. "I'm humongous. How do you still find me attractive?"

"You're you, and you're carrying our child." I run a hand over her stomach, excitement coursing through me. Not long until we meet him. "I'm proud and turned on in equal measure, and I love you. You could be the size of a whale and I'd still wake up hard and needing you."

"Size of a whale," she grumbles.

I laugh and tilt her head back up to mine. Kissing her is slow and languorous and absolutely amazing. Philippa has made this a little rarer and a lot trickier, but all the more precious.

She's breathing hard when I lift my head, her eyes glossy. I trace her bottom lip with my thumb. "You looked just like this when I kissed you, after we said our vows."

She smiles. "You kissed me a lot longer than was appropriate. We had an audience."

"Well, we were already husband and wife. I figured we'd make sure everyone knew it was real."

She chuckles and I turn us around, toward one of the framed pictures on the wall. We're standing in front of the lake where we got married, right where Cecilia had always dreamed it would take place. She looks stunning and I look dazed.

The photo hangs next to the picture from my grandfather's study, my parents and brother along for the ride. Philippa knows the name of every single one of them, including my brother she's named after.

It's not the only picture of them around the house anymore.

"Oh, those were the times, when I fit into my dresses," Cecilia says. "Look how handsome you are. You were born to wear tuxes."

I shake my head. "No, I was not. I hate bowties around my neck."

"That's a shame, because they sure don't hate you."

I kiss her again. Even after years of marriage, Cecilia's unabashed appreciation for me turns me on. She once joked that I was so starved for it when she met me that all she's doing is filling the void. Maybe that's so. All I know is that I still get turned on, like she's flipped a switch, when she says she loves me.

She exploits that to great effect... and I've no complaints.

Cecilia wraps her arms around my neck but can't pull herself close, with the bump in the way. She looks down in frustration. "I want to hug your daddy," she says. "Would you please let us?"

Her belly stays firmly in the way. I chuckle, kissing her

again. My arms are tight around her shoulders. "He can stay. I'm holding two of my favorite people in the world right now."

"With the third seconds away from bursting in here demanding that you play with her. Are you sure you have the time?"

"Absolutely, Mrs. St. Clair. There's nothing else I'd rather do."

Her smile softens, illuminates the face I love so much. The face I couldn't live without. The face I'd once looked at every single day for a year and never truly seen.

I don't miss the man I was back then. Cecilia sometimes talks jokingly about it, about the team we made when she was my assistant, but I can't look back at it with fondness. All I see is someone who was so blind he couldn't recognize the miracle in front of him, let alone treat her right.

"I love you, Mr. St. Clair," she says. "You're the best husband a woman could ever want."

I groan against her shoulder and she laughs, knowing how excited I get. Every time.

But the joyous peal of laughter from the kitchen drowns out my body's needs. "Daddy!" Philippa calls. "I'm coming!"

Want more Victor and Cecilia?

Join my newsletter to read a 7000-word short story told from Cecilia's perspective. She's with Victor in her hometown as they prepare to renew their vows in front of some familiar faces...

after
say yes
to the
boss
OLIVIA HAYLE
after
say yes
to the
boss
OLIVIA HAYLE

GET THE BONUS SHORT

Want more Victor and Cecilia?

Join my newsletter at www.oliviahayle.com to read a 7000-word short story told from Cecilia's perspective. She's with Victor in her hometown as they prepare to renew their vows in front of some familiar faces...

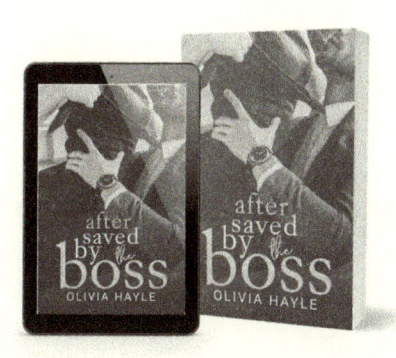

THE STORY CONTINUES

In the final book of the series, Carter Kingsley faces off against a woman immune to his charm.

He wants to win her over.
She wants to bring him down.

But if they're to get a struggling media company back on its feet, they need to work together.

Just not too closely…

**Grab A Ticking Time Boss now
or read on for the first chapter.**

CHAPTER 1
AUDREY

It's the waiting I hate the most. Nerves grow until they're so thick in my stomach that I feel nauseous, my palms turning slick around my glass. Why had I ordered a Cosmo? I've never had one before in my life.

Brian's late. How late is acceptable before I'm entitled to leave? Leaving would be the easier option. A quick text. *Let's rain check.* But that would be fleeing, and I'd promised myself I would face my fears.

Idiot, I think. I should have started with something smaller. Confined spaces, spiders, the concept of infinity.

Just not blind dating.

I can't handle the awkwardness. To see how he looks down at his phone, or worse, to look down at my own in search of an excuse. What if he's visibly disappointed by me? Or worse, what if he wants to grab a nightcap and I don't?

I take a fortifying sip of my pink drink. One drink. That's all we have to share, and then I can say I have to get back home because I have work tomorrow. I'll order some food on the way home to celebrate surviving.

The bar looks good, at least. He'd been the one to suggest it after a week of awkward text exchanges. Dim lighting and patrons in fancy clothes. Music at just the right volume. Not too loud, not too quiet. The prices are just shy of fortune-ruining, which is good for Manhattan.

My phone vibrates against the table with a text. Brian's late, which I already know, and he apologizes profusely.

He actually uses the word *profusely*.

I put the phone down and take five steadying breaths. Maybe I should have eaten something after my job interview before coming here. Maybe scheduling a blind date and an interview for my dream job on the same day was too much. But I'd been caught up in a rush of adrenaline and bravery, and I'd done it.

And now I'm paying the price.

"It's just a date," I murmur to myself. The ball of nerves in my stomach doesn't listen, continuing to spin in nausea-inducing patterns. "Just a date. I can leave if I don't like it. Just leave."

I don't feel better, so I try another argument. One that Nina had said over and over again last night as she talked me back from the ledge of cancelling.

The only way to get more comfortable with it is exposure.

But exposure doesn't seem so harmless tonight, and not when Brian just gave me another fifteen minutes to sit alone and look like a dork while my nerves rise from innocent butterflies to Hitchcock-like birds in my stomach.

I need a glass of cold water.

I leave my Cosmo on the table and head for the bar. It's mostly empty, a few businessmen leaning against it in smarmy suits. Standing up feels good. Moving about feels good.

I lean against the bar and tap my fingers against the glass counter.

The bartender spots me. "Yes?"

"A cold glass of water, please," I say. "Lots of ice."

"Still or sparkling?"

"Still."

"Sure thing." He turns, but stops. "Would you like some lemon in that?"

"Just water. Please." Why is dating horribly, awfully nerve-wracking for me? Everyone else seems to have a breeze doing it. They dance from one date to the next like it's a game.

The bartender sets a tall glass of water in front of me. I drain it, every last drop, until there's nothing but clinking ice left.

A voice speaks to my left. "You doing okay?"

I catch the sleeve of a suit jacket beside me, a large hand curled around a glass of scotch, but I keep my eye on my own. My chest is heaving. "Yes. Just fine, thank you."

"Need another glass of water?" The voice is male, smooth and deep.

I shake my head and close my eyes. The last thing I need is someone to waste all my pent-up small-talk energy on. "Nope. All good."

A small bowl of complimentary peanuts is pushed into my field of vision. "Just in case."

The gesture makes me chuckle. It comes out like a nervous squeak, but it releases some of the tension rising up inside of me like a teapot.

"Thank you," I say, turning toward him.

Light, tawny eyes meet mine. I've never seen eyes like that on a man before. Hair a dark shade of auburn is pushed back over his forehead, rising over a square face. "If you're planning on having a panic attack," he says, "I can think of better places than this bar."

"I'm not having a panic attack. Besides, who *plans* on having one?"

"It's just a figure of speech."

"It's a stupid one," I say, and smooth my hands over my dress. Then I realize what I've just said. "Sorry. I didn't mean to insult you."

He turns toward me, his lips curling at the corner. He's

tall, now that's he's stretched to his full height. "I'm not insulted."

"Good. Well... thank you for the peanuts."

"You're welcome, although I have a confession to make. They were already here."

I snort again. Perhaps this is good. I can blow off steam with this Wall Street banker. "I suspected. Nice gesture, though."

He waves a hand at the bartender, who turns mid-stride to listen to whatever peanut guy has to say. I glance at his suit. He looks like money. It's there in the well-fitting fabric, glossy beneath the dim lights. I don't trust guys who look like him. Too charming to be real, and too rich to be humble.

"Another water for the lady," he says. "Lots of ice, no lemon. You know the drill."

The bartender nods. "Coming right up."

He disappears down the bar and peanut guy turns back to me.

I frown at him. "You didn't say please."

His eyebrows rise. "I'm sorry?"

"To the bartender." I'm speaking more frankly than usual, especially to a stranger, but my nerves have me turned upside down. My cheeks heat up. "I mean, it's just more polite to say please."

"Noted," peanut guy says. He leans against the bar, lips still quirked. "Although, I'm sure that bartender has seen people far ruder than me in his days."

"That's not an excuse to be rude going forward."

"I tip generously," he says. "Always have."

"Flinging money around doesn't make up for a lack of manners."

"So now I'm lacking manners? Interesting."

I shake my head. "That's not what I'm implying. Gosh, can we ignore where I tried to correct you? I'm sorry. That was rude of me."

He doesn't look the least bit offended. "Not particularly."

The bartender returns with a full glass of ice water and puts it down in front of me. I open my mouth to say thank you, but peanut guy beats me to it.

"Thank you," he says, voice dropping. "We really appreciate your help here tonight."

The bartender doesn't stop moving down the bar. "Anytime," he tosses over his shoulder.

Peanut guy turns to me with a triumphant smile. "Am I back in your good graces now?"

"Yes. Sorry."

He rests his suit-clad arms on the bar counter. "So what's got you so bent out of shape?"

"Bent out of shape," I repeat, reaching for my ice water. I drain half of it before confessing. "I'm actually waiting for someone."

"I figured. Is he late?"

"He is, yeah. Is it obvious?"

"Well, you're here and he's not, so yes. Boyfriend?"

"Just a date." I twirl my glass around. "A first date, actually."

"And he's late? That's not a good sign." Peanut guy reaches for an actual peanut, his hand cutting across my vision. It's broad and lightly dusted with dark brown hair. A masculine hand, with long fingers. "How late is too late?"

"I don't know. I don't have a hard and fast rule about it."

"Do you have hard and fast rules about a lot of things?"

I look over at him. It's a bad idea, because he's stupidly good-looking. Square jaw and eyes that meet mine with steady charm. Oddly enough, I'm not nervous talking to him. We're so obviously not suited. He's amusing himself, I'm distracting myself.

Exposure, I think.

"About some things, I guess. I have criteria."

"Let's hear them," he says.

"Well, he has to be a nonsmoker."

Peanut guy gives a nod. "Right."

"I'd like it if he could cook me dinner once in a while."

"So he needs to be a renowned chef," he says. "Got it."

I chuckle at that. "Right. Oh, and he has to subscribe to a newspaper or magazine. *At least* one, preferably more, and they can't just be digital subscriptions."

"Oddly specific," he says. Long fingers curl around his glass, eyes the color of whiskey. "Is that a literacy test? Because I think you can reliably assume a guy your age would be able to read."

"No, I'm a journalist."

"Is that so?"

"Yes. I need someone who appreciates the written word, you know? I want to spend my Sunday mornings arguing over who has what portion of the newspaper." Hearing myself, my cheeks flare up again. "I know how I sound. Like a hopeless romantic."

"Are you one?"

"I'm a realistic romantic," I say. "Which is why I'm on a first date with a stranger."

He lifts an eyebrow again. "This is a blind date?"

"Yes."

"And he's late. Really not off to a good start."

I shrug, feeling the nerves settle into a current in my stomach. Talking to this guy helps. "Well, I'll give him a shot. Something might have happened to him on the way here, you know." I look over his shoulder, but the businessmen down the end of the bar counter are talking amongst themselves, paying him no mind. "Why are you here? Waiting for your own blind date?" I can't say it without smiling. As if.

"No," he says, swirling the amber liquid in his glass around. "I've met her before."

That makes me roll my eyes. "Of course. She's late too?"

"Yes. Often is, as a matter of fact."

"I guess that's not on your list of criteria, then."

"No. Come to think of it, I don't know if she subscribes to a newspaper."

"You should ask her that tonight," I say. "I've heard it's a dealbreaker for some."

His smile stretches wide. "So have I, kid," he says. "Tell me why dating makes you this nervous."

"Kid? We're practically the same age!"

He's still smiling. "Are we? I can't remember the last time I was as nervous as you waiting for someone to show up."

This guy is a roller coaster. "That doesn't define my maturity. I'm twenty-six," I say. Honesty makes me add the rest. "Well, I will be in four months' time. How old are you?"

"Thirty-two," he says.

That's when my phone vibrates in my pocket again. Ice shoots through my veins, freezing me to the spot. Brian's probably here. Has it already been fifteen minutes? God, I hate this. Hate it hate it hate it.

A glance down at my phone confirms it. *I'm outside. Did you grab a table?*

"Is that him?" Peanut guy says.

"Yes," I murmur. "It's showtime."

"For him, not for you," he says. "Just be yourself."

"Right." My fingers fly over my phone. *I have a table inside.*

"Good luck, kid. I'll be over here if you need me."

"Stop calling me a kid," I say. My nerves are flaring up again, making me lash out. "And don't look at me the whole date. That's weird."

He smiles wide, and I catch a hint of a dimple beneath the dark five-o'clock shadow coating his jaw. "Just signal and I'll give you a plausible excuse."

"Um, thanks. Have a nice evening," I say and head toward my table. My disgusting drink stands there, forgotten. I sit down and smooth my hands over my dress. *I can do this.* When I look up, I cast my eyes about for a man striding my way.

Instead I meet peanut guy's gaze.

He's leaning against the bar, glass in hand, and gives me the smallest of nods. There's a hint of a smile on his face.

The arrogant bastard.

But he's quickly eclipsed by the man who approaches me. This has to be Brian. Nina set me up with him, a guy from her old job. She promised he would be nice. That was the word she used. *Nice.*

He looks nice, I think, in a friendly sort of way. He's wearing a beanie that sits low on top of dark curls. He shrugs out of his denim jacket.

"Hey," he says. "Sorry I'm late."

"No worries."

He looks down at my drink, and a frown mars his face. "You've already ordered?"

Yeah, dude. I was waiting here alone for twenty minutes. "I did, yes. I hope that's okay."

He shrugs and sits down opposite me. "Sure, sure. So Nina told me you're a journalist."

"I am, yes. I'd love to work in investigative reporting someday," I say. Hopefully sooner than just *one day*, if the interview today had gone as well as it felt. I'd spent over two hours today at the *New York Globe*'s offices.

"So you write, like, these exposing pieces about government corruption and scandals?" He slouches in his chair, but his eyes glow with enthusiasm. This is promising.

I spin my disgusting drink around and nod. "I'd like to, at least."

"You know, I have a lot of opinions about the press."

"You do?"

He raises a finger. Almost like he's lecturing me. "You guys need to start reporting more on facts, and less with your emotions."

Um... "Yes. Well, reporting on the facts as they are is the hallmark of good journalistic integrity."

"Sure, but so often they don't. You know, I haven't subscribed to a newspaper in years. The facts I care about are all online. I can find them with the press of a button."

I rub a hand over my neck. "Well, a lot of people do that nowadays. Print media is struggling for that very reason."

"It's dying, more like it. But if you reported more on facts, you'd be doing better." He raises a hand, signaling to the waitress. "Over here!"

Oh, dude. That's not okay. My nerves turn to irritation instead. "Say please," I mutter. He doesn't hear me.

"I'll have a beer," he tells the waitress. "Easy on the head, all right? And not a wheat beer. Anything but a wheat beer." He turns back to me, like our conversation was never interrupted. "That's why a lot of people don't trust journalists anymore. It's not that hard of a job, right? Reporting the facts. Not like working in manual labor or, like, working at a brewery."

"Not as hard as your job, you mean?" I say. My hand is tight around my glass.

He shrugs and gives me a smile, like we're sharing a joke. "You said it, not me. Hey, I have a few stories you should write about. I'm sure everyone says that, but I'm serious. I think this could be good for you."

Oh boy. "Really?" I ask. "What are they?"

"I'm a member of an online community. We don't really tell people about it, but we share updates the regular media won't report on. I know exactly how you'll react—but listen with an open mind. Sasquatch was sighted recently, just upstate. Farmers in the area have been covering it up, and a friend of mine online has seen the FBI vehicles." His eyes widen. "This goes all the way to the very top."

I take a long, hard sip of my disgusting drink. *Oh Christ*, I think.

Over Brian's shoulder, I see peanut guy talking to a leggy blonde. Her hair falls in a wave over her shoulder and she has a hand on his arm. He says something and she tosses her head back to laugh.

At least someone's having a good time.

"This is a scoop," Brian says. "Could be really good for your career. I mean, if you want the help."

———

An hour later, I've still not found a way to escape. Brian just won't stop talking. About how my career could go in a different direction if only I had the guts to report the *actual* facts. His ten-minute monologue would be charming, if it wasn't such a blatant example of mansplaining.

He adjusts his clear-rim glasses—I'm starting to wonder if he's only wearing them for aesthetic reasons—and leans back in his chair. "So that's why," he says, "I had to quit that job."

"Because they didn't respect your initiatives."

"Exactly," he says. He looks like he's actually enjoying himself.

Probably because *his* date has mainly been listening to himself talk.

"But strong people like others who take charge. They recognize themselves," he says. His voice has gone weird and soft, and my stomach tightens up in nerves again. No, no, no. This is what I don't like. Turning someone down or having to rebuff them. Conflict-averse to the max, that's me. "Especially women," he continues. "They really like someone who knows how to show them a good time."

"I don't—"

He lunges across the table and presses his lips to mine. It's so unexpected I jerk back, but he follows along, his mouth like a leech.

And oh God, is that his tongue?

I don't kiss him back. I sit there, hands balled on the table, for two long seconds before I push against his chest. He leans back with eyes that are warm.

"Well," he says. "You're a good kisser, at least."

At least? *At least?* This man is unbelievable.

"Thank you for tonight," I say, because I can't find it in

myself to stop being polite. "But I think I'm ready to head out."

"Back to mine?" he asks. "Or yours?"

I reach for my clutch. "Uh, I have work early in the morning. I don't think I'll be able to do that."

"Tomorrow's a Saturday" he says.

Oh, so it is. Shoot.

My gaze travels over his shoulder and locks eyes with the man from earlier. Peanut guy, who called me *kid*, but who'd also promised he would help. He's standing alone by the bar, no blonde in sight. And he catches my gaze.

He raises an eyebrow. *You need me?*

I give a teeny, tiny nod.

"Audrey?" Brian says. "Come on, have a nightcap with me. At least let me take you home. I'll even let you pick my brain for more stories."

The only thing worse than picking this guy's brain would be having him try to suck mine out again through my teeth.

"Oh," I say. "Goody. But, I don't think—"

The peanut guy has reached us. He puts a hand on the back of my chair, his tall form shadowing our table. "There you are," he tells me. His face is serious, no dimple or charming smile in sight. "We've been looking all over for you."

"You have?"

"Yes. Your mom is beside herself. Come on, we have to get going."

"Right now?" I squeak, looking from him to Brian. His eyes are wide on my suit-wearing savior.

"Yes," peanut guy says. "I have a car outside. If we go now, we can still get there in time. Come on." He turns to Brian. "You understand, I'm sure."

"Yes," he says weakly. "Go on, Audrey."

I stand up and peanut guy holds up my thin jacket. I slide into the arms. "I'm sorry. Thanks for tonight."

He nods, and doesn't even say it back. The jerk. Maybe

he's upset he can't keep explaining someone's profession back to them.

"Hurry," peanut guy says by my side. I try to match his long strides through the bar and toward the front door.

"My tab," I whisper to him. "I need to—"

"I've cleared it," he says. "Come on, he's watching."

We emerge into the warm New York air and he lets go of my wrist. My skin tingles where he's held it. "Oh my God," I say, looking over my shoulder at the closed bar door. "That was *awful.*"

"It didn't look great," he says, but he looks mightily pleased with himself. He's even taller out here than he'd been hunched over the bar. Towering over me.

A burst of nerves flitters through my stomach.

"So, what did he do wrong?" he says. "Talk about his mother too much? Compare you to his past dates? Ask you to come back to his and check out his herb garden?"

My nerves die and I laugh. "That would arguably have been worse. No, he didn't do that. He gave me advice about my career."

"That's a bad thing?" peanut guy asks, a raised eyebrow.

"Yes! He knows nothing about it!"

"Ah. Talking out of his ass, then."

"Yes. It was so patronizing I forgot to be nervous. I can't believe I got all dressed up for this," I say, looking down at my uncomfortable shoes. "It looked like you had better luck."

He rubs a hand over his neck, almost as if he's embarrassed, and gestures toward the street. "We should walk. He might leave any minute."

"Oh. And I'm not on my way to my… What was it? My sickly mother?"

"I kept it vague," he says. "Lies usually work better that way."

"You're an expert at it?"

He snorts. "Unfortunately, yeah."

"So?" I press on, shoving my hands into the pockets of my jacket. "How was your date?"

He shrugs. "It went all right."

"I'm sorry if I interrupted it, by needing... assistance," I say.

"Oh, it was already over. I told her I didn't want to see her anymore."

I stop and stare at him. He notices and rolls his eyes. Auburn hair has fallen over his square forehead and his jawline is sharp from this angle.

"Don't look at me that way," he says. "She knew it wasn't going anywhere either."

I think back on the excited blonde he'd chatted to at the bar. "Right," I say.

"At least I didn't lecture her about how to do her job," he says, smiling crookedly. "I know better than to do that."

I rub a hand over my mouth. "God, he kissed me, too. More like lunged at me."

"I saw that," he says, and there's sympathy in his voice. "Didn't look good."

"Definitely wasn't." We've reached my subway stop and I pause, digging through my purse for my card. I doubt he's heading downstairs too. "Thank you for helping out back there," I say.

He nods, eyes on me. "Anytime, kid."

I groan. "Not that again."

"Riling you up is fun."

"You should get a hobby." It's another rude thing to say, but somehow, it feels fun with him. Knowing he can take it and dish it back just in kind.

He leans against a streetlamp, cool and collected and seemingly oblivious to the people passing us. "Oh, this is my hobby," he says. "Rescuing damsels in distress at bars who go on bad blind dates."

"Happens a lot, does it?"

"More than you'd think," he says. "Where do you find these guys, anyway? Dating apps?"

"I've tried a few of those," I admit. "They're not my favorite, but... you get dates, at least."

"I'm sure you do," he says.

I brush past the enigmatic compliment. "But this guy was actually someone my friend set me up with."

"Renouncing that friendship?"

"I really should," I say. "Anyway, this was... nice. I mean, not the date. But the before and after."

He grins. "Happy to help."

"I should probably head home. Had a full day, and all. I actually had a job interview today. For my dream job."

"Is that so?"

"Yes," I say, probably rambling. I inch toward the subway steps. "I never got your name, actually?"

He reaches inside his jacket and pulls out a small notepad and pen. It's a slick move, matching his suit, his demeanor, the moneyed air. I don't trust guys like him. Never have, not since my childhood. But something about him makes me feel energized.

Alive.

"Carter," he says, scribbling something. "I've enjoyed talking to you. Don't see this as having any strings. But if you need to pick a guy's brain or be rescued from awful blind dates again..."

I stare at the paper he's extending toward me. *Carter*, it says. And beneath it are seven digits.

"Your phone number?"

"The very one," he says.

I take it, and wonder why I'm not nervous. He's a man. An exceedingly handsome one, even. But I'd seen the woman he turned down tonight, and she could easily have passed for a model. Looked happy and smiling, too.

This thing, him and me, is so clearly a friendship thing. So I don't feel nervous at all, accepting the piece of paper.

"Thanks," I say. "Might be good to get a guy's perspective on things."

"Anytime," he says, and nods to me. Like an old-time gentleman seeing off a lady. "Get home safe."

"Thanks," I murmur again, and walk down the steps. It isn't until I'm halfway home, dizzy from all the impressions of the day, that I realize I never gave him my name. With shaking fingers, I add his number to my phone and give him the glorious name *Carter Peanuts*.

Then I send him a single text.

My name is Audrey. Thanks for the peanuts.

His response comes just as I've unlocked the room I'm renting on the second floor of a brownstone. I rest against the closed door and read it, feeling endless possibilities stirring around me.

Carter: Anytime, kiddo. Pleasure to meet you.

OTHER BOOKS BY OLIVIA
LISTED IN READING ORDER

New York Billionaires Series

Think Outside the Boss
Tristan and Freddie

Saved by the Boss
Anthony and Summer

Say Yes to the Boss
Victor and Cecilia

A Ticking Time Boss
Carter and Audrey

Seattle Billionaires Series

Billion Dollar Enemy
Cole and Skye

Billion Dollar Beast
Nick and Blair

Billion Dollar Catch
Ethan and Bella

Billion Dollar Fiancé
Liam and Maddie

Brothers of Paradise Series

Rogue
Lily and Hayden

Ice Cold Boss
Faye and Henry

Red Hot Rebel
Ivy and Rhys

Small Town Hero
Jamie and Parker

Standalones

Arrogant Boss
Julian and Emily

Look But Don't Touch
Grant and Ada

The Billionaire Scrooge Next Door
Adam and Holly

ABOUT OLIVIA

Olivia loves billionaire heroes despite never having met one in person. Taking matters into her own hands, she creates them on the page instead. Stern, charming, cold or brooding, so far she's never met a (fictional) billionaire she didn't like.

Her favorite things include wide-shouldered heroes, late-night conversations, too-expensive wine and romances that lift you up.

Smart and sexy romance—those are her lead themes!

Join her newsletter for updates and bonus content.
www.oliviahayle.com.
Connect with Olivia

- facebook.com/authoroliviahayle
- instagram.com/oliviahayle
- goodreads.com/oliviahayle
- amazon.com/author/oliviahayle
- bookbub.com/profile/olivia-hayle

www.ingramcontent.com/pod-product-compliance
Ingram Content Group UK Ltd.
Pitfield, Milton Keynes, MK11 3LW, UK
UKHW030659070525
5801UKWH00021B/119